THE FALL

Book 3 in Rick Fuller's Manchester Trilogy

By

Robert White

www.robertwhiteauthor.co.uk

For my wife Nicola

I have dined with kings, I've been offered wings.
And I've never been too impressed.
(Bob Dylan)

Rick Fuller's Story:

Her skin was cold to the touch, so pale, almost translucent. I held her tight, the only way I could think to give her warmth as we lay together on the cold stone floor of the barn.

Her eyes closed again. I called her name, but she didn't respond.

Strong arms pulled me away from her, rolling me on my back. A guy in an aircrew helmet and overalls jabbed a needle in my arm and held up a drip. The pain in my groin was horrendous, I couldn't move.

"Can you hear me, pal?"

I nodded.

"Can you hold this yourself?"

The same response.

He shot over to where Lauren lay and began to work on her. She had a drip too, and another guy had a blood pressure cuff blowing up on her arm. He was shouting into his headset, numbers and instructions, my brain too muddled to compute them, my own blood loss beginning to dull my reasoning, taking me on the journey into darkness.

The Medevac crew would have flown from Belfast, but would need to fly us to Birmingham, to the Royal Centre for Defence Medicine at Selly Oak. No doubt the guy with the headset was giving the heads up to the medical team there, telling them exactly what they had coming.

I could hear Des barking away somewhere in the background.

Moments later, as I'd expected, things began to get dark.

I had never been a religious man. But just before I passed out I asked the Scot to say a prayer for Lauren North.

Des Cogan's Story:

I watched as the pilot of the Medevac increased the power of the engines for take-off.

Rick and Lauren were aboard the Regiment-supplied aircraft, the Firm providing nothing but the best.

Knowing the on-board crew would be some of the finest trained medical staff in the world, knowing they would be experts in the treatment of trauma injuries and gunshot wounds, didn't help me.

I'll be honest with you right now, Doctor Kildare himself could have been on board that fucking chopper, and it wouldn't have improved my mood.

As the powerful rotors blew snow into my face, filling my nostrils and ears, I couldn't rid myself of my deep sense of foreboding.

Dipping my head and clearing my airways I saw JJ was leaning into the VW van we'd used to gain entry to the O'Donnell farm. He was packing what remained of our weapons and ammunition into a large holdall. Despite deep cuts to his hands, he was keeping busy, avoiding the awkward conversations that would inevitably follow about who may live or who may die.

Off to my left I heard feet on snow.

The crunching sound stopped a couple of feet from me; Cartwright, our MI6 handler had been aboard the helicopter. I examined him as he pulled on a pair of leather gloves that probably cost more than my entire shoe collection.

He wasn't a big man, yet instantly commanded your respect. The combination of his deportment, intelligence and the total lack of any emotion, gave him an air of menace usually only found in more robust individuals.

He gestured toward the Medevac, now little more than a black speck on the horizon.

"They're in good hands," he said, using his finest bedside manner.

There was no need to answer the spook. Staring into his cold blue eyes, I waited for him to get to the point and say what he really wanted.

He gestured toward the devastation we had caused in the courtyard of the farm.

"Talk me through this mess, Desmond."

I knew the drill.

"It's no mess," I said, stepping toward the carnage. "We got who we wanted…so did you."

Declan O'Donnell was the first corpse we came to. He wore a red silk kimono which had ridden up as he'd fallen face down, revealing his bare backside. The massive exit wound in the centre of his back had torn his flesh open like a ghoulish flower. He had died before his face had met the snow-covered cobbles of the yard.

"Declan," I said.

Cartwright nodded.

"And our man Clarke?"

I jutted my chin in the direction of the balcony of the main house. Joseph Clarke, the young man recruited by the Firm to spy on the O'Donnell family, the man who had become Declan's lover and turned against the British Secret Service, lay on his back, his knees drawn bizarrely to his chest. His flesh still smouldered from the phosphorous grenade I had thrown at him. There was the unmistakable smell of burnt human in the air. Rick had put him out of his agony by emptying half a clip into his face; in hindsight, an action that had probably sealed his own and Lauren's fate.

"DNA will confirm the boy's ID," I muttered.

Dead bodies clad in black bomber jackets lay all about the yard, their blood blushing the snow around them, framing each corpse in pinks and crimsons; someone's son, someone's lover, someone's friend. The scene reminded me of so many I had witnessed in my lifetime. Walking through the aftermath of battles or massacres had been part of my world for too long.

"Security," I said. "Hired hands; there are four more in a small copse about a mile or so north of here."

The old spy raised an eyebrow. "The three Irish?"

I stepped over to the VW van that JJ had finished emptying of guns, and pulled open the rear doors. The bodies of Ewan Findley and Kristy McDonald were piled unceremoniously on top of each other in the back, framed like two bizarre lovers caught in a grotesque embrace.

"We think Lauren slotted these two before we arrived." I pointed to the barn. "Dougie's in here."

Cartwright couldn't find the strength to push the heavy wooden door so I gave it a swift kick. It swung open on creaking hinges.

More carnage awaited. Front and centre was Dougie McGinnis; he was on his back, his left leg doubled under him, eyes staring, tongue lolling lifelessly from his open mouth.

Seamus O'Donnell was by the window, the first of JJ's victims with the M24. The back of his head was missing and a mixture of shattered bone and human brain tissue was splattered on the flagstones behind him.

The old spy studied him briefly before turning his attention to the young black guy that lay between the two identifiable corpses. "And the coloured chap with his trousers down?"

"Not sure, but his body temp is lower than Seamus's so I reckon he died first; small calibre bullet to the head, probably Dougie's .38. There's first aid kit in the bag over there, Lauren had a clean dressing on her knee when we got to her, so I'm guessing he was the O'Donnell's' pet doctor."

"So why shoot him?"

I walked to the small table and picked up a half empty bag of cocaine. "The sick fuckers were having a party, a right old knees up eh? Guinness, Grouse, Charlie... Lauren was naked...maybe a sex game gone wrong?"

Cartwright shook his head. "Jesus H Christ."

The door creaked again and JJ stepped into the barn. He was covered in snow.

"I have my M24 now," he said. "We are ready to go, yes?"

I turned to Cartwright. "Is that everything you need?"

He nodded. "For now; there will be a full debrief of course once Fuller is up and about. All your weapons will be returned to a DLB (*Dead Letter Box*) in Manchester. I'll inform you of the location personally."

I shook my head in disbelief. I didn't like the way he thought that Rick would be the only one at the debrief. "Lauren's a fighter you know, Cartwright. She's made of sterner stuff that you think. We'll all be at the debrief, you'll see."

Cartwright gave me that cold look again. "Quite," he managed, before examining his phone, no longer interested in my opinion.

I'd had enough.

"Me an' JJ will take the Toyota in the yard and meet the chopper as planned. I take it the Medevac will drop Rick and Lauren at Queen Elizabeth's?"

Cartwright held up a hand, engrossed in whatever was written on his phone screen. "Elizabeth's, yes, correct," he said.

I gestured to JJ. "We'll be away then."

Reaching the door of the barn, I stopped and turned to the old spy. He may have been a cold fish, and I suppose he had to be in his line of work, but he'd played a blinder with the Medevac.

"Cartwright...I know you pulled a lot of strings for us there, thank you."

He smiled. "No problem...we'll just have to keep our fingers crossed for the other two now, Desmond."

I nodded. "Aye, we will...but, Cartwright, the game's over for us now eh? All debts paid, we're clear?"

He considered that statement for a moment. "Yes, clear," he said, before remembering. "Ah, talking of debts, your fee will be in the same place as the weapons, old boy, in cash of course; we recycled it from what the Irish left in Maxi's club."

There were no flies on the Firm, eh?

The Toyota bounced along the rutted track from the farm toward our RV. I couldn't help but notice Lauren's blood all over the back seat and my stomach churned. The chopper that had dropped us in situ some eighteen hours earlier was six more away, so there was no point in worrying or wondering how she or Rick were. There was nobody to call, nobody to ask. Not yet.

Queen Elizabeth's in Birmingham was the main trauma centre where all the poor bastards coming back from the Middle East with missing arms and legs were treated.

I checked my watch. Two more seriously injured casualties should have just landed.

We made our RV and waited.

Darkness finally fell. The minutes dragged like hours, and we sat in pensive silence as the Toyota's heater dried our soaking clothes on our limbs. I fired up my wee pipe and committed a mortal sin by smoking inside the car.

"Rick would have a fucking fit," I said, doing my best to break the silence any way possible.

JJ manged a smile, and did his best to follow suit, but the cuts to his hands were too painful for him to roll his cigarette.

"Here, let me," I said.

The Turk handed me his makings. "Thanks, Des," he said quietly.

It had been a while but I managed a couple of decent looking roll-ups and lit one for him.

JJ inhaled deeply and inspected the numerous lacerations to his hands and forearms. "My wife, she fix my hands when I get home."

"I have to say, they look sore, pal, you'll be adding a few more scars to your collection there."

He nodded. "Yes, I know. After fighting many years with the knife I have dozens, but Grace, my wife will do a good job."

"Your wife is a doctor?"

"Dressmaker."

I managed a shallow laugh.

Of course, JJ would have no choice but to have his wounds treated at home. Any doctor looking at those hands would be onto the cops in a flash.

"Aye, probably do a neater job, pal...and no daft questions, eh?"

J.J looked out of the window into the ink black night. "I can't wait to see her and my boy. I miss them."

My mind turned to Anne, lying on that awful bed, her hair all but gone, consumed by her pain.

"It's good to be in love, eh, pal?"

JJ flicked his cigarette out of the window.

"Yes, good. It keeps me alive," he said. The Turk cricked his neck. "Lights...chopper's here."

The journey back across the Irish Sea was just as hairy as our outward flight, and we bounced around in shocking turbulence. Luckily, our BMW was exactly where we had left it at RAF Woodvale. Rick had hidden the keys under the front offside wheel-arch and within seconds we were mobile. The snow had failed to make its presence felt on Merseyside, leaving nothing but grey slush on the roads. The German marque negotiated it with ease and we were parked outside JJ's home within the hour.

The moment we came to a halt, the Turk broached the subject we had been avoiding for hours. "When are you going to the hospital?"

"Right now," I said. "I can be there in forty-five minutes. But look, JJ, you know the drill as much as me, pal…"

I swallowed hard, not wanting to even say the words.

"If Lauren's…if she's…if she's gone, they'll search for her next of kin before they tell me anything. If she's still alive, she'll probably still be in surgery."

"I am scared for Lauren," said JJ. "She lost so much blood."

So was I. She was in hypovolemic shock by the time she made the chopper. It's fuckin' nasty. Your kidneys fail, sometimes other organs too. The most severe cases even suffer gangrene in their hands or feet. It all depends how quick they can get fluids and meds into you.

I caught JJ's coal-coloured eyes, and for the first time I saw fear in them. Not fear for himself, but for Lauren.

"She's strong though, eh Des?" he said.

"They both are, pal, and they'll need to be. I'll tell you this much, Rick's wound wasn't so straightforward either. There was something weird about it, I reckon the bullet bounced off his pelvic bone or split in two, maybe it's in his abdomen."

JJ grimaced; he'd been stabbed in the guts in his youth by a drunken nightclub customer. Most unpleasant I'll tell you.

"Maybe I pray," said the Turk absently.

"I didn't know you were religious, pal."

"I'm not…but you never know, eh, Des?"

Being a Roman Catholic raised in the west of Scotland, I knew that when I got the chance, I would go to the chapel and light a candle for Rick and Lauren. My family would expect nothing less, and neither would I.

After all the shocking things I'd seen and done in my life, it was hard to keep my faith, but I clung to it with my fingernails, just in case.

I changed the subject.

"We need to sort your cash out, pal," I said.

Just how much of a fee Rick had promised JJ, I had no idea, but I'd already decided to split whatever cash Cartwright had left at the DLB equally between the four of us. The Turk had saved our arses over there, he was a top bloke.

"I'll get to the drop sometime tomorrow and bring your cash here if that's okay, eh?"

JJ's eyes widened. He was horrified. "But I come to hospital with you now, Des."

I gestured toward his ruined hands. "You need those looking at, mate."

"Yes, I know, but you come into my house now, my wife cook us hot food, good Turkish food, she fix my hands, and we go. You said yourself, Rick and Lauren will be with doctor now. Please, Des, wait for me, just one hour. I want to be there."

I couldn't question the lad's loyalty. "You've done enough, pal," I said.

"Please, this is my way. This is my duty."

Thinking about it, he was right, an hour wouldn't make any difference and a hot meal sounded like heaven.

"Okay, pal, I have to say I'm starvin'." I lifted an armpit and gave it a sniff. "I hope yer missus is the understanding type like. I stink like a pig."

JJ displayed his perfectly white teeth. "Come, you meet my boy too. His name is Kaya, he is four."

JJ lived in Yew Street, Hulme. It was a new build house, rented from a private landlord. Most of the houses in the street had been bought for rental. The area was close to the universities and the city centre. It made good business sense for landlords to buy up whole streets of 'affordable' housing and charge unaffordable rents.

I'd seen lots of JJ's in my time. Guys that had left the army full of good intentions, guys who had tried buying a bar or other business, lost everything and ended up scratching around working twelve on, twelve off for Group4 or some other fuckin' minimum wage security firm.

At least now he had a few quid coming.

The Turk pushed open his door and stepped into the hall. Before he had taken two strides a very attractive blonde, dressed in a blue pyjama top and little else, sprinted down the hall and leapt on him.

Wrapping her legs around his waist and grabbing his neck with both hands, she pulled him to her. Before he could, speak she kissed him deeply on the mouth.

I stood in the cold, feeling uncomfortable and jealous in equal amounts.

She drew her mouth away, and was about to start work on the Turk's neck when she spotted me. Trying to cover an embarrassed smile with her small hand she slid down JJ's body to the floor.

"Oh, I'm so sorry," she giggled.

Realising that her pyjama top did little to hide the skimpiest of underwear below. JJ's wife turned the deepest crimson and ran into the house in fits of laughter.

I stepped in beside him and spoke quietly out of the corner of my mouth.

"You lucky, lucky bastard," I said.

I was shown to a first-floor bathroom by four-year-old Kaya, who solemnly handed me fluffy towels and a set of his father's clean clothes. He was a handsome wee boy, with the look of his dad, but the green eyes of his mum. I took the items and thanked him.

The boy didn't move. He cocked his head quizzically "Are you a soldier?"

"Aye, kindae, I am I suppose," I said.

He flexed a skinny wee bicep and gave me a broad smile. "My dad's the toughest soldier in the world."

On what I'd seen, I couldn't disagree. "He is so, Kaya."

The boy seemed pleased with my response and shot out of the door.

I peeled off my stinking clothes, and stepped gladly into the piping stream of water.

I returned to the lounge to find Grace, JJ's twenty-seven-year old wife, cleaning and stitching his hands.

There was no TV blaring away, no bad news or shite celebrity bollocks disturbing the peace of the household. Turkish music played quietly from an old radio left somewhere in the kitchen, and a wonderful concoction of smells wafted around me as garlic, lamb and basil simmered. I felt as if I was warm for the first time in a lifetime and my heart longed for what JJ had.

Wife, family, love.

Grace knelt at his feet, doing an expert job, without a single question as to how her husband had ended up so badly injured. Kaya watched intently showing no signs of squeamishness. His father must have been in agony as Grace passed her needle through his skin without anaesthetic, yet he never flinched.

My stomach flipped again as I was reminded that the people closest to me, the people that I cared for so deeply, were under the surgeon's knife at best.

JJ jutted his chin toward the upstairs. "Evelyn?" he asked.

Grace didn't look up from her task.

"Gone…she chose the other path. "

For the first time, I noticed JJ's wife was Irish, from the south; that beautiful lilting accent.

The Turk's head dropped. He blew air from his nostrils and nodded in resignation.

Grace finished stitching and began the bandaging of her husband's hands.

"The moment it came on the news that bastard Maxi was dead," she said." She was gone, back to her life, if you can call it that."

Evelyn had been one of Maxi's street girls, hooked on hard drugs, selling herself outside Piccadilly for a pittance, for her next ten-bag. JJ had persuaded her to tell us the layout of Maxi's club and in return he and Grace would help Evelyn get straight.

As it turned out, we never got to use the intel, and now Evelyn was probably in the back of some car earning her next fix. Sometimes, in a heartbeat, life can turn from bliss to bollocks eh?

JJ caught my eye. His glance was as cold and dark as hell itself. "At least she can't go back to that evil man, Maxi eh? I take my knife and gut him like a fish."

Not for the first time, I was glad JJ Yakim was on my side.

Grace stood, smoothed down her clothes and looked at me. Actually it was less of a look, more an examination. It was as if she'd done what was needed, and now she could take a glance at her company. How I'd initially missed her accent was beyond me, for as she took me to pieces with her eyes, the voice was pure blarney.

No more than five foot four in bare feet, trim as a gymnast, she was pretty as a picture and hard as nails. It took me a moment before it came to me. The lack of questions, the no-nonsense repairs to her husband, the calm way with her. Our Grace was from travelling stock.

If young Kaya took after both his parents he'd be a man to avoid in a fight when he was older, that was for sure.

"Yer a soldier so?" she said, her face softening into a smile.

"Was."

"Yer a handsome man there, Desmond, for a squaddie I mean, don't yer think that there, JJ? He's a good-looking fella eh? For his age like?"

JJ caught my increasingly uncomfortable gaze. He knew his wife.

"Don't show our guest up with your talk, Grace."

Her smile grew into a beam and she locked her sparkling green eyes with mine

"You brought JJ home, Desmond. You brought my man back with no more than a scratch or two, an' I'll be thanking you for that."

I shrugged, not knowing what to say.

"Let's eat," she said. "I've made Turkish lamb tagine…you'll like it."

She was right.

Queen Elizabeth's was in Selly Oak, close to Birmingham University. A brand new unit was in the process of being built nearby and it loomed large in the distance as we drove around the old hospital's carpark looking for a space. By the time we located one, it was just before midnight. For obvious reasons, the areas containing our injured servicemen and women had its own security. After all, it wouldn't do for some nutter with a suicide vest to wander into the place and finish the job they'd started in Iraq or Afghanistan, would it?

As we pushed open the main doors two burly RAF MP's eyed us with suspicion, and I instantly clocked two more further along the corridor that led to the wards themselves.

The reception area was little different to any other hospital. Lines of orange plastic chairs were screwed to the floor, and a drinks machine was wedged in next to its snack-dispensing cousin on the wall behind them. Two low tables covered with old newspapers and magazines completed the picture.

Off to my left, sitting bolt upright behind a high desk, was an old guy with a grey crew and a drinker's nose. Peering over half-moon glasses, he sported a neatly trimmed moustache which matched his hair. It twitched as he muttered quietly to himself, obviously irritated by our presence, and the late hour.

As I got closer, I could see that the guy's clothes were as shipshape as his facial hair. He was a civvy, the epaulettes on his tunic announcing the private security firm he worked for, but he'd been in the job, no danger. He had the look of my old Regimental Sergeant Major who had made my life such a misery when I was a young squaddie in training. The guy was well past retirement age, one of those blokes determined to work till they dropped.

Getting closer, I spotted his medal ribbons stitched onto his tunic. Malaya, Aden and Ireland. He had a small tattoo that announced his blood group on the inside of his left wrist. The old boy had done a bit, that was for sure.

When he spoke, he had the deep low London growl of a heavy smoker. "It's too late for a visit, son," he said, sharply.

I'd managed to keep my nerves in check all the way to Birmingham, but the moment I looked into the old soldier's watery eyes, my stomach started again. I asked the question.

"I know that, sir. We're just looking for an update on a couple of colleagues of ours."

He studied me briefly before tapping at his computer.

"Names?" he said.

"Fuller" I said. "Richard Fuller... and Lauren...Lauren North."

He tapped some more.

"No one here by that name, son."

JJ stepped in, his short temper instantly up. "Look again, old man, they are here, we know this."

The old boy was unimpressed by JJ's aggressive attitude. He stared straight into the Turk's eyes.

"Relatives, are we?"

JJ turned away and cursed in his native language. We all got the message, including the two meat-head MP's who were making their way over.

The old soldier raised a hand in their direction and shook his head. He was perfectly capable of handling this one.

He stood, pulled down the hem of his tunic and switched off his computer. "That's me for the day," he said. "Now, you two lads look like smokers to me, why don't you join me for a fag outside?"

JJ reluctantly nodded and we shuffled out of the door feeling pretty dejected.

The night sky had turned clear, and frost formed on the windscreens of the parked cars still dotted around the hospital. I stepped out onto the old tiled pavement, pulling my collar up against the chill and fumbling for my pipe as I walked. JJ stayed by the door, leaning against the wall one-footed. Dressed in tight faded jeans, baseball boots and leather jacket, with his gelled hair scraped behind his ears, he wouldn't have looked out of place in some American movie from the Fifties.

"I don't like this, old man," he muttered, finding his lighter.

"Let's just wait a minute, pal," I said.

We didn't have a minute to wait.

The guy strode from the door, ramrod straight. He'd added a very expensive looking Crombie overcoat covering his tunic, and finished the look with a black trilby. He pulled a pack of Benson's from his pocket, slipped one between his pale thin lips and lit it with a gold Dunhill that cost more than our BMW.

His voice was pure London gravel. "Before we go any further, boys…I'll put you out of your misery…Fuller and North are alive."

I considered kissing the old fucker.

He pointed. "Now…you, and I take it you are Cogan?

I nodded.

"You work for the Firm."

"Well, not exactly…"

"Don't argue…I think it appropriate not to fuck me about. In addition to being on your side, I've seen it all, and done it twice, soldier... or should I say, trooper?"

I nodded. Fair enough.

He took a deep drag. "As soon as your two unfortunate colleagues were flown in here tonight, I got the call. It's about all they use me for these days…the Firm that is… keeping friends and relatives happy. You never quite retire from the British Secret Service, see?"

He stubbed his fag under his brogue and went to light a second.

"Now… assuming, the James Dean lookalike leaning on the wall behind me isn't about to cut my throat…?"

The old boy turned to JJ, gave him a grin and offered his hand.

"Turkish Special Forces I believe? Yakim, isn't it?"

The Turk reluctantly took the old guy's hand.

"I am, most definitely, on your side, son," he said reassuringly.

JJ managed a smile and the ice was broken.

We huddled under the ageing hospital canopy and chain-smoked. It turned out Terry, or Tel to his mates, had served twenty-two years as a Royal Marine Commando, He did his first job for the Firm a month after he allegedly retired and was still in the swim at a spritely sixty-nine.

His deep, broad Cockney accent, made him sound like an old East End gangster.

"You lads must be very fuckin' important to old Cartwright, or you wouldn't be here on this little mission of mercy."

JJ took a sharp drag.

"What you mean, Tel?"

"Well…what I mean is…If you weren't such VIP's, the guys that jumped from the Medevac, the ones that picked your pals up from whatever job you were doing, would have been carrying SLP's rather than syringes, and you'd all be in the same body bags as the rest of the poor sods you left behind."

He was right of course. We were off guard at the time the chopper arrived, and if the Firm had wanted everything cleaned up all nice and bonny, me an' JJ would have been expertly double-tapped to the head. Rick and Lauren would have been left to bleed out in the snow, and the Firm's bean counters would have simply stepped over our corpses to take stock of the horseflesh.

That said, as impressed as I was with Terry's knowledge of the workings of the British Secret Service, I still needed more info on Rick and Lauren. I stuffed my pipe into my pocket and felt for the car keys.

"Well if we can't see them tonight, pal, can you give us some kindae idea when we can get a visit? And what condition they're in?"

Terry turned down the corners of his mouth. "You like a drink?"

I nodded.

He pointed toward the car park. "I'll take you to the man who knows."

As we walked over to the Beamer, the old boy shook his head and made some derogatory comment about the car and how we looked more like drug dealers than soldiers. However, he settled himself into the front seat right enough, lit another Benson without asking the question, and began directing us out of Selly Oak, and toward Cannock, cool as the proverbial.

Tel was taking us to a pub called The Lamb and Packet. Apparently, the consultant surgeon who had operated on Rick and Lauren used the place as digs when in the Midlands. The doc was allegedly very keen on his tipple, and equally enamoured with the landlady of the establishment, a reported beauty by the name of Beyza.

JJ sat up and took notice the moment the woman's name was mentioned.

"She is Turkish?" he asked.

Tel turned and gave JJ a cheeky wink.

"Skin like a princess, my friend."

JJ was impressed. "You know this name Beyza? You know what it means?"

"The pale one," Tel answered.

JJ sat back in his seat, pulled his knife from his back pocket and ran it between his bandaged fingers like an old gambler would a dollar. "The whitest child," he said absently.

Tel turned his head and faced the road.

"She's that alright…Come on, Jock, get your foot down, I don't like working after midnight, it interferes with my valuable drinking time."

The Lamb was apparently notorious in medical circles for staying open until the wee small hours. This enabled member of the emergency services to seek solace in a pint after their shift. The doc would be there. Tel was sure of it.

As we pulled up outside the Thirties-built, yellow-tiled corner boozer, my heart sank. It was in darkness.

Tel was undeterred and set off at a marching pace around the back. The old Marine leaned into the door and we were instantly bathed in light and warmth. The place wasn't just open, it was bouncing.

The old boy pushed his way through to the crowded bar as ACDC's *Whole Lotta Rosie* blasted out from unseen speakers. There were dozens of uniforms dotted about. Paramedics, nurses, cops, lots of blue and green. This was a place to relieve your stress, a place to feel at home.

I squeezed in beside the old boy.

"What yer havin' then, Tel?"

He removed his hat. "Well as you're paying, I'll have a pint of Bombardier and a Ballantyne's on the side, son."

I raised my eyebrows. "Where's the doc?"

He pointed. "With the beauty."

Beyza was indeed pale, her skin was in total contrast to her raven hair and large almond eyes. One look at her and you could understand why any man would travel twenty miles out of town to stay in her rather tired backstreet boozer.

She was in deep conversation with a curly-haired guy in his thirties who just had to be the doc. Crisp white shirt, tweed jacket, deffo the upper-class medical type.

I turned to Tel. "That him?"

He nodded and pushed past me. "Get the beers in, Jock. I'll get you an introduction."

I stopped just short of slapping the old git. Instead, I gave our drinks order to a young barmaid with enough facial piercings to start a jeweller's, and watched Tel saunter over to Beyza and the good doctor.

There was some finger pointing in our direction and the doc looked a little deflated. We were, of course, interfering with his precious time off, and probably more importantly, his window of opportunity with the beautiful Beyza.

I'd have been pissed too, believe me.

Finally, Tel waved us over.

ACDC had given way to Whitesnake as I stumbled across the bar doing my best not to spill my Guinness.

The second I got to the doctor, Tel was off to enjoy his drinks, his job done.

JJ squeezed in alongside me. The doc looked us both up and down before raising his glass. Pissed as the loudest fart in Birmingham, he boomed,

"To the British Secret Service."

Lauren North's Story:

One hundred and eight stitches to repair my leg and thirty-seven to my abdomen.

The curly headed Irish doctor that had 'fixed me' as he put it, was confident that my abdominal injuries caused by Dougie McGinnis's final bullet, were 'minor' and would 'sort themselves out'.

Easy for him to say…my gut was agony, the merest sideways movement in my bed sent lightning bolts of pain through me, and I began to dread toilet visits.

My leg was easier to deal with as I couldn't feel most of it, but according to the most flirtatious doctor I'd had the misfortune to meet since my thankfully ex-husband, this was 'more of a worry'.

They'd managed to get my renal system up and running to somewhere close to ninety percent after my kidneys failed, and I was still drinking my own bodyweight in bottled water to keep the nurses happy.

Rick visited me two or three times a day in his wheelchair.

He didn't care for my Ironside jokes and failed spectacularly to remember our kiss.

I, however, had not.

He was having issues with both his hip and just like me, his intestines. The flexor area where the round had shattered against his pelvic bone was giving him untold grief. However, just like my good self, this was nothing compared to the pain in his abdomen.

Unfortunately, the damage to Rick's intestines had warranted the fitting of a colostomy bag. The flirty doctor had assured him that this was a temporary measure, but Rick looked so ashamed of it, I thought he may tear it out.

By the end of week seven, we were both physically on the mend. Rick moved us to a private clinic on the outskirts of Farnborough to finish our recuperation. He had a yearning for Egyptian cotton sheets and lobster bisque. The place was a palace in all but name.

I'd like to have said I was as good as new, but I'd have been lying. Yes, my stitches were out, and I was walking short distances with the aid of a stick, but nothing prepares you for capture, and for the first time in my life, I understood how sometimes, for some prisoners, survival becomes harder than the alternative.

As I'd dangled by my wrists, slowly bleeding to death in that barn, Seamus and Dougie lewdly fondling my naked body, I almost begged for the end.

There were times when I thought I would be raped repeatedly; times when the pain was just too much.

If I'm being truly honest with you, some days in rehab, I felt so broken inside, that nothing would ever fix me.

I knew I had PTSD. Fuck, I'd had the dreams, the flashbacks; they were one thing, but my waking life had become a much scarier nightmare.

I was improving. The meds helped, no doubt. Yet in the two previous weeks, everything, and I mean everything I did had to be evaluated for risk. Every time I entered a room, familiar or not, I looked for an escape route. I opened every cupboard and checked every space large enough to conceal a person. Once I was inside the place, I sat with my back to the wall. Once outside, I found myself checking every registration plate in the visitor's car park, just in case there was an Irish number in there.

Spring was poking its nose out of its winter blanket, and I spent hours in the stunning gardens, reading endless pulp fiction. Yet the slightest noise sent me schizoid and I found myself shaking uncontrollably whilst scanning the horizon for potential kidnappers.

Rick had been fabulous. I had been pampered within an inch of my life, and although we hadn't had the conversation, I knew things had changed between us. There was no point in beating around the bush anymore. I was falling in love with him.

Rick Fuller's Story:

The first time I experienced being shot was in Ireland. I'd been in the army less than a year. Brand new, straight out of the box.

I'd been sent out on foot patrol with a far more experienced paratrooper by the name of Wilson, a bull of a man, barrel-chested, flat-knuckled, a streetfighter who stank of booze at eight in the morning.

It was Wilson's third tour and he absolutely fucking loved it. For him, it was an excuse to indulge in the two things that mattered to him most, drinking and fighting. He'd take any fucker on. It didn't matter who you were, or more to the point in question, where you were. He'd still have a tear up.

On the long foot-patrols most blokes got to know their partner quite well, but even back then, I was never one for small talk. I do remember Wilson's dream was to leave the army and buy his own truck. I don't know if he ever got one. Come to think of it, I'd be lying if I said I knew if he came back from Ireland alive or dead.

On the day in question, we were on the Shankhill Road, the area of Belfast where the Loyalist Protestants felt safest. Our job was to make them feel even safer, and for the most part, we were welcomed with open arms; even cups of tea and the odd slab of cake were offered. It was a direct opposite to the Falls Road, where the Republican Catholics often greeted you by emptying the contents of their chamber pots over you from the upstairs windows.

As a naive kid, I didn't understand the politics, or the religious divides in Northern Ireland. I had no idea why the Protestants hated the Catholics. I'd been brought up in a kid's home in London, where we all just lived together, with no idea who was Catholic, Protestant, Jewish, Hindu, Buddhist or whatever. You may have knocked seven bells out of each other on a Friday night, but it was more likely to be over a girl or the football, rather than Allah or Jesus.

I watched Wilson's back as we strolled along the road in the sun. We must have looked a right pair. Wilson doing a fair impression of a bulldog, whilst I was just a skinny-necked kid with acne and a fucking big gun.

We passed Frizzell's fish shop, above which the UDA held regular meetings.

The Ulster Defence Association was the largest of the loyalist paramilitary groups and undertook killings of Catholic civilians and PIRA players throughout the Troubles. Despite their obvious involvement in terror activities, the UDA were regarded as a legal organisation by the British and were not banned as a terrorist group until 1992.

Once again, as a raw recruit, I failed to grasp the politics of the situation.

All I knew was, if you walked by Frizzell's at the right moment, the owner would sometimes chuck you a bag of chips and scraps of batter. For a young, permanently hungry squaddie like me, this was a godsend.

The chip shop was to become infamous some years later when the PIRA bombed it in an attempt to kill the UDA men who still met upstairs. In typical terrorist fashion, they missed their targets. They did however, manage to slaughter eight civilians and wound thirty others.

On this day, however, smelling the frying chips as I passed, I looked longingly inside, but this was not my lucky day.

I remember we were passing this row of houses, when some fucker's front door flew open. Out fell a woman with a fat lip and her blouse all ripped. Her old man followed instantly and started to slap her about a bit.

He was a big fucker, all string vest and tweed trousers. Some neighbours watched the show from their windows, whilst others ventured to their front doors. No one attempted to stop the man from showing his missus the error of her ways. Even at my tender age, I got the impression this was a regular incident, and that the locals regarded String Vest as a man not to be messed with.

Nobody, however, had mentioned this to Wilson.

He turned to me, his droopy black moustache twitching with excitement. "Here, son, just take hold of me SLR will yer, whilst I sort this twat."

Now, this was not a good idea. I had my own weapon to contend with and holding a second would render me well armed but totally defenceless.

Wilson's eyes burned into me; I was a sprog, a rookie, I had no choice.

By the time I'd sorted myself out and rested Wilson's weapon on the deck, he was striding over to String Vest, beckoning him over with his balled fist.

The guy hadn't even noticed us. He was too busy ripping the clothes off his wife's back, as she tried to evade his clutches. Now in this day and age, it isn't unusual to see a woman with a tattoo, but back then, the sight of a female with a large red rose emblazoned on her breast was as rare as rocking horse shit.

At my age, I hadn't seen too many bare boobs either and I stood transfixed at the sight of the now topless woman as she began to put some distance between herself and her attacker.

Seconds later, Wilson caught up with his man.

There were lots of tough lads in the military, and over the years, I've met a few, but Wilson was as hard as they came. He set about String Vest with both fists, bobbing and weaving like the boxer he was, slamming each blow into his opponent's body with murderous force, knocking the wind out of the big Irishman. Then he found his range and went for the man's head. The sickening sounds of knuckle on bone reverberated against the walls of the tight terraced street. Most men would have gone down under such a sustained beating, but String Vest was still up there. His nose was broken, along with a rib or two, and he staggered briefly as he spat out a bloody tooth, but there he was, still standing and beginning to throw a punch or two of his own. Wilson had picked on the local hard man.

The whole street was out, enthralled by the contest. Nobody noticed the battered Ford Cortina Estate swing into the Shankhill Road, three up. If the driver had been a little more relaxed and not caused the slightest squeal of tyres as he made his turn, neither would I.

The boy put his boot down and I heard the old engine complain. As the car accelerated, my hackles rose. Squinting against the low evening sun, I readied my weapon. The old Ford was heading straight for the crowd. Men women and children, all gathered together to watch what was an Irish pastime, a bare-knuckle boxing match. The back windows of the car were rolled down, and as it drew ever closer to the onlookers, I saw the unmistakable sight of an Armalite rifle poke out of the offside.

During my initial training, I'd always wondered how I would react in a real drama. I considered shouting to Wilson, but he was a good fifteen yards from me, gripping his opponent in a headlock and punching him repeatedly.

The crowd were cheering and encouraging both men. I ignored them and focused on the car. As I brought my weapon up into the aim, I heard a voice in my head. It was my commanding officer as he drilled us with our rules of engagement. *Never fire at, or from, a moving vehicle*, he was saying.

Fuck that.

I clicked off the safety and put four rounds into the front screen of the Cortina. It veered first left, then right as the driver lost control. The sound of gunfire was not lost on the good people of the Shankill, they knew it only too well, and the crowd began to dive for cover, their interest in the street fight temporarily forgotten.

As the car closed on the gathering, the boy in the back seat let go with the automatic rifle. It was totally random, the car was all over the road, but even so, some of his rounds found human targets, and, for the first time in my life, I heard the screams of the wounded and dying.

Wilson had released his foe and was sprinting toward his weapon as it lay useless on the pavement. He would be too late.

With an almighty crash, the Cortina ploughed into a lamppost, the driver exited via the front screen, already dead from my head shots, but the two boys in the back forced open their doors and rolled out onto the cobbles.

The guy with the Armalite came out firing.

For a split second, I caught his eye. He had that look about him, the same look I saw every time I examined my own face in the mirror. There was something missing in there. Fear maybe? No, it wasn't that, although, even to this day, I can clearly remember the boy showed none.

No, he was missing something else, something I have always had trouble with, he was missing emotion, that was it…emotion.

As the kid drew closer, I found my sight picture and pulled the trigger on my SLR putting two in his chest. I watched his legs buckle under him. The third player ran back along the street in an attempt to escape, but he was chased by the crowd. Within seconds, they became a baying, angry mob.

I stood looking at the blood pooling around the kid with the rifle. Wilson took hold of my bicep and I instinctively stepped back away from him.

"Whoa there, son," he said. "Look…" He pointed at my left shoulder. "You caught one, pal; you've been shot."

The kid that ran away was Sean Patrick Connell. He was seventeen, one of a family of eight. They found his naked body in the gutter four streets away. No one was ever charged with his murder. The boy with the Armalite was a year older, Donal Greenhalgh. He killed two and wounded three more. His youngest victim was a kiddie of six, Peter Black. The boy was out walking with his family when he was caught by one of Greenhalgh's stray rounds.

I will never forget the sight of his mother rocking him in her arms as he bled to death before he could be treated.

Since that day, I have seen that little kid's face thousands of times in my dreams. Whenever I hear of another child dying needlessly, he has always been the one to visit me in the small hours.

Some would comment that I've been a basket case from age nine, a care-home kid, but what I saw and did that day changed me forever. The saying, 'only the good die young,' is a big fat fucking lie.

People die for any number of reasons, good, bad, young, old. Wrong place, wrong time.

Me, I needed eleven stitches, and they gave me a fucking medal I didn't want.

My latest injury however, was a different matter. It had been twenty-seven years since the Shankhill Road shooting, and my rate of recovery was taking far longer than back in that day. The doctor kindly informed me that I would never sprint the same again, but jogging was okay.

Jogging? Fuck off.

It had been over seven weeks and I could just about walk. At least I'd lost the bag and could visit the toilet naturally again.

I'd spent a lot of time stretching my groin area and working my upper body in the gym.

That said, I used up far more time watching Lauren North.

I found myself sitting in the beautifully manicured gardens as she read book after book. She was as stunning as ever, yet somehow, a shadow of her former self.

Thinking back, shooting O'Donnell at such close quarters was a big thing for her. Then, of course, we'd started our business, and had just settled into some form of normality when the Firm came calling, we were back in the thick of it, and she had been captured.

In all my years in the Army, I had never been taken. It had always been one of my greatest fears, and as I watched her read her latest novel in the morning sunshine, I wondered how I would have coped. Lauren had survived. She had used all her training and natural guile to outwit the Irish and to come out the other side. But she had lost something over there. They had taken a part of her away.

I watched her, engrossed in her story, yet as each new car arrived in the carpark, she eyed it suspiciously. If someone approached, she became increasingly tense until they passed by.

Time heals, they say.

I lay back on my chair. The birds sang, and as I dozed in the warmth of the noon sun, right on cue, the boy Peter Black from the Shankill paid me a visit.

Some things, time can't fix.

"Do you always talk in your sleep?"

Lauren was standing over me, hands on hips, silhouetted by the sunshine. I took a moment to grasp reality, shaded my eyes so I could see her face and shrugged.

"I don't know, I sleep alone."

She stepped sideways bathing me in the heat of the day.

"I'm not surprised," she said.

I managed a sarcastic smile.

"Always ready with a compliment eh? What was I saying?"

"Oh, I don't know…you were eating chips and fizzy something."

I half closed my eyes and nodded.

"Ah, the Shankhill, Frizzell's chip shop…the old boy who owned it used to throw me the odd bag of free chips when I was on patrol there."

Lauren grabbed a chair and sat. She rested her chin on her hands.

"When exactly was this?"

I blew out my cheeks. "I was nineteen, I think."

"And you still dream of his chips?"

I sat up and rubbed the top of my head with my palms, in no mood to explain further.

"They were good chips."

Lauren eyed me, her face a mixture of disbelief and mischief.

"Whatever…anyway…talking of food…"

"Yes?"

The words almost tumbled from her mouth. It was as if she'd been holding them in there for so long, she was unable to keep them contained a second longer.

"I want you to take me to dinner."

"You do?"

"Yes, I do. Somewhere nice, and not here, back in Manchester. In fact, I want to leave here soon."

"Soon?"

"Yes soon. I've had enough physio, enough psycho…enough of here. I'm not going to get any better in this environment. I need normality, to get back home, to get back to work.

Please, Rick, take me home…take me to dinner."

I took in her beauty for a moment.

"Okay," I said.

Des Cogan's Story:

I'd been staying over with JJ and Grace on and off for over six weeks. On the first day JJ and I returned from Birmingham, Grace had insisted I crash there until Rick and Lauren were up and about. I had to admit I enjoyed the company, especially the wee boy Kaya, who was a real character and reminded me so much of myself at the same age, always getting into scrapes.

With the news that the pair would soon be out of rehab, I paid a visit to my flat with the intention of moving back in the next day.
Sorting through the three-day pile of mail behind the door, I found a letter with a Glasgow postmark.
I was required to attend the reading of Anne's will, at McCauley and Partners Solicitors, Byres Road, West Glasgow, day after tomorrow.
I must say, this information led to an uncomfortable couple of days. Grace picked up on my mood, but I kept my counsel.

I always take the train to the city. Its quick, easy and a sensible price if you don't mind cattle class.
The train arrived at Glasgow Central on time, and I took a cab to the lawyer's offices, one of many on the street. The reading was due at 1230hrs and as I stepped out into a rare sunny Glasgow day, I was twenty minutes early.
I had a quick look up and down the street, found a wee independent coffee shop, bought a latte to go and stood outside McCauley and Partners' gaff, having a smoke on my pipe.

Just after 1220hrs, a nice shiny new Audi convertible with the top down pulled up in front of me. Driving was a middle-aged, bleached blonde, with most of her tits on show. Sitting in the passenger seat, was none other than Anne's widower, Donald.
He was so in awe of the driver's ample assets, he didn't even notice me standing in the doorway. The woman gave Donald a wee peck on the cheek as he stepped out onto the pavement, almost bumping into me.
"Alright there, Donald?" I said with a knowing smile, blowing smoke in his direction.

He took on the look of a hare in the headlights, before regaining some of his composure. "Still not packed in the fags then?" he said glibly.

I pushed my pipe into my pocket and gestured toward the convertible being parked over the road.

"Seems I'm not the only one with a bad habit though eh, Donald?"

He turned down the corners of his mouth. "I don't see how Mary is any of your business," he snapped.

"No?" I countered. "Really, pal? Is that right? Well I'll have you know, I think it is ma fuckin business. My Anne is hardly cold in her grave, and you're swanning about with Marilyn Monroe there."

Donald saw my anger rising. I'll say this, I always had the guy down as a decent sort. Even though he'd fucked off with my missus, I still didn't bear him a grudge, but this? This felt fucking wrong.

Donald's tone was conciliatory. "I know what you're thinking, Des, but look, you must understand that Anne was ill for a very long time. Be honest, you were only there for her final hours. I'd nursed her for months." He looked over toward the approaching blonde. "Me and Mary are just good friends, that's all."

I shook my head. I was ready for punching him right in his smug kipper. "Aye right, of course you are. Funny how you both have a nice wee suntan there eh? You didnae get that walking around Strathclyde Park did ye, pal?"

The woman was getting closer. Donald hopped from foot to foot. "Be reasonable here, Des. A man has needs, you know?"

I prodded the wee jobbie in the chest. "Needs you say? I'll show you fucking needs, pal. Remember our chat in the garden, the day Anne died? Remember you said you couldn't put her out of her pain, because it was a sin…against the Commandments ye said…remember that, pal?"

Donald's voice was no more than a whisper. "Yes, I remember, but…"

I got right in his face. "But fuckin' nothing, Donald. Unless my bible class was seriously flawed, adultery is firmly on that list, eh?"

The blonde reached us. "Everything all right here, Donald?" she said in a sing-song Edinburgh accent.

I turned, and gave her a big beaming smile.

"Everything's fine here…Mary, isn't it?" I held out a hand which she took. "I'm Des, an old friend of the family…did you and Donald have a nice wee holiday, hen?"

The woman relaxed instantly. "Oh, aye, we did so, Des, thank you." The girl wasn't backward in coming forward, I'll give her that. Attending the reading of the will of a woman whose husband you'd obviously been shagging for some time, was bare-faced cheek. "Barbados is lovely this time of year, Des…you should go yourself," she cooed.

I could have slapped her. Instead, I kept up the smile and nodded toward her ample cleavage. "Well, you've a bonny tan on ye, I'll say that, Mary."

She placed a hand over her chest, pretended to be coy, and turned to her lover. "We need to go inside now, Donald, it's nearly time."

I gave them both another look at my shiny new gnashers. "Why don't we all go inside together eh?"

The office was a small affair. Three chairs were set out, and a portly woman, who I knew to be Anne's Aunt Bessie from Cork, took up one seat. The other two were obviously for Donald and me. I have to say I was shocked at the lack of other relations, but it was obviously Anne's choice.

Mary stood looking uncomfortable and disgruntled in equal amounts. The brief who was about to start the reading was blunt. "Are you a relative, Mrs…?"

"McGowan," said Mary, filling the gap. "No, I'm just here to support Donald… as a friend."

"Aye right," snorted Bessie. The old girl was obviously as pleased to see Mary as I was.

"Well, I'm sorry, Ms. McGowan," said the brief stonily. "But I'll have to ask you to wait outside during the proceedings."

Mary looked crestfallen, but realising she had no choice, turned on her heels and was out of the door.

Bessie turned to Donald and gave him a look that would have turned most to salt. "A pity we can't do the same with you…you fuckin' bollocks," she spat.

I gave the old girl a smile, we all sat, and the will was read.

Bessie had been left a portrait, some china and some silver, which seemed to please her.

There was over thirty grand in a savings account, that was going to Donald. It seemed like he'd expected that. I reckoned he'd already spent most of it on a car and a holiday.

Then the brief turned to me.

"Mr Cogan," he began, "It was Anne's wish that the dwelling, known as Hillside Cottage and all its contents are left to you."

My mouth must have dropped open. Donald's chin hit the fuckin' rug.

"That can't be right," blurted Donald, standing up, attempting to see the will itself.

The brief was cool as a cucumber, obviously used to these kinds of antics at readings.

"Sit down, sir," he boomed. Then turning again to me, he said, "Copies of the deeds will be sent to your home address, Mr Cogan. The property is mortgage free and there can be no challenge to this ruling as your ex-wife owned the property outright. There is also a letter from Anne that she wished me to pass to you. I will send that along with the legal documents." The guy stood. "That is all, and I'll bid you all a good day."

Donald flew into a rage.

"This is a damned disgrace I tell you," he bellowed. "A disgrace I say."

The noise attracted Mary from downstairs and she stuck her orange face around the door.

"Is everything alright, Donald?" she asked worriedly.

I stood, pushed past the blonde and said, "Everything is fucking peachy, Mary."

Lauren North's Story:

When I saw my white Audi RS6 parked outside the rehab centre, my stomach did a little flip. I'd had to hide the car away after we used it to chase the three Irish through the streets of Manchester. The boys obviously deemed the car useable again, but as glad as I was to see my most expensive purchase to date in pristine condition, I was even more thrilled to see Des and JJ leaning against it.

Rick struggled with his luggage as he negotiated the steps to the car. Neither Des nor JJ moved or offered to help him. They both knew he was still in pain and his injuries were causing him grief.

Nonetheless, they watched him fight with his matching Louis Vuitton numbers, pointed, made very un-PC cracks about old men and cripples, and smoked. I was unsure which annoyed Rick most, but I was glad the boys were on form.

My single case and I fared better than the big fella, as my physical injuries were in far better shape than the inside of my head. The grand steps negotiated, I was hugged by both boys, and told how good I looked.

I eyed them both suspiciously. "Why are you being so nice?"

JJ shrugged. "You want we call you cripple too?"

Rick was at my shoulder, "Fuck off, JJ…" He turned to Des. "and you …you Scotch twat…"

The Scot was beaming, secretly bursting that he had his best pal back. "Now, now, less of the 'Scotch.' As you well know, Scotch is a fiery wee tipple named thus by you Anglophiles, unlike the correct term for us superior beings, which is Scot or Scottish.

'Scotch' has no bearing whatsoever on the fine race of people living north of the wall that Italian bloke built…So fuck off yersel, ye bollocks."

Rick dropped into the back seat, slammed the door like a petulant child and muttered away to himself. If there was something I'd learned about Richard Fuller, it was that until he was back in physical shape, he would be murder.

I gave Des a second look. He was looking well…really well. He'd dropped a few pounds, sported a tan, he'd visited a barber, and wasn't wearing his usual Marks and Sparks numbers.

I cocked my head. "You are looking…fit, Desmond."

He smiled to reveal his new, now permanent teeth, after he too had suffered at the hands of Dougie McGinnis.

"I have been getting some in, like."

JJ pushed forward and gave me a theatrical wink. "Desmond has joined a gym," he said.

I raised an eyebrow. The Scot was an unlikely health club member. "A gym?"

Before Des could explain, JJ was in there like swimwear with the gossip. "Lauren, this place is more than a gym, it is health club, private health club, many women there, you know what I say?"

I locked eyes with the Scot. "I see, and has our celibate Scottish friend been making use of *all* the facilities at this club?"

Des smiled, his natural embarrassment almost hidden by his pride. "Actually, it was Grace, JJ's missus, who suggested it like. I think she was gettin' fed up with me loiterin' round at their place."

I heard Rick bellow a huge 'Ha!' from inside the car.

Des ignored the grump.

His smile fell away. "She kindae told me I should be out living a bit, you know? After everything with Anne and that, she said it was time for me to meet new people."

"She's right," I said.

Des's smile returned and lit up his face. I couldn't help but love him.

"Well," he said. "I did, I joined, and it's no' bad."

I looked into his sparkling eyes.

How could such a lovely kind guy not have someone?"

Rick knocked on the window of the car and gestured us to hurry.

And how come I always pick the difficult one?

I ignored Mr Happy.

"And…and have you met anyone?"

Des pulled up the collar on his polo shirt.

"I may have been a trifle fortunate in the female company department of late."

I hadn't seen Des since we left Birmingham for Farnborough, and it was so good to see him smile.

However, JJ was listening intently, and couldn't help himself. "She a stripper," he gabbled.

Even Rick couldn't contain himself at this news. He opened the car door and descended into howls of comic laughter.

Des scowled. "She's no' a stripper!"

For a briefest moment, my heart went out to the Scot. I was just about to feel sorry for him and admonish the other two for being so cruel, when Des burst into fits of laughter himself.

"She's…she's… a professional lap dancer."

Des cupped his hands suggestively in front of his chest and |I got the picture.

The banter continued as we drove. It felt good to have the team together again. More to the point, I felt good.

After an hour of motorway, the car fell quiet and I reached over to Rick and took his hand.

He didn't flinch, now, I felt marvellous.

The lads dropped me at my flat. I stood stock still at the garden gate whilst my car disappeared out of sight, leaving me with nothing but the birdsong for company.

I listened for a moment before setting off along the path to the front door, dragging my case with me. Within three strides, I began to shake. By the time I made the porch, my legs were jelly and it took three attempts for me to punch in my entry code.

My pulse was banging in my head, my breathing equally rapid, and I knew I was having a panic attack. People who have never experienced this phenomenon are lucky. Even though you know what is happening, and the chances are you're physically fine, within seconds, your body convinces you you're fucking dying.

As my legs appeared to have given up the ghost, I clambered the stairs on my hands and knees, leaving my suitcase in the hall. Struggling to open my flat door, I dropped my keys for a second time and cried out in frustration.

Finally, I was inside.

Doing my best to control my breathing I staggered to the kitchen for a glass of water. Eventually remembering I'd turned off all the utilities before I'd left the last time, I fumbled with the stop cock under the sink.

The water ran grey for a few moments before the glass filled with clear liquid. I drank greedily.

Peering out of the kitchen window, I hoped against hope the view would relax me. The front lawn had been cut, the gardener had potted pansies, yet all I imagined were men in suits with guns, talking into radios and pointing toward my flat.

I stepped away, found my bag, and inside it the small packet of pills given to me by my doctor. I threw two into my mouth and finished the remaining water before wandering to my bed.

Within minutes, the drug did its job, and I slept.

Rick Fuller's Story:

The drive seemed to take forever, but I was finally home. I'd had to find alternative accommodation after Goldsmith and his crew managed to sell my old apartment on the Quays, but after weeks of searching, I discovered a stunning three-bed penthouse in Bowden. It was a fully managed house within a house, enclosed in what had been a country manor, a great lock and leave.
I loved the roof terrace and the fact it had secure parking for the Aston and MV Augusta.
The décor, however, was far too fussy.
Still, beggars couldn't be choosers and as my budget had been limited to £450,000, I couldn't complain.
The moment I stepped inside, I changed into my running gear and set off to take in the sights of Devisdale. I was particularly pleased with my latest Asics runners, they had a lime green flash which matched my Nike joggers perfectly
My doctor had insisted I should jog every day. He, however, didn't have to go through the pain, which was shocking even on the flat. Negotiating steps…don't even mention steps.
I ran as hard as I could past Denzel House, which had once been owned by a guy who died fighting the Zulus, and followed the tracks that ran through the historic grounds. Bowden Wakes had been held here since the seventeenth century. Heading out toward the forest, I turned up my iPod and found encouragement from Don Henley's *Boys of Summer*.
Running made my problems feel small and insignificant against the towering history that surrounded me.
I fell into the rhythm of the ex-Eagles drummer and drank in the warm early evening air. The pain in my hip faded and I hit autopilot.

My mind, however, took me back to another place. To the night all this got started.
To May 1997.

Cathy had been gone six months, and I'd run north, to Manchester. I was a drunk, and a paranoid one at that. I needed to hide, just as much as I needed to seek.

My shrinking bank account was not going to cover the bills so I needed a job. But before I could even consider sticking my head above the parapet, I knew I had to buy a new name, passport, driving licence, National Insurance number, the lot. Once I had that, I could work under the radar.

Five grand later, I had become Stephen Colletti, but the Greek who'd sorted it all out for me had cleaned me out.

I'd worked some doors, but was drunker than most of the punters, which didn't go well.

Finally, I'd got a break and bumped into a guy I'd done a couple of ops with back in the day. He gave me the number of an agency who wouldn't ask too many questions, and as a result, I got some body-guarding work. Nothing big or clever, but, I was thankful for small mercies and all that. As I'd been drinking straight from the bottle most days, and topping up in the local bars at night, I was lucky to be in work at all. The job paid the rent and put clothes on my back, so it was good enough for me.

By the night in question, I'd done eight or nine babysitting jobs for them, and been dry for almost a month. Sobriety, however, did little for my irrational behaviour, and away from work, I spent countless hours frantically searching for any information that might draw me closer to the man responsible for Cathy's death. The man, who I now know, was Patrick O'Donnell.

This night, I was in the Hacienda club on Whitworth Street West, Manchester.

I'd been given the job of guarding some no-mark actor, Ronald Cruise, (no relation.) Ronnie, as he preferred, had heard from his posh mates in London that Manchester was as rough as a bear's backside, so his 'people' booked me, to carry his man bag. It paid okay, but nowhere near enough.

My, would-be 'soap star,' had been recording a bit part for ITV in Salford, and wanted to visit the so-called 'iconic' Hacienda venue, so he could tell his luvvies in London how fucking 'cool' he was. He was one of those people back then who used his fingers to make stupid quotation marks as he spoke. I instantly hated him and wanted to cut his throat.

I remember the place was a shithole. It had been something to do with Tony Wilson back in the day. Allegedly, New Order's record sales had kept the place afloat for a while, but recent, well-publicised violent incidents had all but finished the place.

As it turned out, I was about to deliver another.

This was the night that I took my first steps into the criminal underworld, a place I was to stay for another nine, very profitable years. Thinking about it, that £450k I'd just spent on a flat in need of decoration, came from those ill-gotten gains.

A major contributor to those very coffers was a man called Joel Davies.

To most of the outside world, he was a bona fide businessman; an antique dealer of international renown. His business made him millions, yet Joel had a dark side. He supplied cocaine, amphetamine and cannabis to a major part of the city of Manchester.

This too made him rich.

It also made him very fucking dangerous.

I didn't know who he was when he arrived in the Hacienda that night. It was obvious he was a face, as the door staff almost kissed his arse as he walked in. Add to that, he was dressed in a pale pink Armani silk suit, and flanked my two flat-nosed knuckle-draggers. I instantly got the picture. The only thing missing was the word 'gangster' tattooed on his forehead.

To be honest, I was so bored watching my actor pal chewing his own face off after he'd dropped his third E, I really didn't give a fuck.

It seemed every player in the bar knew who Davies was, and what he did, except of course, my TV star chum, who is completely off his head.

The DJ sticks *Billy Jean* on the decks, just as Joel walks by, and my dumb bastard actor only throws half a pint of Strongbow and black over his pink number whilst trying to fucking moonwalk.

There was momentary chaos as Knuckle-dragger One started to dab the incandescent Joel with a bar towel and number two launched himself in the direction of my charge.

Now, my client may have been a twat, he may have been talentless, and he certainly couldn't moonwalk, but nonetheless he was my twat, and I was being remunerated to ensure his physical safety.

I chopped number two Dragger to the throat, and he went down gurgling like a drain.

I then did what all good bodyguards do, grabbed my useless actor by the neck, got him to the door and pushed him outside into a waiting cab.

Job done?

Oh no.

By the time the taxi sped away, both Joel's muscle boys were on the pavement and within touching distance. To add to my woes, it was looking like one of the bouncers fancied it too.

Three to one in a street fight are never good odds. I realise that in the films, the hero usually manages to win the day using all his Kung Fu moves, but actually, three six-foot-five lumps, onto one, often means the solitary chap gets a kicking.

My only thought was the nearest guy. Drop him, then worry about the next one. He came to grab my leather jacket with his ham of a fist, but I stepped away and he lost balance for a second. It was enough time for me to slip to the side and kick his legs from under him. It's a technique used a lot in judo, but not many think about it in a brawl. It works a treat. The guy cried out in shock, did his best to break his fall with his hands, failed miserably and landed flat on his back on the flagstones. I added to his misery by penalty-kicking him in the jaw with my Timberlands.

Number two guard was the guy I'd already chopped in the throat and I could see in his eyes he didn't fancy it now his pal was bleeding all over Whitworth Street West.

I was about to go in with my head when Joel barrelled out of the door and everything stopped.

He stood in the middle of the street in his pink fucking trousers and a black shirt and started to lay down the law to his minions.

I could barely stifle my laughter.

Then he turned to me.

"You," he said. "I want a fucking word with you, at the bar…now."

I shrugged. "Fair enough."

Joel was a bull of a man, and was possibly the hairiest bloke I'd ever seen. I found it difficult to take my eyes from his Adam's apple. It was bigger than your average walnut and it danced between his chin and the hirsute abyss of his chest as he spoke.

"Fuckin' amateurs," he bawled over the shitty Indie dirge the DJ had started to play.

"Who?" I said.

Joel turned his head, his eyes bulged, his face red with anger.

"Who? Those fuckin' morons outside, that's fuckin' who."

I shrugged. "Either you don't know the right people or you don't pay enough."

He glared at me. "Really? So, who the fuck are you then?"

I met his eye "A professional."

Joel laughed. "You got some bottle, I'll say that…tell you what…Mr Fuckin Professional…you do a little job for me, and they'll be more work for you. And I'll pay the right money."

"What are the terms exactly?"

He smiled to reveal expensive teeth. "Guy in here, right now, in this bar, owes me ten large for some sniff I provided for him and his celeb friends. He's a slow payer, get me the ten and I'll drop you five hundred."

"I take twenty-five percent of the whole sum I recover."

Joel almost spat out his Peroni. "You want two-and-a-half grand for a simple muscle job?"

"Who said I'd just get you ten?"

Joel raised his brows and pointed a stubby finger.

"Now I like the sound of that. Okay, clever boy…Freddy Garratt's over there, table on the left, blonde bird with her tongue in his ear."

Freddy was indeed lounging at a table with a very plastic blonde, a typical Altringham boy, the type who enjoyed slumming it with the working classes.

He was flying, on cloud ten. The poor sod was probably so stoned he'd forgotten he owed the most feared gangster in Manchester money in the first place.

I sat without being asked. His blonde lifted a silver case from her bag and started chopping a line out for herself, there and then on the table, oblivious of the violence in the air and fuck the consequences.

She looked up, saw me and said, "Sorry, did you want one, darling?"
Me? I am the epitome of polite viciousness. I ignore the
entertainment and go straight for the money man.
"Mr Davies's ten grand, Freddy? You got it or what?"
Freddy shrugged his shoulders, bent forward and devoured the line
his girl had just chopped. She turned to him, considered complaining
for a moment, thought better of it and started the process again. It
seemed there was a constant supply of the Bolivian marching
powder.
I was about to ensure her lover-boy paid for it.
Freddy wiped his nose, dabbed what remained of the line with a wet
finger and rubbed the last of the drug on his gums.
"I told Davies, I'd pay at the end of the month. He knows I'm good
for it."
I promptly hated him even more than my failed TV star I'd just
shoved in a cab.
Much to my annoyance, the prick wasn't finished.
"Now," he slurred. "I don't know who you are, and quite frankly, I
don't give a fuck, so off you go and tell your boss that I'll pay next
week or something."
He flicked the fingers of his left hand toward me as if brushing some
fluff from his sleeve. "Go on, trot on, sonny."
Freddy's left hand interested me more than he knew.
I stood, smiled politely and said, "I'll tell him that, Freddy."

Joel had moved away to the far side of the bar and was in deep
conversation with a young Chinese guy. He looked up, saw me and
waved me over.
"So, where's my ten, clever boy?" he says, all cocksure of himself.
"What car does Freddy drive? I said, unimpressed.
Joel shrugged. "Last I saw, was a Bentley Continental."
I turned on my heels and slid out of the door.
The bouncer, who minutes earlier had been fancying his chances
with me on Whitworth Street West, eyed me with suspicion.
I stepped in close and stuck fifty quid in his jacket pocket.

"You go in there and tell that fuckin' hooray Henry, Freddy, that the
alarm on his Bentley is annoying the neighbours, okay?"

He looked like a puzzled bullfrog. "Freddy? You mean the guy with the blonde bird?"

"That's him, son."

"Now?"

"You want the fifty or not?"

"Yeah."

"Now, then."

At that, he turned and disappeared into the club.

I scanned the street and sure enough a nice shiny black Continental was parked not fifty yards away.

Stepping across the road to my own very modest VW, I rooted in the boot until I found what I wanted, then sprinted to the Bentley and gave it a swift kick to the rear light cluster.

The car started to howl like a wounded banshee.

Sure enough, out came Freddy, all concerned for his pride and joy.

He was so out of it, he was zig-zagging down the road, whilst trying to point his expensive remote at the British marque and shut off the alarm.

Finally, he made the driver's door. The sap still hadn't seen me standing at the boot.

I took three steps, grabbed his left wrist, tore a gold Rolex from it and quickly slipped it in my pocket. Then, lifting his hand upward, I twisted it into the position I needed. Freddy tried to focus on my face. He should have been looking at my hands.

I found the pair of tin snips in my jacket.

I don't think Freddie even felt me cut off his little finger at the second knuckle.

Back inside the bar, Joel was holding court with faces from around the town. Never one for publicity, I caught his eye and waited for him to sidle over.

Once in a quiet corner, I pushed a plastic bag into his pocket.

"If you can't get twenty large for that lot, you are in the wrong game, Davies… You got my five on you now?"

He pulled out the bag. Even Joel winced when he saw the claret pooled in the bottom. That said, he quickly recovered and closely inspected the watch.

"Nice," he said, before eyeing the ring on Freddy's severed digit. It was platinum, with three solitaires, twenty grand all day long. He gave me a knowing look and offered,

"I'll give you three."

I was losing patience.

"The Rolex is a Sky-Dweller, worth twenty-five grand alone. Give me the bag back, and I'll give you your ten."

Joel smirked, pushed the bag in one pocket and pulled out a wad of notes that would choke a horse from the other. He slowly peeled off my five grand, making a show of what a big hard, rich gangster he was.

You see, guys like Davies needed people like me, people who could make him look ruthless, people who would spread fear around the city.

The thought of Freddy sitting on the pavement outside, with a paramedic looking up and down the street for his finger, made Joel's dick hard. That, and the sure knowledge that Freddy would now never dare tell a soul how or why he went on to acquire the nickname 'Four-finger Fred.'

I pulled a twenty from the stash, wrote my untraceable number on it and gave it him back.

"Name's Colletti," I said. "Stephen Colletti."

Davies pushed it in his pink trousers, and I went for a late dinner with his money.

Am I the same person now as I was then? I don't call myself Colletti anymore, but that's for you to decide.

I opened the door to my home, sweating from my run. The wound to my groin ached and made it difficult to even walk. My phone was flashing on the kitchen table.

Spiros Makris was missing.

Des Cogan's Story:

When Rick's call came, I was just about to sit down to my dinner. This consisted of a twelve-inch hot and spicy pizza, a portion of garlic dough balls, large chips with garlic and chilli sauce, and four cans of Guinness extra fuckin' cold. Now some would say this was a most unhealthy meal, and that, as I was spending a not inconsiderable amount on my gym membership, also counter-productive.

And I would retort, that you don't have to sleep with a twenty-two-year-old stripper that arrives at your flat at four every morning after work as lively as a kitten on ketamine. I was eating like a horse and getting thinner by the day.

Anyway, apparently Spiros Makris, the infamous Greek forger, had done a runner and Rick was not a happy bunny. He wanted to meet, go to the guy's gaff in Hale, and have a snoop about.

Makris was Rick's contact. I'd never met the guy, but my mate thought highly of him and that was enough for me.

Apparently, on the face of it the Makris family were importers of olive oil, yet I knew Spiros had provided Rick with a new identity in his early days in Manchester. I was also aware that he had supplied us with passports and weapons for our jaunt to Gibraltar via Puerto Banus.

As a result, Stephan Goldsmith had paid Spiros a visit for his trouble, beat him within an inch of his life, and shot his little girl Maria.

Rick, felt he owed the Makris family a debt. The younger brother had called and asked for help. It was a no-brainer, pal.

I ran down the steps from my apartment stuffing pizza in my gob. Rick wound down the window of his Aston.

"Don't think for one fucking second you are getting in here with that."

I stood on the pavement and pushed the last of the slice in my mouth.

"You're getting very tetchy and judgemental since you've been shot, pal," I said, doing my best not to spit tomato sauce on his swanky motor.

He handed me a wet-wipe out of the car window.

"Hands and mouth," he said with a sarcastic smile.

Like a toddler, I did as I was told. "Yer a wee fuckin' shite, I'll say that." I stuck my head through the open window. "Am I clean enough to enter, sir?"

Rick rolled his eyes. "Get in, numb nuts."

I sat, and pulled on my seatbelt. "You want to fill me in before we get there?"

Rick turned down the corners of his mouth, set the Aston in gear and hit the gas.

"You know about Goldsmith and the little girl?"

"I do."

"Well, I met with Spiros and his brother Kostas, just before we left for Belfast to slot O'Donnell. We owed him money for the weapons he'd provided for Gib, and I felt the need to go see him and give my condolences, yeah?"

I nodded.

"Well, he didn't want Joel's 911 as part of the deal, hence it languishes in the lock-up. His price was Goldsmith."

"But Goldsmith was already dead, he topped himself in jail."

"That's what I told him."

"So?"

"So, Kostas the younger one, he's an angry man. He says he wants absolute proof that Goldsmith is dead. Prove it, and we are square; one document for the price of the car. So, when we did the last weapons deal, just before the Maxi fuck up, I gave Kostas something to put his brother's mind at ease."

"Something?"

"Stephan Goldsmith's death certificate."

"And where might you have obtained this document?"

"Never mind that. Kostas says, ever since he gave his brother the certificate, he's been like a man possessed, missing for days at a time. This time, it's been over two weeks."

"So, you think he's been checking on the authenticity of the certificate?"

"Would figure."

"Mm…I'll ask you again, where'd you get the documents?"

"A friend."

"You don't have friends."

"Well, this *acquaintance* of mine, works in Manchester Register Office, and has a weakness for Victoria's Secret underwear."

"What's his name?"

"Very funny, Des…*She* is called Amanda, and is always very eager to help."

"I'll fuckin' bet she is…Does our Lauren know anything about the sweet Amanda?"

"It was before Lauren."

I couldn't hide the shock on my face.

"Oh, I see…before...So you two have finally got it together?"

"Shut the fuck up, Des."

The conversation was over.

We pulled up outside the Makris home, well, as far as the electric gates. I mean, these were not just gates, they wouldn't have looked out of place outside Hampden Park, eh?

I stepped out of the Bond-mobile, but couldn't see much of the gaff as it was surrounded by a high wall. Mature trees, swayed above my head.

The place stank of money.

Rick was out beside me and pressed the intercom to the right of the impressive wrought iron monsters.

"This is all new," he murmured, half to himself. "Always used to just drive in."

I figured, if I'd had my wee girl shot in front of me, I'd be moving out, not installing a big fuck-off cage at the front of my house.

Anyway, as if my magic, a guy appears, he's a big fucker, with a look of Desperate Dan about him. He sticks his face through the bars and asks us, none too politely, who we are.

I'd already clocked two CCTV cameras above us hidden in the trees. They were both PTZ's (Pan, Tilt and Zoom.) If someone was watching the screens, they knew exactly who we were. Nonetheless we went with the flow, and after two or three stupid questions, we were back in the Aston, through the monstrous gates, and crunching over the marble chippings to the house.

"Bit like Joel Davies's old gaff," I commented.

"I hope we get a better welcome than our last visit to that house," Rick snorted.

I couldn't have agreed more, "Jesus, you're right there, mate."

I remembered that little soiree. I was covered in plaster dust and deaf from automatic gunfire, before I'd left the kitchen. It had been the setting for Lauren's first kill, and I remembered her tears. Stephan Goldsmith had escaped that night. It was as if he'd been bulletproof. To think, had we managed to kill him in that battle, we wouldn't be here, the scene of his horrific crime against the Makris family.

The place was a 1940's Accrington brick-built affair, all big bay windows and heavy drapes. An impressive arched entrance door was half open. Standing in it, framed by the yellow of the hallway lights, was a shaven-headed guy. He was only my height, but a real gripper.

"Kostas Makris," explained Rick as he killed the engine. "The younger brother, the Mr Angry I told you about."

"Ah," I said. "Any chance of a wee smoke before we go in? I've just had my tea."

Rick thumbed a remote, and the Aston responded with a flash of its indicators and a satisfying bleep.

"No, you fuckin' can't…" He turned and acknowledged the big bloke at the door. "Kostas!"

The guy just jutted his chin in acknowledgement of our presence and walked inside. I looked to Rick for confirmation that we should follow.

He spoke through his teeth, which was never a good sign. "Come on then, look sharp…and don't fucking touch anything."

Rick Fuller's Story:

Kostas marched us along the hallway of the family home.

On my last visit, the whole house had been a cacophony of noise, smells and clutter. Yet as my John Lobb brogues rattled along the pristine mosaic floor to the stairs, all I could smell was bleach.

I recalled feeling almost jealous of the untidiness of the place, and the genuine comfort Spiros enjoyed, sitting alongside such chaos. To me, that night, his world had been strangely desirable.

I had delivered Joel's old 911, as part payment for the weapons that Spiros would provide for the Puerto Banus job, and entered his bombsite of a study in awe. How the man could ever find anything in such pandemonium, was beyond me.

Now, however, everything was in order.

I turned to Kostas. "You tidied the place?"

He motioned to the desk. "We were looking for the envelope you gave to me."

I nodded.

"I gave it to Spiros," said Kostas. "That very night. Even though I knew it would be about that animal Goldsmith, I did not look inside. My brother took the envelope from me, and never revealed its contents. I thought that if we found that envelope, or what was inside, it may lead us to him."

Des chipped in. "So, it's not here then, pal?"

Kostas shook his head. "No...but there is something else."

"Like what?" I asked.

He looked at us both in turn. "We need to talk outside. "

Kostas led us out to the gravel drive. Even in the warm evening air, with the birds giving it their all above us, he looked about him, nervous and on edge. He pushed his hands into his jeans and began. "From the first day Spiros have the envelope, his wife Maria, she tell me, he is like an insane person. He disappear for one, two, sometimes three days at a time. He is so crazy, Maria come to my house and ask for help."

"When was this?" I asked.

"Two weeks ago...maybe more. Anyway, I come here to the house, but Spiros... he's gone. So, I take a few of our guys and we search his study… everywhere, for this envelope…for anything to do with Goldsmith, but there is nothing. We even check his computer."

Des took advantage of being out in the open and pulled out his dreadful pipe. He spoke as he prodded tobacco into the small bowl. "And you don't think Spiros…your brother…I mean…there's no possibility he's just…lost the plot and done one?"

Kostas looked about him for a second time, removed one hand from his pocket and pulled out a small object with wires attached.

"When we search and clean the house, we find this."

I took it from him, and removed the battery.

Des picked the unit from my hand, held it between thumb and forefinger and took a closer look.

Once he was happy he'd correctly identified the device, he lit his pipe and blew a plume of blue smoke into the night.

"You sure you've searched all the house for your brother, Kostas?" he asked.

The Greek gave a withering look. "Positive. My brother is not here."

Des looked like some kind of stage hypnotist, as he dangled the small black object by its two wires in front of Kostas's face, I almost expected Debbie McGee to dance down the drive in a fuckin' leotard.

"Where'd you find this wee baby?" he asked.

Kostas stepped back to regain his personal space. "Inside a cigarette packet… in the trash…the litter bin…in my brother's study."

Des eyed him. "You know what it is?"

Kostas turned down the corners of his mouth and gave a trademark Corfiot shrug. "Of course, I know, you think I'm stupid? You think we are amateurs here? It is a bug, a listening device."

"So," says Des. "I'm sure the man who planted this wee packet, is looming large on your rather posh CCTV system."

Kostas waved a hand. "Maybe, you can look, the system is very complicated and need passwords I don't have."

Des threw the item to me. I caught it and slipped it into my jeans. They were Diesel, but last season's cut, as I considered we may end up searching the house ourselves, and I had no intention of ripping my latest pair.

On cue, the Scot confirmed my suspicions. He turned to the Greek. "So, you won't be minding if we have a look around then, pal?"

Des Cogan's Story:

I'd never consider myself a detective, or even a run of the mill plod type, but I knew a few basics. I'd had a mate who'd joined the Met after he'd done a nine in the Paras, and he'd swapped a tale or two with us over a pint and a curry when I lived up north.

One thing I did know was that in the event of a missing person, the first job the cops did was search the home address, and I mean, everywhere.

The cellar, the cupboards, wardrobes, loft, you name it, they look. The reasoning being that one in every ten missing persons are found in their own gaff.

Weird eh?

Well, not as weird as you think, as those statistics often involve small children and teenagers. Oh, and dead people.

Under normal circumstances, you would say, Spiros was a grown man, and perfectly capable of looking after himself. Even if he'd been sniffing around where he wasn't wanted, asking questions about dead gangsters, it wasn't the end of the world.

In all probability, the most likely explanation for his disappearance was because he'd suffered a massive blow in his life, he'd lost a child, and his head had gone. He was depressed, not receiving medication and vulnerable. Anyone with any common sense would reckon he was entitled to fall apart and do a dusty.

But they'd be wrong though, eh?

The moment I saw the wee gadget the Greek boy was holding in his hand, my heart sank.

That little homemade bug and transmitter gave a whole new meaning to the mystery.

The first time I'd seen one, was in the early eighties. The Det guys used them over the water in Northern Ireland. The Det, otherwise known as 14 Intelligence Company, a unit set up and trained by the SAS to find out what the naughty Irish terrorists were planning next, used these little babies on a daily basis back then.

The boys from 14 Intelligence were recruited from all areas of the armed forces, and were either very brave or very crazy.

They wandered in and out of the most dangerous clubs and bars of Belfast, looking like someone out of Status Quo, and dropping fag packets everywhere.

It was a simple ploy, if you had the balls.

First, nip into the 'Flying Bottle,' some PIRA or UFF stronghold, where the jolly locals would kneecap you just for ordering the wrong fucking lager.

Next, insist on zero close military backup, just in case the locals got the jitters.

Then, sidle up to a known player of some repute, casually finish your pint of Harp, and chuck your 'empty' fag packet into the ashtray in front of him.

The beauty of the fag packet bug, was its simplicity. The Det guys used to make their own they were so basic.

The things only worked for about twenty minutes, and transmitted barely fifty feet or so. But the beauty was, you could sit outside the boozer in your Vauxhall Cavalier, without any other kit, tune your car radio to medium wave and hear every word the bastards said till the waitress emptied the ashtray or the battery ran out.

So, what did Detective Des deduce from this mine of information? Well...

Firstly, the Det had long since been disbanded, and any modern spy worth his salt would have far more sophisticated tools at his or her disposal. Therefore, the person in question, the dropper of the bugged cigarette packet, was old school, probably from the developing world of surveillance. At a guess, I'd say, Chechnyan, Serbian, or maybe even Albanian.

If Makris had some information that one of the aforementioned groups of psychotic gangsters wanted, it meant our Greek forger friend was in the deepest shit

And that was not good.

It took us over two hours to search the house from top to bottom. Finally, we stepped out into the night, sweating and dusty. Rick had managed to get grease on his shirt and was close to breaking point.

He stood a strategic ten feet away from me as I lit up, rubbing his sleeve angrily. The birds had gone to bed and all I could hear was distant traffic.

Rick looked about him, resigned to throwing his hundred and twenty quid designer number in the bin. "He must have taken his little green car," he said absently.

I inhaled gratefully and tapped my temple with my finger. "We didn't check the garage…where is the fuckin' garage anyway?"

Rick turned on his heels. "Around the back."

This garage was bigger than my fuckin' house, built out of the same brick as the main building; it sported an impressive slate roof, and boasted not one but three remote-controlled up and over doors.

They were locked and we had no way in.

"I'll ask Kostas if he has a remote," said Rick.

Whilst he sought out the brother, I inspected each metal garage door in turn, running my fingers around the edges. Finally, I put my nose to the gap between one door and the brickwork and took a good old sniff.

Taking a step away, and emptying my nostrils as best I could, I managed to keep my spicy pizza down, but only just.

We'd found Spiros alright.

Rick Fuller's Story:

I clicked the remote with a heavy heart. Kostas stood by my side, his eyes fixed on the heavy, garage door. As we'd suspected, the electric motor slowly whirred to reveal a battered Ford Ka.

I stepped forward. Flies buzzed from somewhere inside the little vehicle, and the smell…well, there is nothing else in the world like it. Death has got its own personal aroma.

Kostas stayed put. His voice about to break. "You…you look, Richard," he said.

I looked.

Spiros Makris was sitting in the driver's seat, bolt upright, seatbelt fastened. The two front windows of the car were rolled down. The reek of exhaust fumes fought for precedence over the stench of rotting flesh.

I trod ever closer.

Where you find flies, you find maggots.

They take the eyes and the tongue first. It's their gateway, their roadmap, to your insides, your brain, your lungs, your last meal.

Des joined me and grimaced. "He's been here a wee while, but no two weeks. It's been warm for close on a month now. With the temperatures we've had, I'd be guessing a week tops."

I nodded, steeled myself against the stink and pushed my head inside the window. Horrible tiny popping sounds emanated from Spiros's skull, and I could only imagine what was going on inside.

The little Ford's keys were in the ignition and had been left in the second position. The car had been running until it ran out of fuel, the battery flattened.

Spiros had indeed been asphyxiated. Even in his state of decomposition, his lips were blue. Everything pointed to a suicide…well, not quite everything.

I stepped toward the fresh air, and pulled on the open, up and over garage door. It didn't budge.

I had confirmation.

There was no remote on Spiros's car keys.

Meaning?

Meaning, he couldn't have closed the garage door without one.

There was an emergency button on the inside of the garage to let you out, but no manual means of closing the doors. I'd just tried it.

It had to be closed by the remote, and Kostas had found that in Spiros's study.

Therefore, I now knew one thing for certain, Spiros did not die alone.

Another deep breath, and a quick look around his neck and throat for any kind of injury, revealed nothing.

Noting the sound of leather on gravel, I looked up to see Kostas making his way toward the garage.

Without me saying a word, Des stepped away, grabbed Kostas by the arm and led him toward the house. This was not the way to remember your brother.

I had one last look, said goodbye to my friend, and called the cops.

Lauren North's Story:

I woke with a stiff neck and a banging head. Whatever was in those pills the doctor had given me knocked me out, but left me feeling like I'd had a night on the tiles with the England rugby team.
My phone flashed silently on the bedside cabinet. I opened Rick's text message.
Dinner's off for a while. Meet at the office, 0900hrs
Checking my watch, I realised I had three hours.

As my surgeon had suggested, I ran until the pain was too great. That said, I'd managed 10k for the first time since I'd sustained my injuries. The natural endorphins that my body produced during strenuous exercise were better than any drug. I showered, changed, and caught a cab to the city. Even though the workout had made me feel slightly better, the closer I got to our office, the more my stomach tightened. As much as I wanted normality, my head wasn't going to make this easy.

Following Rick's very disappointing text, I'd had a short and rather stilted conversation with him. It appeared, due to recent events, our romantic meal for two was most definitely off...for now at least. He'd given me a quick brief about his and Des's visit to Hale, and I wasn't at all impressed.

On my arrival at our office, I found that we'd inherited a dippy receptionist by the name of Estelle.
Des and JJ had figured that leaving a temp in charge of our body-guarding business whilst Rick and I had convalesced was a good idea. This was anything but the case. We'd gone from clearing four grand a week each, to practically zero.
Ours was a hands-on business, clients needed guarding there and then, not next week or next month.
With that in mind, I'd figured it was time to knuckle down, put the past behind us, and concentrate on building what we'd started. It would help the business, our bank balance, and my head.

As the four of us settled into a room I'd previously used to interview our clients, Estelle brought coffee and croissants. It was the first time she'd seen Rick, and I noticed her eye him appreciatively as she handed him his black Americano.

I smiled at her and waited until she had closed the door.

"Pretty girl," I commented.

None of the boys answered. They just munched away and slurped their Neros.

Feeling slightly stupid at my immature comment, and realising I wasn't going to get a response, I changed the subject to the matter at hand, the reason we had been summoned.

The unexplained death of Spiros Makris.

"So, you didn't stay around until the police came?" I asked.

"Nah," said Des, "I had the CCTV module away, and we were on our toes like."

I found it hard to hide my irritation.

"Don't you think stealing the CCTV unit was a bad idea? I mean, wouldn't whatever was on that hard drive be better in the hands of the law…in the hands of the people that are paid to investigate this kind of thing?"

Des immediately fed on my exasperation, his tone sharp and dismissive. "We didnae steal the unit, Lauren, Kostas wanted us to take it. It's him that wants us to look into this…this, wee incident. And he's paying a very healthy fee for the privilege too, I may add."

"Well isn't that nice," I said rather too bitterly. "We certainly need the money, looking at our books."

JJ was calm. "This can be fixed, Lauren, now we are all together again, we can build things, yes?"

I didn't know what was coming over me, but I was unable to control myself. My anger boiled.

"Okay, Spiros may have been Rick's friend, and Kostas is paying us well, but we have a business here. We can't expect to make a profit, and just run it as and when we feel like it. I mean, what exactly are we? Are we a body-guarding business, or are we private investigators?"

I found myself waving my arms around like a demented TV chef. Maybe I should have taken my meds before I set off.

"I'll tell you what I think. Well, I don't think, I know this for a fact."
I pointed. "You lot… can't let this shit go, can you? You can't leave
it alone for one fucking second…any of you.
You crave the guns, the bombs, the bullets…"
I added a good dose of sarcasm to my tone. I was going overboard
and I knew it, but I just couldn't stop.
"Well you aren't Special Forces anymore, boys. You are civilians,
just like me."
Des squirmed in his seat holding his tongue, whereas my mouth ran
away with itself.
"As for you, Rick, all those big ideas back in Abu Dhabi, it was just
bollocks, wasn't it? As soon as the opportunity arrived, it was any
excuse to get the Glock out, play soldier again, and fuck the
consequences."
I grabbed my croissant from the table and tore into it. My hands
were shaking.
"And this." I spat flakes onto the table. "This whole business
now…If you want my opinion…well it's just another fucking
revenge mission."
I felt a hollow laugh emanate from my throat.
"And you are *so* into those, aren't you, Rick?"

Rick drained his coffee and caught my eye. Those beautiful
chocolate pools of colour were flat and lifeless. I'd seen the look
before. That night in Belfast, the night we went to the Nest bar
across the street from the Merchant Hotel. The night of the, 'I'm not
Cathy' conversation.
I felt a prick of conscience.
There was menace somewhere inside him, and I got the impression
that had I been male, I would have been a bloody mess on the carpet.
Silence fell on the group, a tight, uncomfortable silence, nobody
willing to break it.
Finally, Rick laid his hands flat on the table and took a deep breath.
Everyone else released theirs.
"Okay, okay, we all know what's going on here. Just sit back a
minute, Lauren, just take a breath. We know, you're struggling."
He addressed JJ and Des in turn. "And we've all been through it…
eh, boys?"
Both nodded.

I felt a bead of sweat drip down my back.

Des did his best. "They used to call it 'shell shock,' in the first war," he babbled. "Fuck me, they shot dozens of lads at the battle of the Somme thinking…"

"We know your problem, Lauren, and we want to help," chipped JJ. Rick leaned in. "We have all been touched by this…this disease, this syndrome, whatever you want to call it. What about me, eh?" He pointed at his chest. "Yeah, me, you know I was there, in that fucking horrible dark place. You of all people know I had the dreams, the flashbacks…. Look, what I'm trying to say is…stop fighting us. We want to help you get to the other side."

Lifting his cup to his lips, he realised he'd finished it already and dropped it on the table. Rick spread his palms, exasperation in his voice.

"Look, are we… are we all okay here?"

My heart raced so hard I could feel each beat in my head. Finally, I managed,

"…Yes…sorry…we are okay…but can I ask one thing?"

Rick eyed me suspiciously. "Go on."

"Do you think the cops will come to the same conclusion as you? The conclusion that Spiros was murdered?"

Rick paused. "No."

"And why is that?" I asked.

He held his chin and stared at the table in front of him.

"Because someone doesn't want them to."

I raised a quizzical eyebrow. "And that someone…is who we're looking for?"

As was his wont, Rick ignored my question and instead addressed us all.

"I believe Spiros Makris was murdered, because he found evidence that Stephan Goldsmith is still alive."

He waited for the information to sink in. JJ, of course, was impassive, never having met the guy or suffered at his hands. Des raised a suspicious eyebrow.

Me? I felt sick.

"Just a fucking minute here," I barked. "If I recall, we were told by none other than Sir Malcolm Harris, the head of MI6, and Anthony

Cyril Thomson, the serving Home Secretary of this country, that Stephan Goldsmith was dead…hanged in his cell."

Rick nodded. "We were also told, by the very same people, in that very same office that, and I quote, 'Stephan Goldsmith has been a very reliable and informative witness'."

I folded my arms. "And by that, you mean?"

"I mean," said Rick, obviously finding it difficult to hide his irritation. "That we were given that information by a politician and a spook. Both as reliable as a fox in a chicken run. They also happened to be in the company of a silent guy in Ray-Ban sunglasses."

"The CIA dude," said Des.

Rick waved a dismissive hand. "Let's forget the CIA, and big conspiracies for a minute. At the time, I believed them too. So much so, I promised the Makris family proof that Goldsmith was dead. After all, he had murdered Spiros's daughter trying to get information about *our* whereabouts. It was the least I could do."

"So?" I asked.

"So, I obtained Goldsmith's death certificate and handed it to the family."

Rick stood and filled a paper cup at the cooler. He drank it in one and continued his theory.

"I believe Spiros took that document, and from that moment, began his own investigation into Goldsmith's alleged suicide. Now, a death in police custody is not an easy thing to sweep under the carpet. It entails a coroner's enquiry. Lots of witnesses, and a perfect paper trail, so at first, I had my doubts. After all, Spiros was a troubled soul, and I know only too well how an obsession can take over your life."

"I still have doubts," said Des. "It could be pure coincidence. Let's face it, the Makris crew are no angels, eh? They're arms dealers…that and forgers. In their game, it's easy to make enemies. Spiros could just've upset some Eastern European nutter. Whoever dropped the fag packet bug was old school."

Rick was about to speak, but Des was on it.

"So maybe, just maybe, he ripped someone off, the wrong kind of person, some Chechnyan gangster type… People get greedy, mate, even your pal Spiros."

Rick opened his laptop and tapped a few keys. "Spiros hadn't done a deal since his girl was killed. He was a broken man, I don't believe he'd rip anyone off, and I don't believe in coincidences."
He found the document he was looking for.
"So…this is what I know to be true."

"Officially, Stephan Goldsmith was taken from Gibraltar by military aircraft. That transport landed at RAF Mildenhall."
"That's a US Airforce facility." said Des.
Rick nodded "Exactly, but the Firm, not the CIA, got to him first. From there, he was taken by car to be debriefed at Canary Wharf. Of course, the Americans were pissed that they didn't get first crack at their man, especially as technically, he'd landed on US soil. It must have been a very hot political potato, but before the Yanks could speak to him, he was transferred up north and held in the high security wing at Strangeways."

I shook my head. "Someone of his profile would never be transferred up north. Why risk taking your prisoner long distances? He'd have been lodged in Belmarsh for sure."
Rick nodded. "I agree, but according to his death certificate, he died in Strangeways."
I met his gaze. "So, the Firm are at it again?"
He closed his laptop. "There is no doubt, it would take the influence of people in high places to fake a death in prison. It's a possibility MI6 have their hands dirty again, yes."
I took the deepest of breaths. "So where do we start?"

There was an awkward silence.
"Not *we*," he said.

His words hit me like a bullet. I couldn't believe what he was saying.
"Lauren, you need stability right now," he began. "That, and to take some advice you may not like."
He rubbed the top of his head with his palm.
"You need to stay here with Estelle, looking after this end.
Look…you were right about that side of things. The business needs a hand on the tiller and you are the best person for the job…so."

He looked to the boys for support.

"Me, Des and JJ will look after this little matter. It shouldn't take too long, no more than a week or two, and you can get the business back on track while we're away."

I wanted to punch him. I wanted to hurt him. Did he not understand this was the very last thing I needed?

My right knee bobbed up and down at a rate of knots, my mouth as dry as a bone.

I licked my lips.

"I didn't ask for fucking well-meaning advice, Rick, I asked where do we start? What is the first job?"

Rick sniffed and shook his head. "I don't think so, Lauren."

I eyeballed him. We were like two boxers waiting for the bell to sound. "Well I fucking do think so, Rick. You are not going to do this to me." I pointed an accusing finger. "I'm telling you, I can still function, so…just stop pretending to be my fucking shrink and tell me what is the first objective in this fucking…investigation?"

He cricked his neck, left then right. At the second attempt it cracked, loud enough for all to hear.

"That would be to locate the prison officer who allegedly found Goldsmith dead in his cell," he said quietly.

I nodded furiously, swallowed acid in my throat and tapped my chest a little too hard with my finger. "I'll do that."

Standing on ferociously wobbly legs, I reached the door and turned.

"And you will not be fucking taking this away from me."

Des Cogan's Story:

There was a long and disconcerting silence as we listened to Lauren slam about in the outer office. Estelle did her best to make pleasantries, but to no avail. Finally, we heard the front door open and then close with an earth-shattering bang.

She was gone.

Having a spooky feeling that the mood needed a wee lift, I looked at my watch.

"Well, I don't know about you boys, but I'm ready for a beer or two. How about we have a nip over to The Thirsty Scholar?"

My old pal Richard was troubled. Lauren meant more to him than he was letting on. In a way, it was good to see him show some emotion again. After all, the last time he'd known love, Gazza was making a fool out of Scottish defenders at the Euros.

He visibly pulled himself together.

"No…no beer for me, I need to get that CCTV unit over to Egghead and access the footage…besides, it's only eleven-thirty, and…"

I cut him off.

"Aye right. That baw-faced shite Egghead will still be in his pit dreaming about circuit boards and stuff, so you can forget about him for a wee while. And anyway, my body clock has never recovered from that two weeks we had in Benidorm circa 1986, so to me, it's constantly two hours ahead of GMT.

That makes it, half-one in the blistering sunshine pal. The Spanish clock has controlled my drinking habits for over twenty-years."

Rick was about to argue, but I was in again.

I lowered my tone. "Look, I know Spiros was your pal and all, but the whole crew have had it rough lately. Look at the state of you. You aren't getting any younger, this isn't the old days."

I pointed at his gut.

"You're still struggling just to jog and walk down steps, mate. Come on, take a breather. You need one." I motioned in the direction of the front door. "And so does that wee lassie."

Rick scratched his head.

"You think I should call her and see if she wants to join us?"

JJ and I were in unison.

"No!"

The Thirsty Scholar was a funny little boozer which sat under the arch of the railway bridge that ran over Oxford Road adjacent to the station. Smack bang opposite was the very swanky Palace Hotel, and although the Scholar boasted a stone floor, a vegan menu and seventeen draft beers from around the world, I considered not many of the hotel's guests ventured inside.

Personally, I quite liked it.

Rick took a sip of his Red Stripe, sat back in his seat, scratched his head with both hands, and with more than a hint of sarcasm said, "Well my chat with Lauren went well, eh?"

I couldn't help myself. "You always were a useless twat when it came to women, pal. I never really understood how Cathy put up with you."

There was the merest hint of his prickling temper. I figured I was still the only man alive who could mention his wife's name without getting a smack in the mouth for my trouble.

Time heals, they say, and there was the merest hint of a smile as he remembered her.

"I know what you mean, Des. I think it was because we were opposites you know? She was so chilled out all the time, nothing fazed her. I just spent my whole life being wound up like a clock."

How could I not agree?

Over the following three hours, we got steadily pissed and talked more shite than should be allowed.

More worrying, and much to our vegan landlord, Martin the Mod's consternation, JJ had ordered a bottle of Jameson.

By five o clock, he was halfway down it. I think Martin considered calling the cops when the Turk pulled his knife from his back pocket and began to clean his nails with the razor-sharp blade.

I pushed a twenty in the Mod's pocket and read him his horoscope. Nobody likes a grass, eh?

JJ slid the knife away as swiftly as a magician with an ace of spades, and leaned in. "You know, when I was in the army, I never had a woman?"

"You were a vegan?" slurred Rick.

I bawled laughing. "No a fuckin' vegan…Martin the Mod's the vegan…you mean a virgin."

"That's what I said," Rick pointed.

JJ's eyes flashed. "Don't make fun. I was good boy until I meet my Grace."

Even I turned my head at that one. Despite the pock marks and scars, JJ was a good looking fella, and it would never have occurred to me that Grace would have been his first lover.

Then I thought for a moment. "You know; Anne was my first too."

JJ sank another Irish. "See, is not so crazy."

I couldn't argue. "Yer right there, pal…Grace is a fine woman, you're a lucky man, you have a nice family, JJ... very nice."

Rick spoke half to himself, half to his empty beer glass. He wasn't drunk, but he'd consumed just enough for him to let that notorious guard down a notch. In ten years, he'd never admitted once to being lonely. There had never been an ounce of emotion. Until now.

He looked at us both in turn. With the hint of a slur in his voice, he said, "I still miss her, you know?"

Lifting JJ's bottle from the table, he poured whiskey into his empty beer glass. "Cathy, I mean… you know what I'm sayin'? I mean, I miss her every single day. The weird thing is, for weeks now, the dreams have stopped. The dreams that have haunted me for ten years and more, they've gone," He snapped his fingers. "Just like that. Since her death, I've never gone longer than a day or two, without one."

He sipped the whiskey. "Now, even they have left me."

He caught my eye, and suddenly, he was that lanky kid I'd met in Belfast, who looked too skinny to carry his gun.

"I know this is going to sound crazy to you," he muttered. "But I even miss the nightmares."

He took the rest of the spirit in his glass, grimaced and sat back as if exhausted by the effort of telling his short tale.

I stood. "Well I reckon it's time I nipped to the little boy's room…so, lads… whose round is it?"

Rick held up a hand and nodded, eyes at half-mast. "That will be me."

I staggered to the loo, pushing past students, mixed with a more mature crowd who'd just finished their shift, edging my way through the swathes of midweek normality.

I did what I had to do before standing at the solitary sink to wash my hands. A polished plate of stainless steel was screwed to the wall above it. This makeshift mirror would not be smashed by drunken revellers.

As I plunged my hands under cold water, I peered at my distorted reflection. The lines on my face were deeper, grey hairs dominated where brown had once reigned. Lauren was right, we weren't soldiers or troupers anymore, we were middle-aged men playing a dangerous game. Yet I wasn't willing to let it go.

Not just yet.

Lauren North's story:

How dare they? I mean, come on, I know I'm not quite on point, and maybe I did go over the top in the meeting, but couldn't they just cut me a bit of slack?

Not only that, I knew they'd gone to the pub without me, and that hurt.

I walked through town to the library and spent three hours looking for any articles relating to the death in custody of Stephan Goldsmith, together with any clue as to the identity of the officer that had found his body.

The sum total of my search revealed two column inches on page five of the *Manchester Evening News*. The headline was obviously written with a more prominent position in mind, 'Another unexplained Strangeways fatality.'

The reason for the lack of column inches was obvious, the writer didn't even have the name of the 'deceased,' and described him only as, 'a prominent drug trafficker of Dutch origin'.

The name and title, 'Rupert Warwick, Chief Crime Reporter,' sat in bold print below the text that told me next to nothing.

Okay, Rupert, let's see what you really know.

I rang the paper.

"Rupert Warwick is on holiday," I was told in no uncertain terms.

"So how do I contact him? I have a story he will be interested in."

The woman on the other end of the phone would have done a great job in a doctor's surgery, but at a paper desperate for news stories, this was not her true vocation in life.

"It's against company policy to give out personal information, madam, I'm afraid you will have to wait until he returns from leave."

I couldn't hide the irritation in my voice. "And when might that be?"

Mrs Helpful spoke down her nose. The longer the call went on, the more she appeared to relish her task of being unhelpful.

"Unfortunately," she whined, "I am not at liberty to divulge that information either, you see…"

I ended the call in frustration. It was only as I uttered a few choice expletives, that I realised just how hushed the library was.

Sitting opposite me was a middle-aged man dressed in tweed. He gave me a withering look, and gestured toward a nearby sign. It sported a picture of an ancient mobile phone with a bold red cross through it.

I pocketed my Samsung, smiled at him, and held up both palms in mock surrender.

He didn't smile back; my day was not going well.

I figured that I had one last card to play. Most big business have their own email server, so, as I stepped into the Manchester sunshine, I wrote a quick message to rupert.warwick@men.co.uk. There was a slim chance that I had the right link and that as Rupert was a 'chief crime reporter,' he would be the conscientious hack type and have his work phone with him. I headed the message 'Urgent' hit the 'send' button and set off towards Deansgate and refreshment.

Finding an empty table in the sun outside Mocha a coffee and chocolate lover's paradise just off the main street, I plonked myself down, ordered a grande latte and watched Manchester's well-heeled go about their business. My Columbian drink was delivered by a handsome boy who temptingly left the cake menu alongside it.

I was about to give in the delicious offerings, when my phone buzzed.

I opened the email icon and found a message from our diligent reporter Rupert. It read: *Re: info on Strangeways death, very interested, call 0778992351, Rupert.*

As I was using my work mobile, I had no intention of using Goldsmith's name, or divulging any other information over the network. It was bad enough that all calls, text messages and locations were logged by the phone companies, but having no choice, I sent him a text and hoped he'd take the bait: *Meet me in Mocha, off Deansgate, now, Lauren.*

I didn't have long to wait for a reply:

On way, how will I know you? Will you be carrying a newspaper? Lol.

Well, at least he had a sense of humour, something I was in need of.

I played along:

Outdoor table, ponytail, Gucci glasses.

Twenty minutes later, Rupert sat down alongside me and failed miserably to hide the top to toe examination of my figure. I wouldn't call it lecherous, more…appreciative.

As I was feeling a little lacking in self-confidence, it was quite nice. It's always baffled me how some women found the equivalent of the builder's wolf whistle demeaning. For me, it's always given me a little lift, that, 'well, you've still got it girl,' feeling.

Each to their own, I suppose.

Anyway, Rupert was more Harry Potter than Harrison Ford, so ticked none of my boxes. He was however, passionate about a string of suicides that had occurred at the high security wing of Strangeways prison.

We talked for close on an hour. I spent as much time being vague about the prisoner's pressure group I was allegedly part of, as he did examining my cleavage. He wasn't a fool, and quickly realised I was giving him zero other than a nice view and a coffee.

However, I did come away with the name of the guard who'd found Goldsmith dead in his cell.

Colin Reed.

Result.

Now all I needed was to find him.

One thing Rupert had been right about; I would get nothing from the prison itself. I came away from the crumbling old jail with something amounting to a flea in my ear, and a deep sense of foreboding. Strangeways was a ghostly place. It had been an executioner's prison and the bodies of convicted murderers had once been buried in unmarked graves within the prison walls.

It gave me the creeps.

Being a category A prison, it had housed the most dangerous criminals in the country, infamously Ian Brady and Harold Shipman amongst its guests.

And, of course, Stephan Goldsmith.

My next port of call was the nearby pubs. Just as with hospitals and police stations, there is always one local, the staff would use post shift.

When I walked into the tap room of the Berwick Arms on the corner of Carnarvon Street, a pub just far enough away to avoid friends and relatives of the inmates but close enough to walk to, I knew I'd found that place. Half a dozen white-shirted guys and a couple of very beefy looking women were gathered around the old Victorian bar, drinking and talking shop.

Their conversation stopped the instant they heard my heels on the tiled floor.

My first impression, that outsiders would not be welcome, was to be well-founded, and the only snippet of information offered was that Colin Reed was on long-term sick leave due to work-related stress. Posing as his long-lost niece, I pressed for his address and was unceremoniously shown the door.

As I was determined to prove Rick wrong and find our first piece in the jigsaw, this left me with only one option that I could think of, and it wasn't the best idea I'd had in a while.

Levenshulme Police Station was almost as grim as Strangeways jail. I couldn't decide if my stomach churned because of the stink in the public waiting area, or the company I was about to keep.

I checked my reflection in the two-way mirror, for the tenth time. I'd taken out my ponytail, applied some lipstick and considered I looked pretty good. Even so, Detective Chief Inspector Larry Simpson kept me waiting for just over an hour.

Finally, the door opened and there he stood. His lean frame only served to accentuate his height. He wore a crisp white shirt with an open neck, his sleeves rolled to the elbow, revealing his muscular forearms. He was indeed a handsome man, yet as my butterflies did back flips, I felt nothing but disgust.

I instantly hated myself for lowering myself to this visit. I wanted to slap the smug look from his face.

He read my mind. "Still not forgiven me then, honey?"

Even though the waiting room was empty, I didn't trust Lawrence not to have his broken-nosed partner snooping behind the mirror to my right.

I straightened my back, pushed my hair behind my right ear and managed a smile of my own.

"I think, should I decide to make an official complaint regarding your unscrupulous undercover policing methods, forgiveness wouldn't come into it, Lawrence."

He waved away my bravado.

"Whatever it is you are here for, sweetheart, it isn't to make a complaint, so I think it best we talk in my office eh?"

He turned before I could answer and I was compelled to follow. He had me at a disadvantage, and he knew it.

Two narrow corridors that bustled with uniforms, a flight of stairs, a sharp left and we arrived at a door that proclaimed Lawrence's name and rank. He pushed it open, strode around his desk and flopped in his chair. The old boss's trick of forming a pyramid with his fingers came straight out of the box and he gave me a big beaming smile.

I felt sweat drip down my spine for the second time in a day, and every bone in my body screamed at me to turn on my heels and leave.

I sat.

"Now," he said, "please tell me that you are here to give me that bastard Fuller's head on a plate."

I was totally off-guard. My recent trouble with concentration and lack of nerve under pressure hit me like a Ricky Hatton body-shot.

"I…I'm not here for that…no."

The pyramid disappeared and his hands lay flat on the table

"Then off you go," he said, his smile disappearing like drain water.

I forced the butterflies to settle somewhere inside me and dragged some of my lost confidence from deep in my gut.

"Look…you owe me, Larry." I said. "You deceived me, you lied and betrayed my trust. And as I don't seem to have a single criminal conviction…not so much as a parking ticket, your behaviour was unscrupulous at best, if not fucking illegal." My self-assurance flooded into my core. I pointed at him. "As I understand it, the IPCC guidelines are very clear when it comes to 'relationships' in undercover operations."

Genuine anger rose in my throat. "How far would you have gone, Larry? Would you have had sex with me? Slept in my bed? Told me you loved me? Made plans for the future? Have you any idea how that made me feel?"

There was the merest change in his face. His ice blue eyes narrowed. "I did what I had to do, Lauren. I didn't want to hur…"

"Don't!" I couldn't believe what he was about to say. "Don't you dare go there, Larry. You knew exactly what you were doing and why. You thought we were common criminals, when in fact, we were working for the Firm." I snorted a derogatory laugh. "You lost and we won, it's as simple as that."

Larry was not so easily defeated. Raising his tone a level, he pointed at my face.

"Richard Fuller is nothing more than a drug-dealing murderer, that you helped escape police custody."

I almost guffawed. "Oh, come on, Larry. Rick is a war hero that served his country well. And if he has ever taken a life since the day the service betrayed him, you should be bloody grateful, as I would wager they were the scum of the earth and made your life easier."

Larry shook his head.

"You can't just take the law into your own hands and top someone because you don't like their morals, Lauren. There are laws…rules."

I had him.

"Yes, Larry, there are laws, and rules…and you broke them too."

He sat back in his chair and blew out his cheeks. There was an awkward silence before he leaned forward again, his tone conciliatory.

"I'm not a bad person, Lauren."

"Neither is Rick."

Another silence.

"What do you want from me?"

"The address of a prison officer that works at Strangeways."

"Why not ask the Firm?"

"This isn't Firm business, it's personal."

"Are you going to tell me why you want it?"

"No."

"Are you going to hurt him?"

"No."

He bit his lip and considered his options. He knew I had no power over him. He knew he could just throw me out on the street.

Finally, he spoke. "Give me the name…it will take me an hour or two. Meet me in the Old Monkey on Portland Street…let's say nine o' clock."

He broke into that smile of his. The one that made me date him in the first place.

"It's your round."

Des Cogan's Story:

We piled out of the Thirsty Scholar, much the worse for wear. Rick caught a cab, and a rather cross-looking Grace collected JJ. She had his wee boy in the back of the car in his pyjamas, obviously ready for bed. I reckoned JJ was in for a mouthful.

This left me smiling stupidly to myself, standing under the arches, surrounded by half-pissed students.

My head was telling me to go home and sleep, but my seemingly endless appetite forced my legs to walk across Oxford Road toward a banquet for one.

The night was warm and the city bustled with theatregoers, tourists and the usual mix of street dwellers.

I bought a *Big Issue* from a guy on Princess Street and strode onward toward the mixture of casinos, lap dancing bars and restaurants that is Manchester's China Town.

I was about to cross Portland Street when I was stopped in my tracks.

Standing on the pavement outside the Old Monkey was Lauren. I liked the place myself. It was a good old fashioned boozer that served real ale. What stopped me dead was her company.

Facing her, gently holding both her hands and looking deep into her eyes, was none other than Detective Chief Inspector Larry Simpson. I hurried to the nearby tram stop and hid myself in the crowd of waiting travellers.

From my new vantage point, I watched Larry bend his head slightly and kiss Lauren on the cheek. Seconds later they both turned and went their separate ways.

Now, I know what you are going to say here. 'Don't jump to conclusions', and I didn't. But I'll tell you this for nothing.

I'd fair lost my appetite.

Rick Fuller's Story:

My head was thumping like my mother's old twin tub, but I forced myself to take my morning run.

I'd earmarked the second bedroom in my new apartment as a gym. Thus far, I'd only managed to get the floor reinforced and some plastering done, but it was a cool, empty room to work out in.

After my 10k, I stepped into the half-finished space, and spent another thirty minutes doing Ashtanga Yoga, a form developed in the Forties where you take up a sequence of postures and use breathing and internal muscles to get your results. There's a risk of hamstring injuries, but the increase in upper body strength you can achieve far overshadows traditional weights.

A shower, four-egg omelette, a black coffee and, I was starting to feel my old self again.

My plan, was to go and visit Egghead, otherwise known as Simon, our friendly tech support officer, and see if he could access the Makris CCTV unit.

He lived in a one-horse town called Ramsbottom, just off the M60/66 junction. He and his elderly mother were the only residents in a house that was more suited to the Adams family than one of the brightest and best paid hackers in England. To make matters worse, Simon's mother Ethel was a cat lover. On my last visit, I'd stood for three hours, rooted to the spot in a very nice Hugo Boss suit, surrounded by mewing hordes.

I came out smelling like a litter tray.

Even though I had the suit professionally cleaned, I could never bring myself to wear it again.

This was not a dress-up day.

I walked into bedroom three…my wardrobe, and selected Levi 501's, a black Ralf Lauren polo and a casual collarless bomber I'd picked up in Ted Baker for a mere £239, and pulled on my trusty brogues.

I called Des to tell him my plans for the morning and arranged to meet him at our offices after lunch. He sounded troubled and a little reticent. I didn't ask why. Looking back, I should have pressed him.

Hearing the sound of a horn outside, I strode out into the sunshine. The Aston was staying put, I was not about to chance hairy sharp-clawed beasts sitting all over it, so a cab it was.

It was a tad after ten as the surly taxi driver dropped me outside Egghead's house. After an eternity of knocking, Mother finally answered the door.

"He's in bed," she announced, before disappearing back into the old farmhouse, leaving me surrounded by the cats from hell.

I'd made it halfway up the long staircase, gripping Spiros's CCTV unit, tiptoeing around various deposits on the carpet and bawling Simon's name every three steps, until he finally emerged on the landing.

Simon had the physique of a man who sat in front of a computer all night, and the pallor of an individual who slept the remainder of the time.

Behind each of his ears sat tiny electronic devices; these little gems were specially designed to keep his equilibrium. You see, Simon had revelled in a much misspent youth, his favourite pastime during his formative years being to indulge in copious quantities of class A drugs, beg, borrow, and quite often steal, high performance cars, and crash them into trees.

Simon had more steel in his head than grey matter.

I couldn't imagine how brainy he would have been if he'd not had three fractured skulls.

He scratched his crotch and then disgustingly sniffed his fingers.

"Hey, Mr Fuller, well this is a surprise."

He held out the same hand for me to shake. I opted to put the CCTV unit in there. "How soon can you have a look at this for me, Simon?"

He took a quick glance at the unit.

"Windows based?"

"I think so."

"Password protected then?"

"Yes."

"Username?"

I shook my head. "I don't have anything, but it is urgent."

Despite his poor hygiene, Simon was always amiable once awake.

He chuckled to himself.

"It always is, Mr Fuller, always. You'd better come up to my room."

I was hoping to turn on my heels and return once the task was completed. I'd never visited Simon's bedroom, and had no desire to, but it seemed it was going to be necessary.

"It will be a bag of sand, Mr Fuller."

Simon also had this odd sort of rhyming slang going on. Being a London lad, I'd pretty much heard it all, but Egghead had some all of his own. This particular snippet however, translated into him charging me a thousand pounds for his work.

I nodded. "Okay, Simon, just get on it."

To my surprise and not inconsiderable delight, Simon's 'room' was not only cat free, but scrupulously clean and tidy. Neat benches held various monitors and gizmos that I could only guess at, whilst others had component shelving with alphabetical ordering labels on each.

He pointed to a hair-free swivel chair in one corner.

"Have a seat, Mr Fuller, while I get this baby plugged in."

Seconds later, Simon sat in front of a monitor showing the entry screen to Spiros's CCTV recorder.

"Now," he said, cracking his knuckles. "What's the mush called that owns this baby?"

"Makris," I said.

"First name?"

"Spiros."

Simon typed in SPIROS in the username box. Then hit 1234 for the password and the screen changed from entry mode to the menu box.

"There you go, Mr Fuller, all done."

I was well pissed. Firstly, because I hadn't even thought to try the simple option first, and secondly, I had just paid an arm and a leg for ten seconds' work.

"And you expect me to pay a grand for that?" I blurted.

Simon shrugged his shoulders and beamed.

"Mr Fuller…some of these jobs take hours, some minutes, and some, like this one, seconds." He gave a childlike chuckle. "Now, would you like to have a nosey at the content while you are here? I can leave you in peace…smells like Mum's on with my full English downstairs."

I nodded and ruefully handed Simon a thousand in cash.

He beamed again, kissed the money and pushed it in his back pocket.

"If you want to print anything, Mr Fuller, just pause the screen and hit Ctrl + P on the keyboard. It will come out over there under the window."

He winked and made a strange clicking sound with his mouth.

"No charge for the paper."

I didn't know whether to laugh or slap him, so did neither and began to search through the footage.

As I'd expected, the unit had somehow been switched off externally on the day that Spiros had met his death. In the few hours prior, there were no suspect vehicles at the gate, and no one about the house other than the Greek himself, shuffling from his study to the kitchen. I scrolled further and further back until I found who I was looking for.

The guy that dropped the cigarette packet bug in Spiros's trash basket.

I paused the footage at various points, showing the guy at the door, in the hall, in the study, and leaving the house. Spiros had let the guy in and there didn't appear to have been any altercation between them. That said, pictures only tell part of the tale.

I printed the images as Simon had suggested, then laid them on the table in front of me and studied the man.

As I scanned the shots, the door opened and Simon entered rubbing his stomach. "Hey, Mr Fuller. I'll tell you what, the old girl does a mean full English. Two bacon, two sausage, egg, beans, tomato and fried slice...bloody marvellous."

"Nice," I managed.

Simon looked over my shoulder at the images spread on the table. "This the mush you are looking for then, Mr Fuller?"

I gave him a look.

Simon held up his hands. "I know, none of my business, Mr Fuller, just saying like, cos, that mush is in the car game like, mean fucker he is, foreign and..."

"You know who this guy is?" I snapped.

Simon shrugged and took a step back. The lad was definitely not one for the physical contest. However, Egghead knew how to make money and recognised every opportunity to do so.

"Now then, Mr Fuller, opening boxes is one thing, information on the contents of said boxes is quite another."

I gritted my teeth. "Another five hundred?"

Simon hopped from foot to foot.

"I don't know, Mr Fuller, I mean, if this guy ever found out I'd…"

I was losing patience.

"Okay, look, another bag of grain or whatever you call it."

"Sand," said Simon with a sudden smile. "A bag of sand, Mr Fuller."

Lauren North's Story:

Larry had been the perfect gentleman. He'd given me the address of
Colin Reed and hadn't asked any awkward questions; there'd been
no sarcastic remarks, no references to our business or past
misdemeanours, rather, he'd made conversation about anything but
our lines of work and had kept me entertained throughout the
evening. I wasn't quite at the forgiveness stage, but it hadn't been as
much of a trial as I'd thought. That said, this morning I'd driven my
Audi to our office riddled with a mixture of anxiety and a goodly
portion of guilt.
Why can't you be as keen, Mr Fuller?
JJ was waiting outside the front doors and jumped inside carrying a
holdall and two coffees. He smelled of booze, and I took it the boys
had been on a bit of a bender.
We crawled out of town in rush hour traffic in silence.
Eventually JJ handed me a Starbucks, leaned back in his seat and
pushed his Ray-Bans up his nose.
"Did you tell Rick and Des where we go?" he said.
"No, why?" I offered.
He shrugged, obviously not wanting to involve himself in the
internal wranglings of the previous day. He simply leaned forward
and removed two Glock 19s from his bag.
He checked them both, pushed one into the waistband of his Levis
and slotted the other into the glovebox.
"Someone kill the Greek for looking for this guy Reed," he said
coldly. "Someone professional. If we go with just two, it is best to be
careful, no?"
Finding a gap in the traffic, I put my foot down. The V10 engine in
the RS6 growled like a caged tiger. I turned up the Blaupunkt;
Stereophonics blasted.
"Nothing we can't handle, JJ."

Rick Fuller's Story:

Simon had identified the guy in the pictures as 'Red George'.
I'd heard the name many times over the last ten years, but had never seen his face, hence my inability to recognise him. There were differing stories about how the guy had got the nickname 'Red'. As with most of Manchester's gangland folklore, it depended on who you spoke to. Some said it was purely down to the fact he was Russian and therefore a Communist.
He was neither.
Others affiliated him to an infamous Manchester United football hooligan crew that organised mass vicious brawls across the city.
He actually hated the game and had never been to Old Trafford.
Then, there were those who were convinced it was down to his love of the machete when fighting at close quarters, and the amount of blood he spilled.
Close. He did like to use a knife, and was so big he could easily use his brute strength to overpower his opponents before slicing them like a Sunday roast. But the real reason for his nickname, was his love of the Russian made, Kalashnikov AK-47.
His name was Gjergj Dushku and hailed from Kosovo. He had fought for the KLA smuggling arms from his parental home of Albania. He battled the Serbs in the Kosovan war, and when the conflict ended in 1998, he fled to Greece to avoid being tried for his part in the rape, torture and subsequent slaughter of dozens of civilians. From there he made his way to the UK, claiming asylum from the Milosevic reign of terror.
We patted him on the head and probably gave him a council flat for his trouble.
Now, there could have been all manner of reasons why Spiros Makris would indulge Red George and invite him into his home.
After all, the Makris family were indeed gun runners, and, being Corfiot, had close connections with the Albanians whose home sat less than a mile from their island. Indeed, there was every possibility that Spiros had done arms deals with Red George, who in turn had supplied half of Moss Side with death and destruction.
Was this the nutter that Des had suggested Spiros had upset and therefore ended up spitting out maggots in his garage?
I wasn't convinced.

Why?
Because Red George was like me. He was a hired hand.

Lauren North's Story:

Colin's house was situated on an estate of 1980's semi-detached houses in a small town that sat between Bolton and Salford.
I wouldn't have chosen Walkden as my ideal place to settle, but I'd seen worse, and I supposed Colin got a lot more bang for his buck when compared with Manchester city prices.
The house was set halfway along a short cul-de-sac. Wrought iron gates secured a small paved driveway which led to an integral garage. As with most houses in the street, Colin's highly polished Nissan Micra sat on the drive rather than inside his garage.
The small front lawn had been recently cut and summer flowers planted in neat rows around it.
It appeared Colin had been using his long term sick leave to good use, at least in the DIY department.
As I grabbed the door handle of the Audi, I turned to JJ. "I don't think I'll be needing the Glock on this one, mate."
The Turk didn't answer, just shrugged his shoulders, pulled his own SLP from his waistband, checked it all over again, and reinserted it in position.
I shook my head and stepped into the street.
As I opened Colin's gate, I noticed the neighbour's curtains twitch.
It reminded me so much of the street I grew up in in Leeds.
Everyone looking out for each other.
I had to admit, JJ did look a little on the menacing side, but it didn't stop the rather large lady responsible for the twitching drapes barrelling out of her front door the split second I knocked on Colin's.
"I think he's out, love," she said in the thickest Bolton accent I'd heard in a while. "Window cleaner were here ten minutes back and he didn't get his cash."
I smiled sweetly but didn't comment.
The woman folded her arms across her considerable assets.
"You from the prison too, then?"
I instantly felt my hackles rise. "We are…umm…we're from the occupational health unit actually, just checking on Colin's welfare."
The woman eyed JJ with some suspicion. Even I couldn't pass the Turk off as a health visitor, so I changed the subject.
"So, Colin's had another guest then?"

The woman leaned across the fence conspiratorially. "Oh aye, yesterday morning I think."

She put a finger to her lips. "Or could've been the day before...see I like a can or two in the afternoon like, and I forget...anyway, he were from the prison I reckon. Right big bloke, all muscles, shaved head." The woman pouted. "Ooh aye, just my type he were...massive."

I smiled again, feeling slightly sick.

"And did Colin let this man in?"

She pulled a face that told me her alcoholic afternoons made that a difficult question.

I pressed on. "So how long is it since you saw your neighbour, Mrs...?"

She pushed out her chest. "It's Miss actually, Miss Morrison, like the supermarket."

I was losing the will to live and heard JJ mumble something in Turkish. It was my cue.

"Really...Well, Miss Morrison, I don't suppose you have a key to Mr Reed's, do you? I mean, I couldn't live with myself if something untoward had happened. After all, Colin is off work with a mental illness."

Miss Morrison's jaw dropped. "Mental? You mean you think..."

She was on the hook and I wasn't going to let her off. I put on my best senior staff nurse face.

"Stress is the number one killer in men Colin's age, Miss Morrison." The woman covered her gaping mouth with her hand for a moment before pointing at her front door. "Oh my...I do have a key, yes. Colin leaves it with me so I can water his plants when he's on holiday, I'll...I'll go get it."

By the time the woman had returned, I'd visited the Audi, taken JJ's lead and recovered my Glock. Big guys with shaved heads are never a good sign in our line of work.

Miss Morrison lumbered her way around the fence to Colin's front door. She too had recovered some poise.

"I can't let you in on your own of course. I mean, I should ask for some form of identification really."

JJ lifted his Ray-Bans to reveal those black eyes of his. "Open the door, lady," he said.

I wouldn't have argued either.

Miss Morrison pushed the key into the front door and it swung open on well-oiled hinges.

I took the lead.

The hallway had a pale laminate wood floor. Pictures of smiling children adorned spotless white walls. There was no clutter. Just as with the car and the garden, Colin liked to have everything in its place. To the left, the lounge door was open, the room empty; ahead the kitchen door was closed. On the laminate, in front of the white glossed door were three spots of bright blood.

I turned to JJ, pointed at my eyes with fore and middle fingers, then to the claret.

He nodded, drew his Glock and clicked off the safety.

Miss Morrison who was almost stuck to my back, let out a gasp. I pulled my own weapon and whispered.

"Step outside, love."

Rick Fuller's Story:

As I reached our office, Estelle was busy taking a call. I acknowledged her before slipping into the back, carrying the offending CCTV unit.

Des was working on a shift pattern for some of our guys who were about to depart for Saudi on a shockingly boring but lucrative babysitting job.

"Any luck?" he asked, dropping his pen and stretching his back.

"Well," I said, "I've identified the guy that dropped the bug in Spiros's litter bin, but there's no footage of anyone at the house after that. He must have topped the Greek, managed to disable the system on the day, but didn't have the sense to nick the fucking unit."

Des shrugged, "Or it wasn't him, it was someone else?"

I pulled the printed pictures of Red George from my bag and handed one to Des.

"Way too many coincidences for my liking…This is our snooper, he's a real sweetheart called Gjergj Dushku, an Albanian. Big lad, eh?

Des let out a low whistle. "Yeah, he looks a proper handful. I was out in Kosovo in 1997, one of my last jobs in the Regiment. It was a horrible conflict, almost as bad as Columbia, mate. The Albanians are evil fuckers."

"Simon…our Egghead, who is on a better hourly rate than the PM I might add, is looking into his background for us. Apparently, he will be able to tell us the horrible bastard's shoe size by teatime."

Des absently felt for his equally horrible pipe.

"So, I take it we're going to pay old George a visit then? See if he's dancing to Goldsmith's tune?"

"That's the plan…where's Lauren and JJ by the way?"

Des shrugged. "When Estelle rocked up early doors, she said JJ was waiting outside the front of the office. Said he jumped into a white Audi, didn't see who was driving…I'm betting that was our Lauren's RS6. Reckon she's doing just what you asked her not to."

"Looking for the prison guard that allegedly found Goldsmith's body?"

"Yup."

I shook my head and began my plan to find Red George.

Lauren North's Story:

I admit I'd been sceptical about Rick's theory, but Spiros Makris was indeed dead, and now, fresh claret on Colin's polished oak laminate did not bode well for our first possible witness to the alleged suicide of Stephan Goldsmith.

Had the three spots been bone dry, that would have been an altogether different matter, but whoever had spilled that blood had done it fairly recently. If the big muscled visitor had been and gone, well so be it, but this was not a time to take chances.

If Rick was right and Stephan Goldsmith was indeed alive, he would be intent on keeping the fact a secret, and equally keen on seeing our little team out of the way.

And that was really not good.

I shuddered as images flashed in my head, and I saw myself rolling on the cobbles of Puerto Banus, fighting Goldsmith for my life.

I felt instantly terrified.

Our nosey neighbour had legged it to her house and was no doubt opening her third premium cider of the day, whilst ringing the cops. There was no time to worry about her or them, we needed to open the kitchen door, clear the house, and get away clean.

My right leg shook as I stood in the lounge doorway with no more than a stud wall and a wooden casing for cover. The door in question was ten feet in front of me, outward opening, handle to my left.

JJ was in the kneel to the right of the door, tucked halfway under Colin's staircase, his Glock punched forward and upward. He looked at me with those, lifeless pools of his and gave the slightest of nods. I felt sick but tucked myself in, brought my weapon to the aim and nodded back.

JJ inched forward, keeping low, stretching slowly for the handle, all the time keeping the centre of the door covered.

My other leg began to shake, and for the first time since the gun battle at Joel Davies's house, I started to doubt myself.

I knew that when JJ opened the door there would be a split second where he would be blind until he rolled to his left, so it would be up to me to deal with any threat on the other side.

Bile pricked my throat. My palms felt so wet I was convinced I would drop the Glock. I inwardly screamed at myself to get a grip.

Before I could worry anymore, JJ reached the handle and pulled downward.

The door swung open, JJ rolled as I expected and by the time I'd stepped forward, he was at my right shoulder.

Colin Reed was sitting at his kitchen table.

A pool of thick congealing blood surrounded his chair. The room smelled like an abattoir.

I somehow managed to keep down my Starbucks. JJ concentrated on clearing the kitchen as I stood motionless.

I really did need to grow some… and quick.

Colin's bare arms lay palm up on the table. A small steak knife with a bloodied blade lay close by. His eyes were closed, mouth slightly open. He looked almost peaceful. Well, he would have done had it not been for the slits in each arm running upward from the palm, almost to the crook of his elbow. The incisions were so deep it was as if he'd attempted to butterfly his forearms. If you were determined to slit your wrists and ensure certain suicidal success, this was the way to do it.

All, and I mean all, of Colin's blood, was on his immaculate kitchen floor.

I'd seen dozens of 'slit' wrists in my previous life as a nurse. Leeds had been full of young drug-dependent street people who regularly found their way to A&E on a Friday night with everything from a slight graze to wounds that needed stitching. I'd even witnessed the PM of a young woman who'd been successful in her quest. She had copied the Hollywood stars by drinking a bottle of Scotch, lying in a hot bath and slicing her veins open with her unfaithful husband's razor.

Even so, I'd never witnessed any kind of self-harm that had been carried out with such gusto.

JJ reappeared from clearing the rest of the house. For some reason, he checked the washing machine, but there was no time to ask why. "We go now," he said, pulling his Aviators from his head and covering those eyes of his. "I think the fat lady from next door will call the cops, yes?"

I shook my head. The Turk was definitely lacking in the odd social skill.

"I think it's a good thing that poor Miss Morrison didn't nip in to water Colin's plants after a few cans of Strongbow eh?"

I pointed at Reed's corpse. "Have you seen this, JJ? I mean, you're the man in the know when it comes to knife wounds. I've seen enough in my time, but I've never seen anything like this."

He grabbed me by the elbow.

"Yes, I see," he said. "I see everything...I also hear police siren...let's go."

As he pulled me along the hall, I was drawn back to the grotesque scene at the kitchen table. Colin Reed at peace?

No, Colin Reed... posed.

Rick Fuller's Story:

Our newfound and very attractive secretary was waving a post-it note above her head like a linesman on Fergie's payroll.

She smiled, revealing perfect teeth. "You have a message, Mr Fuller."

This spoiled my mood further, so I ignored the information for a moment.

The fact that Lauren had deliberately gone against my wishes was irritating to say the least. Add to that, JJ had trotted along with her, without so much as a 'by your leave'. This saw me particularly tetchy.

"Have you any idea where Lauren went?" I asked.

Estelle checked her nail polish and rudely spoke to her fingers. "Sorry, no."

My temper got the better of me. "Give me the note," I barked, and snatched it from Estelle's hand.

Estelle jumped in fear.

I shook my head in disbelief. "Oh don't be so fucking sensitive…who's it from?"

Estelle's face showed all the signs that she was about to cry.

I figured I'd gone too far.

She recovered a little too quickly. Jutting her chin, she raised her voice, her secretary accent slipping to reveal her actual broad, flat Mancunian.

"I told him right, you'd just walked in and you would be two shakes yeah, but he hung up and just left his number… didn't leave a name…posh bloke, he was."

Scanning the note, I didn't need a name, I recognised the number immediately.

Estelle questioned my parentage under her breath and with a flourish, dropped the plastic cover over her desktop monitor. She then stood, smoothed down her skirt, collected her bag from under her desk, and stepped around it until she was inches from my face.

Was she going to do one?

Oh yes, but not quite yet.

"No one…" she started. "And I mean nobody speaks to me like that…and you," she spat. "Mr 'big I am' Rick Fuller, can stick your job."

She prodded me in the chest with a scarlet nail to accentuate each last word.

"Up… your…fuckin'… arse."

And with that, she was gone.

Des wandered into the front office, pipe in mouth, lighter in hand, headed for the street.

"Dickhead," he said, and stepped into the sunshine.

I stood in the office like a fuckin' naughty schoolboy whilst he gave himself lung cancer on the pavement outside.

Finally, he returned, the smell of tobacco, following him like the Grim Reaper. I stood, eyeing the offending post-it.

Des was not pleased. He gestured toward the offending yellow note.

"So, what's so fuckin' important that you lose our secretary for it?"

I didn't get chance to answer, it was his turn to go off on one. He pointed towards the street.

"That Estelle was a good girl, you big fuckin' bully. While you were getting your bollocks rubbed by private nurses down south, she held this place together. Me and JJ were like headless chickens when it came to the admin side. Estelle worked all fuckin' hours…and now…you've fucked things up…again!"

He was right, I was wrong. Was I going to admit it?

Never.

"She's ten a penny, pal, a pretty girl in cheap shoes."

It was Des's turn to step in close, a whole new and very dangerous ball game. I had a good four inches over him and maybe three stone, but I'd seen him fight men twice his size. This wasn't going to be pretty if it went off.

He curled his lip.

"You and your fuckin' fashions get right on my tits, pal. See that wee lassie? Well, she earns fucking eight quid an hour. What d'you think she's going to wear to work, fucking Jimmy Chong at a grand a time?"

"It's Jimmy Choo," I corrected.

You could have cut the air with a knife. I thought he was about to butt me. Instead he poked me sharply in the chest and wound up the tempo further.

"Ye think that kid shops in Selfridges, don't you eh, matey? Ye need a reality check."

Things were about to get out of hand.

I wanted to tell him that when someone suffers a trauma, real trauma, obsessive behaviour is a common side effect. It's a medical fact.

My obsession is clothes, don't laugh, yes, clothes.

I mean…how can you kill a man without a Paul Smith suit?

We both turned as the office door opened with a swish.

The very recently deposed Estelle dropped her handbag on her very recently ex-desk.

"What are you two up to?" she managed, head down, hiding her eyes. "Having a dance?"

We stood in the middle of the room doing fair impressions of goldfish.

Estelle sat, removed the cover from her monitor and switched it on. She started to type.

A silent minute passed, then without looking up she said quietly. "I need this job, Mr Fuller. I have a mum at home on disability and a brother in the nick. So, if you're going to sack me, so be it, but I'm not walking."

Finally, she raised her head and there was a trickle of a tear. Her bottom lip trembled.

She was definitely going to fucking cry this time.

Des shuffled over. He was about as good as I was with a distraught female. The dopey Scottish bastard started to rub Estelle's back with the flat of his hand; he looked like he was fucking winding her.

Add to that, he made various angry comedy faces at me in a vain attempt to involve me in the process of making Estelle feel wanted.

Thankfully, we were all saved by a further swish of the door. This time, the noise announced the arrival of Lauren.

Looking pale as she stepped in from the late afternoon sunshine, she wore a pastel pink silk blouse and cream combats I knew she'd bought from Warehouse, together with pair of classic all white Adidas tennis shoes. Her hair was held in place by Gucci dark glasses that I hadn't seen before, but quite liked. Despite her pallor, she looked good enough to eat.

In fact, she looked so good, for a moment, I forgot I was pissed off with her.

JJ stepped in behind carrying a holdall.

"The screw's dead," he said, and strode in the back.

Estelle burst into floods of tears.

Lauren North's Story:

I stepped into the back room to find JJ unloading our two Glocks. He checked the safety on each, removed the mags and pulled back the action of each weapon to eject the chambered round, then laid the two bullets to one side for destruction.

It wasn't something you might do if you were out in the field or short of ammunition, but the theory behind it is that once a bullet has been chambered, the working parts may have left some very small indentations on the shell casing, therefore if reloaded, may increase the chance of a misfire. It was a belt and braces exercise, but better safe than sorry.

"How's Estelle?" asked Des.

"I called her a cab," I said, before turning to our esteemed leader Richard Fuller.

"She told me what happened. Sometimes, you are a proper twat, Rick."

He tapped at his laptop and feigned ignorance before finding a retort. "If she can't take a joke, she shouldn't have joined," he said.

I was about to find a witty reply myself when he looked up, those dark chocolate eyes of his so full of anger.

"So, where the fuck have you been... exactly?"

Any confidence I'd found on the way back to the office drained from me in an instant. Opening my mouth, I tried to speak, but nothing came out. As I bit my lip with embarrassment, JJ saved me.

"We go to see the prison guard who find Goldsmith hanged. He work at Strangways many years, his name Colin Reed. We go his house, but when we look inside, he is dead."

Rick thought for a moment before turning to me.

"How'd you find him so fast...this Reed guy?"

I thought I would be sick on the spot. Of course, nothing happened between Larry and me that evening, but I knew Rick would never have agreed to me contacting the cop or using him for information. I went with a half-truth.

"A reporter...a journalist. I went to the library, looked for newspaper articles around the date of Goldsmith's incarceration and found this guy who had been investigating suspicious deaths in the high security wing at Strangeways."

For some reason Des turned away and looked all uncomfortable. Rick didn't notice. "This guy have a name?"

I squared my shoulders. I wasn't going to be so easily intimidated. The fact was, I'd moved the investigation along.

"Warwick," I said. "Rupert Warwick."

"And he works for?" pushed Rick.

"The MEN," I said with a little more confidence, my white lie gaining in credibility.

Rick frowned to show his displeasure but to my relief moved on to JJ, who was next for the treatment.

"So, pal, you and Lauren go to this guy's house…then what?"

JJ shrugged before slouching in his chair and taking up his standard 'fuck you' pose.

"This fat woman next door, she let us in the house with key. We find the guy, this Reed guy, sitting at his table with his wrists cut open…dead, like I said… and before you say anything bad to me, Lauren ask me to go and watch her back…what the fuck you expect me to do eh?"

There was a brief eyeball standoff between the two men.

Rick broke it. "How about letting the rest of the fucking team know?"

JJ gave another shrug and Rick's irritation began to show.

"So, this guy Reed…he killed himself?"

JJ and I spoke in unison.

"No."

I gave my impressions of the crime scene. How the horrendously deep wounds to Reed's arms could not have been inflicted by the small bloodied knife conveniently left on the table top. How the body was deliberately posed and how only three tell-tale drops of blood by the kitchen door had been spilled outside the pool around the body.

As he took in my information, I caught Rick's gaze. "So," I said. "If me and JJ can suss this isn't a suicide, then the cops are definitely going to be onto this one."

Rick thought for a moment, pulled a yellow post-it note from his pocket and studied the writing on it.

"I'm not so sure," he said.

"What's that?" I asked.

Rick tossed the note into the bin. "Nothing important."

He stood and walked over to the window, which overlooked the small yard at the back of the building. Gazing out, he addressed us all.

"One thing is for sure now, we can't rule out the Firm having a hand in all of this. If they, as I suspect, did a deal with Goldsmith and had him in some kind of witness protection programme, we will have to watch our backs even more."

Des was in. "You think the Firm have Goldsmith?"

Rick shrugged. "I think they did. Whether they still do, is another matter. That's why, from today, we work from the lock-up. Leave your usual work and personal phones here, pull the SIM and switch them off. There is a stash of pay-as-you go non-GPS phones in the cabinet over there. Remember, good surveillance people can still triangulate your position when you use any mobile phone, so short calls only. Take one each before you leave. I want you all to start using anti-surveillance measures wherever you go from now on. We're in lockdown until this is all over."

He checked his watch.

"Our next job is to find a guy called Gjergj Dushku. He is our connection to Stephan Goldsmith. RV at the lock-up in two hours, say any goodbyes you feel the need to, and bring enough clothes for a week."

He turned to me.

"You sure you're up for this, Lauren?"

"It would be nice to know exactly what I'm up for," I said. "But yes."

He studied me then nodded.

"Two hours," he said.

Rick Fuller's Story:

So Colin Reed, the man who allegedly found Stephan Goldsmith hanged in his prison cell, was dead. And I had a sneaking suspicion that the more we looked for answers to that incident, the more the body count would rise.

It was one thing I didn't need on my conscience, so our lines of enquiry had to progress, and fast.

I'd asked JJ to stay behind. The others left for their respective homes to sort out their lives and a bag of clothes.

Once we were alone, the Turk ran the whole scenario of the visit to Walkden by me in intricate detail.

I quickly realised that the man who I had once thought of as a one-trick pony with a bad attitude, was far more.

The attitude was still there of course, but that made him what he was, it was an essential part of him, and without it he and I would probably be dead.

"We go in the house and find the body in the kitchen," he began.

"He is sitting at the table, hands rest on top like he is meditate, no? His feet flat to floor, but one shoe is missing.

"The cut to each forearm is made by a big knife, I mean hunting knife or Kukri, you know, the knife Gurkha use."

I nodded.

He continued.

"A big thick blade, and the cut is made from the elbow down to the wrist in one movement. Very clean, very accurate. I know this is so, yet no blood is on the table top, not one drop. All the blood is on the floor around the corpse in a perfect circle yes?"

I thought I was getting his point. "So, he couldn't have lifted his own arms up onto the table, because he bled out with his arms at his side?"

"This is one part, and this takes time, Richard, a lot of time, because on purpose our guy doesn't cut the artery. When I see Colin sitting there, this is the first thing I notice, the first piece of puzzle."

He tapped his nose with his finger. "His missing shoe, the other one, is on the top landing, I see this when I clear the house. I think maybe he was taken from upstairs, maybe he try to run up there to escape. Someone big and strong drag him down, tie him to the chair, cut his veins and watch him die slow."

"Tie him with what?"

"I think bed linen. One bed has no sheet and one single was in the washing machine alone, still wet. I don't think you wash just one piece, no?"

I couldn't help but smile. "You're a proper little Hercule Poirot, eh?"

"I don't know this person," said JJ flatly.

I gave in. "Okay, mate, anyway, why do this to him?"

The Turk shrugged as if the answer was obvious.

"He ask him questions of course."

I had to say, it wasn't an interrogation technique I'd ever come across, and I'd seen a few nasty ones in my time.

JJ had the answer.

"In the fourteenth century the Ottoman Empire invaded Greece, but some parts remained under the control of Venice, yes?"

"You mean Italy?"

"No, I mean the Most Serene Republic of Venice."

I was at a loss. My London comprehensive hadn't run to fourteenth century history, so I kept quiet. JJ, however, knew his stuff.

"The Republic of Venice was a separate entity to Rome and very powerful. She controls the Ionian Islands of Corfu and Kefalonia whilst us Turks have Crete and others, yes? The Venetian also invade the coastal areas of what is now Serbia, Croatia and most of Albania."

I tried to keep quiet and waited for the punchline.

"So, when these fighters take the Greek island of Corfu and cleanse whole villages, they find they have no one left to work the farms, no food to feed their army. So, they use labour from the closest country they control…Albania.

The men of Corfu hate the Albanian for stealing their land. But they will not lie down and die like animal. They form small militias…kill many soldiers and many Albanian, raiding the small villages around the north coast. The Corfiot are very brave men."

Much to my horror, JJ started to roll a cigarette as he spoke. But as I'd never heard him speak more than two or three words and a grunt at any one time, this was a special occasion.

"So," he continued. "When the Albanian, he catch one of these Greek fighters, this was the way they interrogate him. They cut him bad along the forearm or sometimes the calf, but not enough to kill. The prisoner slowly bleed to death as he is questioned.
Inside his mind, he know that if he answers, there is a chance he will live, no?"

"But they never did?"

JJ nodded. "The Albanians would leave the corpses of the Greek fighters in a chair surrounded by a circle of their own blood for the local women and children to see. This was a warning.
They call this, 'the pool of shame'. This is the Albanian way of marking a man, saying they make him inform on his own people. What they say here in Manchester? A grass?
I tell you, Richard, Reed was killed by an Albanian."

I rooted in my case and found one of the pictures I'd printed out at Egghead's house.
I laid it on the table.
JJ looked at it for a long time, then said, "The fat lady next door say a man with shaved head and big muscles call at Colin Reed's house before we go there. One day before, maybe two."
I had all the conformation I needed.
"So, he's at least a day in front of us," I muttered half to myself.
Tapping the picture, I said, "This is Red George. The man who left the bug in Spiros Makris' house. He's Albanian and I know he likes to use a machete as his preferred close combat weapon."
JJ handed me back the photo. "You think this man lead us to Goldsmith?"
I nodded. "I think he is working for Goldsmith, yes."
"Then we find him…and kill him," he said.
And they say great minds think alike.
JJ went to light his roll-up.
I caught his wrist. "Smoke that outside, pal."

Des Cogan's Story:

Of course, I knew it wasn't going to be as simple as slotting Red George, dumping his body in the ship canal and going for a pint in O'Shea's.

Oh no, never mind that we had to take on a seven-foot, machete-wielding psychopathic, Albanian. Our Richard had far bigger fish in his sights, Rick's ultimate aim was to see Goldsmith dead. He was convinced the Dutchman was still alive and that the big Albanian would lead us to him. And this time, there would be no rest for anyone until he'd seen Goldsmith's body…personally.

The thing with Rick Fuller, and I feel I can share this with you as we are so far into this tale...he never forgives and never ever forgets. Goldsmith tortured Rick, scalding his legs with boiling water. He forced him into giving me up; forced him to show weakness. The fact that Goldsmith was on his third kettle, didn't come into it. The animal had got one over on him. So…the biggest mistake he ever made?

Not putting a second round into Rick's head up on that moor.

As I packed my carry-on, I have to admit that I felt a twinge of excitement. The mixture of trepidation and anticipation had never left me, and I was pretty sure that it never would. I pushed a spare pair of jeans and the usual mix of T-shirts, skids and socks into the rucksack. Never bothering with shaving kit on a job, there was just a toothbrush, paste and soap. After all, it's not a beauty contest. I fastened the zip and sat on the end of my bed.

My flat wasn't up to much, don't get me wrong, the place itself was okay, but other than the bed I sat on and one of those zip-up wardrobes, the room was bare.

In the lounge, was a sofa, TV, and a Sky box.

The kitchen had a good beer fridge. To my detriment, the cooker was brand spanking new and had never been switched on.

There were no paintings on the walls, no little souvenirs from days gone by. This was my life, this was what it had come to.

After writing a note to my lap dancer I shouldered the sack, wandered down the hall and stuck my only goodbye on the outside of the door. Both my parents were dead, and after Anne and I divorced, my staunchly Catholic brothers made it clear that I was persona non grata.

I shook my head in the realisation that the young lady who visited me in the early hours was the lone person I felt the need to tell I was going away, and I didn't even know her surname.

I was just about to leave when I noticed a letter on the mat. I wasn't sure how I'd missed it, but there it was, and it boasted a Glasgow postmark.

I dropped the sack and ripped open the envelope. It was headed 'McCauley and Partners Solicitors.'

Inside, were the deeds to Hillside cottage.

Sitting behind the legal documents that needed to be signed and witnessed was another envelope; the one the brief had mentioned at the reading of the will.

The script on the front had been written by a shaky hand, yet I recognised it immediately. If Anne's hand had shaken though illness, my tremor as I opened the pale pink packet was caused by pure emotion.

Dear Des,

By the time you read this, I believe we will have met for the final time. As you will have witnessed, my illness took its toll on my body, but not my mind.

I will have asked you the hardest of questions, and you will have given me your answer.

You always were the strongest one.

I know how hard I fought to keep Hillside, but I cannot bear Gordon to have the house. No doubt, you will find out my reasons soon enough.

I could go on about mistakes made, but there is no time for regret now.

Do with the place what you will. If it holds too many painful memories, then sell it, take the money and run. It is your time now, Des.

You have weathered the storm all your life, my love, now it's time for you to dance in the rain.

Anne.

I smiled at that one. The little saying at the end came from a small wooden plaque that used to dangle on our kitchen wall. Anne had bought it when we were on a rare holiday in Cornwall.

I read the letter again, folded it carefully and slipped it into my carry-on.

Leaving the legal stuff on the mat, I stepped out onto the landing.

Lauren North's Story:

I had no idea why Rick was being so obtuse, but it wasn't unusual. We would be briefed at the lock-up where he felt safe and all would be revealed.

I managed the short walk to my building without shaking legs. I liked to think that it was down to my returning mental strength, but it was equally probable that the good doctor's 'happy' pills had worked some magic.

Either way, I'd binned the rest of the course. It was time to see if I could cope without them.

I showered and inspected the recent scars to my body.

Were they worth it?

I thought so.

Two hours wasn't much time to get my bag together. I lived forty minutes away, for God's sake. Having all my fighting kit stowed at the lock-up was one thing, but it was the personal stuff I lacked, and knowing Rick, I would need everything from jeans to that little black dress in my rucksack.

I dressed in the heavy stuff… jeans, hoodie, some nice boots I couldn't resist, and used the sack for some skirts, posh tops, good shoes and the LBD.

I brushed my hair into a ponytail and applied some slap.

As I checked my face in the mirror, the tap on my front door made me drop my lippy.

Heart racing, I stepped silently toward the door. Nobody had ever knocked on my door before without buzzing up from the main entrance. Holding my breath, I managed to reach the spy hole.

It was Larry.

"You frightened the life out of me," I barked at the closed door.

"And I see my welcome hasn't improved," he said with a laugh in his voice. "Any chance you can open the door?"

I didn't feel like I had the choice, flicked the lock and took a step backwards.

"Ah," he said. "That's better."

"Hello, Larry," I managed. "This is a…"

"Surprise," he added for me. "Yes, I know. I mean, I can guess…erm..." He noticed my bag on the floor behind me and pointed. "Going on a trip?"

Larry was dressed as he always was, in a suit. This time a pale grey three-piece. His tie was pulled away from the neck of his shirt, his hair tousled probably by his own hands during the course of his day. Handsome didn't come into it.

I was briefly put at odds with myself and couldn't think of an answer. Finally, I managed, "Oh me? Yes, I'm off to my mother's."

He furrowed his brow. "You're visiting your mother dressed in jeans, a Helly Hansen hoodie, and taking the rest of your wardrobe in a rucksack?"

I nodded too many times.

He stepped inside without being asked, purposely brushing my shoulder, smelling even better than he looked. "Nice place you have here, Lauren. I never got to see the inside on my last visit."

"No, erm…well…sorry about that, but, well, you know."

He turned.

"But things are different now aren't they, Lauren? I mean, you and your pals are working solely on your body-guarding business eh? No more gangsters, guns and bombs?"

More nods.

He pretended to be examining my bookcase but was expertly taking me apart.

"So, the fact that the guy whose address I gave you last night, is currently in the morgue with his forearms slit open has…"

I got myself together at that one. "…has nothing to do with me, yes…correct."

Larry moved a box of wallpaper samples from my sofa and sat. "I know," he mused. "Doc says he'd been dead over twenty-four, maybe forty-eight hours."

There was no point in any further bullshit. "The blood spill looked fresher than that to me."

Larry leaned forward. "So, you were inside then? Are you going to tell me why you wanted to talk to him?"

I shook my head.

"Official Secrets Act and all that eh? Still in the pockets of the spooks?"

I let him make his assumptions, shrugged and kept my poker face.
"Like the old Eagles song, Larry. 'You can check out any time you want'…"
Larry stood and stopped inches from me. He took my arms gently and looked into my eyes.
"Yeah, I know the song, but you *can* leave, Lauren. You can get away, and I can help you …Want to help you."
My head swam. "Look…Larry, I…"
He didn't let me finish.
"I know what you are going to say, but just hear me out. What I did to you was inexcusable and I'm sorry, genuinely sorry. But I'm not here because I'm a cop or I want to know about the Firm, I'm not here for any of those reasons. I'm here because…because I think that me and you could… well you know?"
Larry leaned forward and kissed the corner of my mouth.
I pushed him away, avoiding his gaze, "You'd better go."
He took a step back, but gently lifted my chin until our eyes met.
"The other night in the pub, I felt something I hadn't done in a long, long, time, Lauren. I'm not being all soppy here. What I'm saying is I felt at ease, able to talk to someone who genuinely understands what it's like to be in the job. What it's like to be away from the nine to five routine…We could be good together, me and you."
I started to shake my head, but he was having none of it.
"Don't say no now, Lauren…look, I can see you are going somewhere, and I know it will be with him, with Rick. All I ask is that when you get back, you call me…Okay? Promise me that."
He kissed me again, this time full on the mouth, and I kissed him back.
I drew away, tasting him, smelling him, my head all over the place.
"No promises," I said. "After all, Larry, I never know if I'll make it back, do I?"

Rick Fuller's Story:

I'd always demanded the highest standards from my teams and measured my own performance against the best of them. From the early days as a lanky kid walking the streets of Belfast, through to the jungles of South America and burning African villages, for me only the best and bravest had been good enough.

The men and women who failed to reach those standards were left behind at my request; some however, lay dead on the battlefield. Although I knew my own talents were fading with each passing year, I found myself wandering around the lock-up, surrounded by memories of past adventures with a growing expectation.

Just as back in those days of combat and conflict, in the darkest moments just before the call finally came, the call to fall thousands of feet into the night, the call to detonate that charge on that door, I felt the same excitement rise in my belly.

Bring it on.

I had spread our largest table with every single weapon that remained at our disposal. Four Bergans sat against the wall, filled with clothing, rations and meds. The old wooden slab virtually groaned under the weight of weaponry, ammunition and auxiliary kit, yet none would be of any use until we could identify the whereabouts of our prey, Gjergj Dushku, Red George. Therefore, a second and equally crowded table top sat under the television, packed full of binoculars, cameras and other electronic surveillance kit that I'd begged borrowed and stolen over the years.

Why had I demanded the team double their own anti-surveillance efforts?

That yellow post-it, that's why.

JJ was the first back.

He slumped into a comfy chair and rolled his knife around his hands as was his wont. I'd almost gotten used to his ways, and I would never forget the bravery and toughness he showed when it really mattered. He'd saved my life not once, but twice.

He gestured toward the table full of cameras and lenses.

"This is not my thing, Richard. I have no patience for watching, unless with a rifle."

"Me either, pal, I've never been one for sitting still for too long. But we won't be using that gear just yet. Not on this first job anyway."

The door was pushed open. Des strode in and dropped his day sack alongside his Bergan. He went straight to the weapon table, selected a Sig, checked the safety and removed the full clip. Then picking up two spare mags and a box of rounds, he sat and went about pushing 9mm into each.

As there was no greeting, no sarcastic comment and a definite lack of eye contact, I presumed there was an issue that he wasn't going to share with the group, so I left him to it.

Seconds later Lauren appeared.

If Des had got a face on, she was a contender for the 'lost a quid and found a penny' contest.

I shot a glance at JJ. He just shrugged.

She too dropped her bag alongside her fighting kit, but chose to attack the fridge rather than the weapons. After selecting a chicken leg, she bit into it and found a chair.

There was no time for babysitting, so I cracked on.

"Okay…Lauren, Des, JJ…heads up."

On the wall above the Bergans, I'd stuck a blow-up shot of a street on the Anson Estate, Longsight, Manchester. An area of town that you visited if you liked being shot at.

Longsight was bordered by Ardwick to the north, Rusholme to the west, Levenshulme to the south, and Gorton to the east.

If you were the social worker type, you may have said that Longsight was an ethnically diverse area, with high levels of poverty, deprivation and crime.

I'd just describe it as a shithole.

The area had been plagued by gang-related violence for years. Just like Moss Side, the viciousness came from tensions between just two rival gangs fighting over turf.

Last year, 2006, there were a hundred and twenty gang-related shootings between the two small districts. Even fucking Chicago couldn't match that.

Egghead had identified Red George for us and was also able to give us his last known place of work.

The Albanian monster had been working for Jimmy and Kevin London, a pair of high end car thieves, who also transpired to be the heads of one of the aforementioned two gangs, that regularly caused so much chaos, smack bang in the middle of Longsight.

Fortunately, Egghead, in his previous life as a coke-head-cum-car-thief, had sold the odd knock-off motor to the London gang, and knew the lay of the land. That gave us a place to start, even if it was in the arsehole of the city.

I pointed to the picture.

"This is Jimmy and Kevin London's house, or should I say houses. They reside in the two semis on the left, numbers 18 and 20…both council-owned three-beds. As Jimmy and Kevin are cash rich, you might think they would try and find a little more salubrious area in which to live. Not these two; apparently, they like it in Manchester's answer to the OK Corral and religiously pay the twenty-nine quid a week rent for each of these proverbial palaces out of their benefits. Yes, unbelievably, they still sign on.

Jimmy was born in 18. His uncle Trevor and cousin Kevin had number 20. In 2002, Uncle Trevor was shot in the face trying to steal a Range Rover from a farmer in Cheshire. Shortly after that the two cousins felt the need to be closer to each other, and knocked out the walls to make one large house. No one from the council dared complain about the building work.

Jimmy and Kevin are old school. They have never worked a day in their lives, have never been out of England, and still drink in the same pub they had their first pint in. That said, they are rich beyond most of Longsight's residents' dreams.

The information we have is that our main target, Red George, the man seen in Spiro Makris' house just before his murder, and the man we believe Miss Morrison saw at Colin Reed's house around the day of his demise, has been working for Jimmy and Kevin as recently as last month. I'm guessing that the Albanian has been acting as some kind of go-between, helping move stolen motors out of the country. The London's empire is built on stolen cars. They make Nicolas Cage look like Miss Daisy when it comes to knocking off motors.

Their people only steal high end vehicles and most of these will be rung, and end up in Eastern Europe.

Now, don't let the car thief tag faze you. Jimmy and his cousin Kevin are a couple of Manchester's most violent criminals. Both were sentenced to a nine stretch for kicking a student to death outside a Manchester nightclub. All the kid had done was puke on Jimmy's car. Apparently, they took it in turns to kick the boy in the head, fracturing his skull in eleven places.

The murder charge was dropped to manslaughter at Crown Court, on the proviso of a guilty plea. Both served only three years of the nine, all of it in Strangeways, from where they not only ran a landing, but their stolen car business too.

Since then Kevin has been arrested four times, twice for wounding with intent, and twice for rape, one on a sixteen-year-old schoolgirl. In all those cases, the witnesses have failed to attend court to give evidence and he's walked.

Jimmy seems to be able to keep his dick in his trousers, but was pulled for possession of a firearm in 2004. He served three months. These two choirboys are the only connection to Red George we have, and we need George to get to Stephan Goldsmith."

Lauren dropped her chicken leg into the pedal bin and returned to the fridge for further supplies. She seemed to have recovered some of her composure.

"Where's the intel come from? How good is it?"

"Egghead…Simon that is, the guy who hacked into Spiros's CCTV unit. He finds out current intelligence quicker than the boffins at the Firm. The detail is superb. Also, he was a car thief long before his interest in computers saved him from a lengthy prison term. He worked for Jimmy and Kevin London back in the day so the intel is good and reliable."

She nodded and crunched a celery stick.

Des had finished loading mags. He still had the look of a man with something on his mind and I finally realised I'd seen that very look before. Whatever his problem was, I reckoned it had something to do with his ex-wife, no danger.

"So, we're going to pay these wee bastards Jimmy and Kevin a visit then?" he asked.

"We are," I said.

He pointed his finger and gave me a look that told me I was crazy.

"At their house? That one there in the picture?"

I shook my head. "No, not the house…for two reasons.

One, the ongoing gang war between the London crew and their rivals has meant a massive increase in their security. Simon describes the house as Fort Knox, all internal gates and reinforced doors. Also, Jimmy and company, have joined the rest of Manchester's gangsters and recruited the usual group of teens to ride around the surrounding streets on BMX's, clocking strange cars or faces and reporting to their main security.

These guys form their real security cordon, older faces, more experienced, often armed, working foot patrols in four-hour shifts around the house. According to Egghead, most of their muscle live on a diet of Clenbuterol and Charlie. The last thing we need is a gun battle with a group of muscle-bound blokes who think they are ten men, especially on their turf."

"And the second reason?" asked Lauren.

I began pinning up pictures of The Anson pub.

"Because we know exactly where our target will be and when.

The intel is, that it's Jimmy who does the hiring and firing, and he will be the one with the knowledge on Red George. So… it's Jimmy we want, forget Kevin, we take Jimmy, alive, on the street…here…outside his local."

Des Cogan's Story:

The Anson reminded me of a few pubs I'd visited over the years. You found them in inner city shitholes wherever you lived. They tended to be big red brick-built, corner plots with lots of rooms and massive car parks, which nobody with a brain cell ever left their car in.

The Anson was one such venue. At some point in its life, some entrepreneurial soul had taken over part of the main building and turned it into a take-away. I suppose it gave the clientele a change of scenery in which to stab each other without the need for public transport.

Rick had used Google Maps to show all the possible routes from Jimmy's house to the pub.

I could see the job was a non-starter straight away.

"There are too many ways he could go, mate. I mean, there's only us four eh? And he could take five, maybe six ways there. He could go on foot or drive, and anyway, the moment our crew set foot on the estate, the jungle drums would be banging, nae bother."

"I realise the issues," said Rick, pointing at the pile of binos and kit on the table under the TV. "That's why we are not going to use the usual surveillance methods."

I didn't like the sound of this little soiree, and I was right not to.

"Aye…go on then, pal."

"I want you and Lauren to sit inside the pub, clock Jimmy as he arrives, and take him on the carpark. Me and JJ will be sat just off the manor, and as soon as you give us the nod, we'll come and complete the lift."

I couldn't help but smile.

"You want us… me and Lauren… to sit inside that shithole and wait for this bad boy to turn up?

No chance, pal. Me and Lauren will stand out like spare pricks at a wedding in that boozer. Everybody in the place will be either related by birth or have lived on the Anson for donkey's years. The only thing you'd be lifting from the car park would be our battered bodies."

Always one for a plan, Rick just pointed at the picture of The Anson and waved away my concerns.

"If you two keep yourselves to yourselves, you'll be fine."

"Oh aye," I said. "That's just fine and dandy. It's okay for them to knock the fuck out of the Scottish lad eh? It will make a change from fuckin' Sky Sports for the wee boys."

"Now you're being awkward," said Rick. "You'll have Lauren as back-up."

I couldn't believe what I was hearing.

"Awkward, am I? Well, how about this then? How about you go into the boozer with JJ, and me and Lauren wait outside in the car?"

It was Rick's turn to shake his head. "Can't do that," he said.

"Why?" asked a very uptight Lauren.

Before I tell you what he said, let me point out that he was deadly serious.

He laid his palms out flat.

"Firstly, Jimmy and Kevin may recognise me from back in the day…and anyway, no one would ever believe I lived on a council estate."

Lauren North's Story:

I wanted to slap him. Just who did he think he was?

JJ sat and smiled to himself. If it had been a joke, it may have even been funny, but Rick had no idea he'd just insulted us. To him it was just…obvious.

I closed my mouth and gritted my teeth.

Rick ploughed his furrow regardless. "Okay so, Jimmy always visits the Anson on a Wednesday night," he began. "He's captain of the pub darts team and never misses a match."

Des was incredulous.

"You're thinking of doing this tonight, aren't ye?" He checked his watch. "In the next two hours?"

Rick nodded.

"That's fucking crazy, pal," said Des. "We don't even know what this guy Jimmy looks like. Do you have a mugshot?"

"No," said Rick flatly. "But Egghead says he looks like an older version of him out of Oasis."

Des shook his head, "Fuck me…Liam or Noel?"

Rick pulled his face. "I don't fucking know, both of them maybe. He's all mop-haired and John Lennon glasses. Always wears an army-style jacket with lots of pockets, neck full of tatts, bad attitude, stupid walk."

Des stood, he wasn't a happy bunny, and I knew why. "Oh, that's great. A big fucking help that is.

Is this gaff, a City or United pub?"

"City, I think," said Rick.

Des laughed. "Hah! So, half the fuckin' customers will be dressed like the Gallagher brothers, and walk like they've shit their pants. The other half will be a mixture of shaven-headed nutters with shiny black tracksuits and rolled gold accessories, mixed in with skinny crack heads who are barred from every other pub in the north of England.…how the fuck do we ID the wee bastard, when half the pub resembles his description?"

"You won't be able to miss him," said Rick. "He'll be with cousin Kevin, who's a skinny little runt with dyed black hair, and a guy called Paddy Devlin, the London's bodyguard. Paddy is a big fucker with a carrot top. Ex 2 Para."

As if it wasn't obvious what a shit job this was already, Rick added, "You'll need to avoid Paddy like the plague, he's a very nasty piece of work and is always armed. Kevin won't be a problem.

Apparently, he's that skinny he'll stand out like Buddy Holly at a Meatloaf convention. That said, he is known for attacking guys when their backs are turned."

Des scratched his head. "I dinnae know about this, pal…How far away will you and JJ be? How long do we have to hold onto this wee shite before the cavalry arrive?"

"Four minutes." he said.

Des eyed his best friend for a moment.

There was no doubt that Rick intended to go ahead with his plan, and there wasn't the slightest uncertainty that Des and JJ would simply find a way to achieve it.

That said, even I knew four minutes was way too long.

"You need to halve that," said Des. "Even if Lauren covers big Paddy and the skinny lad, I've still got to overpower Jimmy, who after about ten seconds is going to realise that this is a kidnap and not a hit. He's going to kick off…I want you there in two minutes max."

Rick instantly nodded his agreement, then turned to JJ. "We'll just have to risk being closer."

JJ shrugged at the obvious and went back to playing with his knife.

I couldn't believe what I was hearing. All my training told me we needed more time. Feeling rather jelly-legged again, I did my best to focus on the real issues.

"Are you really suggesting we do this without any preparation, Rick? I mean, even you must agree that we need to see the layout of the pub; entrances, exits, stairs, just basics. And I'd want a physical check of the area outside the venue too for any obstacles, that kind of thing. We wouldn't want to be dragging Jimmy to the car by his ankles and run straight into fucking big hole the council had dug that afternoon, would we?"

He remained impassive.

I shook my head in disbelief. "Come on, Rick. You know standard operating procedure would call for at least three exit strategies in case it all goes to hell in a handcart, I mean, what if...?"

At that, he stepped in.

"We haven't time for any what ifs."

"Oh, come on," I barked. "What's the hurry? Why not next Wednesday? Do the job right for God's sake. We'll still get to George, still get Goldsmith."

Rick held the bridge of his nose between thumb and forefinger and squeezed his eyes tight as he began.

"Because we have no time, Lauren. I reckon that Goldsmith has instructed Red George to eliminate everyone who had any part in the investigation of his so-called death."

I held out my palms. "And where is your evidence of this?"

Rick locked eyes with me and slowly laid out his stall. "I reckon Goldsmith discovered Makris was investigating his so-called suicide...He sends George to top Spiros, but that wouldn't be enough for Stephan. He would want more insurance. That means the silence of any possible witnesses Spiros may have contacted."

JJ opened his knife with a flick of his wrist. "Colin Reed is the first witness, yes? Like he was going to be our first."

"Exactly," added Rick. "And if we don't act now, there could be other innocent victims; prison officers, paramedics, doctors, even undertakers may be on the list."

Nodding toward JJ in appreciation, Rick added, "We know that an old Albanian torture technique using a machete type knife was used to cause Reed's slow death. What we don't know is what the poor fucker told his tormentor, but you can bet that he would have given any names he knew."

Rick squared himself.

"Look...the murders of Makris and Reed are definitely the work of Red George...Gjergj Dushku, a UK resident since the Kosovan war in '98 and as dangerous a man as you are likely to meet.

As far as I knew, he was a freelancer. But according to our friend Egghead, he's recently been working for Jimmy London.

Now, our George speaks fluent Russian, Polish and Albanian...handy to have around in the stolen car game eh? He's also built like a brick wall and was trained by the KLA.

The description from the neighbour points to him being at Colin Reed's gaff one or even two days before we discovered his body. We could confirm that by showing his picture to Miss Morrison, but I think we have the answer already. I believe with every day that passes, George will be out there looking to cross off another victim. I'm sure of it. I wouldn't ask any of you to do this, if I didn't truly believe there is no other option."

He caught my gaze again. His eyes were full of passion and determination. "This is not just about Goldsmith, Lauren, Spiro's kid, or even me. It's about saving those poor sods who just get up for work every day at Strangeways jail. We have to do this, and we have to start tonight."

There was a long silence and some knowing looks, but what was there to say? Rick was right.
I wandered over to the weapons table where the Scot was sorting himself out.
"I've done this a time or two," he muttered, pushing the two spare magazines he'd loaded into the inside pockets of his coat. "No prep, no plan."
"And?" I asked, out of earshot.
"Normally goes to shit," he said quietly, checking the safety on his Sig and finding it a home in the waistband of his jeans.
"Bit warm for a leather jacket, isn't it?" I asked.
Des smiled; he was his usual dry self, "Probably right, but, unlike yourself, I've no choice. I'm not walking in The Anson carrying a fucking handbag. As there is every chance my teeth, that I've not long since paid a small fortune for, will be all over the pub floor within an hour or two, the last thing I need is to give the fuckers an excuse to inflict any further damage eh?"
He smiled and squeezed my shoulder, appearing relaxed. This was good, as I felt anything but.
I'd gone cold turkey all day. I felt sharper, but my hands shook as I opened my bag.
The ASP that I'd used on the streets of Ireland sat on the large table laid out with other weapons. I remembered giving Fat Barry a few good cracks with it whilst playing prostitute on Linen Hall Street. I also clearly recalled how Siobhan, the young prostitute, had repaid

me for saving her a beating. Alongside it was a neat looking silver-coloured Colt SLP with a pearl inlay grip. I'd not seen it before, but it was small, just a six-round mag, and it felt good in my hand. After a quick check, it went in the bag alongside the expandable baton and some loose 9mm.

Rick wandered over.

"You got everything you need?" he asked.

I managed a smile for him. This was no time for anger or argument. He was never going to change, whatever the occasion, however dark things got.

"I suppose we have," I said.

He handed me a set of keys. "Good...good. Those're for a red Golf GTI. It's parked on the Arndale, Floor 3. Registration is on the fob."

I nodded and studied his dark eyes. They weren't cold, they were just... elsewhere. Would there always be this distance between us?

"We never got that dinner," I said gently.

His face softened and he bit his lower lip. Something flashed in those chocolate pools of his. "No," he said. "Maybe next time, eh?"

Having no answer, and feeling suddenly tearful, I turned to Des. "Come on you, let's get a move on, or Jimmy will be in the boozer before us."

The car was exactly where Rick said it would be. It was a bit of a wreck and smelled of cigarettes, but once on the road it was quick and nimble to drive. The main point being, it was disposable.

With no map or navigation system, I had to drive the route from memory. I think Des was as surprised as me when I pulled into The Anson's car park without a single U-turn.

The reason I'd wanted a walk-through of the job became obvious the moment we arrived. Half the carpark had been taped off by contractors, who had left for the day. There were piles of rubble everywhere, and a mechanical digger and a generator were chained to a solitary lamp post. This was apparently a bid to stop them from being stolen during the night.

Two huge skips, one full, the other empty, blocked the main entrance of the pub.

"Dinnae worry about the skips," said Des, reading my thoughts. "It only means our man will have to come in through the side door over there. I reckon he'll park here, near us. That gives us fifty feet or so in which to take him."

I looked at the cloudless sky. Manchester was experiencing an early heatwave.

"That's if he's driving at all. He could walk here, it's a nice evening for it."

"Maybe," said Des. "Like most of these jobs, hen, it's a wait and see."

Unsurprisingly, there were no outdoor tables or pleasant sun shades outside The Anson. Over time, they had probably found their way into the various back gardens of the locals. Even so, pitched between our car and the door were half a dozen youths lolling about drinking pints, soaking up the last of the evening sunshine. They all sported skinheads, black tracksuit bottoms and the essential gold chains. The hot weather ensured that they had removed their T-shirts revealing skinny arms and sunken chests.

Clocking us instantly, they stopped their banter, and took a long look at our red GTI.

Des pushed open his door, looked over at me and raised his eyebrows.

"Showtime," he said.

Rick Fuller's Story:

I always knew my old Escort van would come in handy. I hadn't used it since I'd had to transport one of Joel Davies's employees back to his flat and throw him off his balcony. He'd been riding around in his boss's 911 and putting Charlie up his nose he hadn't paid for.

Big mistake.

I seemed to recall that unfortunate soul was called Jimmy too. Our new shiny Jimmy was much richer, but equally stupid. If everything went according to plan, I knew exactly what was about to happen to new Jimmy, and it wasn't going to be pretty.

We needed a safe place to deal with our car-stealing murderer, and I'd asked the only person I could trust outside the team for help, Kostas Makris.

The Greek had given me the keys to one of his industrial units in Haigh Park, Stockport. It gave us a nice easy run from the pub, straight down the A6 through Levenshulme, a left at Heaton Chapel, and we'd be there. Well that was the plan.

The unit itself was on a self-contained site and didn't run twenty-four hours. Kostas said it was nice and quiet with no security or CCTV to worry about.

We could interrogate Jimmy there without interruptions.

My initial idea was to park out toward the Apollo, but Des was right, we needed to take a chance and get closer to the pub.

We tucked the van in nice and close to Saint Chrysostom's church, just off the Anson Road. I estimated we could be on the Anson carpark within ninety seconds.

I don't know where he'd got the idea from, but JJ had decided that there was the chance that things may go wrong. Rather than an SLP, he'd brought an MP7 along with him, one kindly recovered from the O'Donnell conflict by the Firm and dropped at our DLB. Pushed into the inside pockets of his leather were two spare mags and a suppressor. I considered he could do enough damage with his knife, but with the H+K he could take out the whole fucking estate. With the suppressor fitted, the MP7 would be as quiet as his blade too.

I'd opted for my personal Sig Sauer 1911 Fastback as it didn't stick in your back whilst driving. We both carried hoods and plasti-cuffs in our back pockets. These were intended primarily for Jimmy of course, but, should any nosy kids on BMX's come sniffing about, it would be a way of keeping them quiet for an hour.

I checked the time, and felt mildly irritated that I'd not changed my watch. Glowing perfectly on my wrist was one of my latest purchases, a very nice TAG Heuer Carrera, a snip at £4,500.

In all the excitement, I'd forgotten to swap it for a more workmanlike unit.

JJ noticed my annoyance. He pulled out the twenty-quid phone I'd insisted all the team carried. The screen announced 19:03.

"I have the time," he said with a smile. "I think you leave this very nice watch in the glovebox, no? Things may get a little rough."

Des Cogan's Story:

The wee laddies blocking our entrance to the Anson were nothing to worry about. As we closed on the crew, the thick sickly smell of weed hung in the air. I noticed one pass a joint to the other, and he openly pulled on it, laughing as he did so.

I thought it unlikely that the local boys in blue would be turning up to arrest these errant youths any time soon.

When the cops visited pubs like the Anson they would be mob-handed, and it would be out of absolute necessity, not to bust some kids for smoking a joint.

I've never been one for drugs myself, apart from the legal variety that is, but one thing I will say about cannabis users, once they'd had a smoke, they were fucking useless in a fight.

As we approached the lads, they moved without issue. The closest guy had eyes like slits and wore a big smile as we went by.

"I wouldn't leave that Golf there, man," he said.

I turned to him and gave him my finest welcoming Glasgow look.

"I think it will be fine, pal…especially with you boys looking after it."

The kid looked blank for a moment, before nodding fiercely as the penny dropped.

"Oh yeah, man…sure…we'll be here, man."

"That's what I thought," I said. "I knew you were good boys."

Lauren smiled to herself and shook her head as she stepped into the pub.

"You are a bad man, Des Cogan," she said.

I ordered a pint of Stella as I knew the Guinness would be shit.

Lauren opted for the same. The sight of a woman drinking pints was a daily occurrence in the Anson, however one that looked like Lauren North was a different matter.

The room was already half-full with early evening drinkers. There was more of a mix than I'd thought. A good few old boys with their halves of mild, rubbed shoulders with the expected meatheads and Oasis doppelgangers.

No one seemed to notice us, except the half a dozen women of varying shapes and sizes that populated the bar. They jealously watched Lauren's every move.

I've been in some rough pubs in my time, and one thing I learned is, don't mess with the girls. The women in places like these are worse than the blokes.

Two girls in particular eyed Lauren with something between envy and hatred. They muttered to each other. I couldn't hear, but could guess.

Lauren had clocked them too.

"The two sweethearts in the corner are lovely eh?"

"You can kiss and make up another day," I said. "We need to get a seat with a clear view of the carpark."

Lauren gestured toward a circular Formica-topped table and two, once comfortable, chairs available against the window.

I parked my glass and checked the view. "Perfect," I said with a smile. "And you thought this job was going to be shit, didn't you?"

Lauren North's Story:

We'd been sitting less than ten minutes.

"I need the loo," I said, knees trembling.

Our table shook with me. Our drinks shuddered in concert.

"You okay?" asked Des, knowing the answer.

I nodded unconvincingly.

"Has the doc got you on anything?" he prodded.

I shrugged. "Stopped taking it."

Des took a breath. "When?"

Another shrug. "Today."

He took a sip from his pint and tipped his head to one side. "Good move."

"I know…look…whatever…I still need the loo, and the Andrews sisters over there are going to follow me into the Ladies, sure as eggs are eggs."

Des gave the two feral females a cursory. "Don't make a mess," he said casually. "Leave your bag, just take the ASP, and don't be too long in case our body turns up."

Realising that I wasn't going to get any special treatment did me good. I think if Des had tried to protect me in any way, I would have folded there and then.

Even so, my confidence wasn't quite strong enough to stop my stomach doing a flip as I slipped my hand in my bag, gripped the baton and pushed it up the sleeve of my Levi jacket.

The ASP is a weapon regularly used by the police, particularly support groups. They are the guys and girls you see on the TV wearing NATO helmets, looking like Robocop, smashing down doors in drug raids.

When collapsed, the ASP is not much longer than a pencil. Imagine the old-fashioned car aerial pushed down to its smallest size and you aren't far away. The difference being that, with a flick of the wrist, the ASP extends and locks itself into a solid tungsten bar capable of breaking bones.

I strode to the toilets, with half an eye on the two sweethearts that were checking my Italian Loriblu sneakers, I'd recently bought them from Forzieri, a very nice Italian designer Rick had introduced me to. It was my own fault. I should've stuck with my Adidas trainers rather than a £600 pair of fur cuffed numbers, but it was too late for that.

I opened the loo door, to be assaulted by the smell of ammonia. The once white tiled floor was wet with goodness knows what; the walls were covered in foul graffiti.

To my horror, the two toilet cubicles had no doors.

It was just as I was coming to terms with the lack of privacy whilst taking ablutions, that I was joined by the first of the two shoe admirers.

She was tall, maybe five ten…well over six feet in her killer heels. Her peroxide white blonde hair with the inevitable dark roots was cut to shoulder length. Good figure, lots of makeup.

Without a second thought, she pulled down her jeans and knickers and sat to pee in the open cubical.

I did my best not to stare.

"They took 'em off a few months back," said the blonde. "The doors like."

She pulled tissue from the roll, wiped herself and stood revealing, well, just about everything she had.

"Knob heads were shooting up inside," she said as she restored her modesty. "That or doing lines, or shagging. So Frankie, he's the landlord like, unscrewed 'em and took 'em away."

I did my best to push the images of the locals' drug-addled romps from my mind.

Despite it all, I still needed the loo, so bit the bullet, stepped into the next cubical, wiped the seat and went about my business.

Seemingly unfazed by the fact that I was half naked, the blonde stood at the opening and continued her conversation.

It was exactly how I'd expected it to go.

"Not seen you before," she started.

I wanted to tell her to go away in short sharp jerky movements whilst I did what should be done in private. Instead, I played on my Leeds accent.

"No, my other half has been looking at a car around the corner, so we just nipped in for a swift drink. We'll be off after this one."

I buttoned my jeans and felt slightly less vulnerable.

"Nice shoes," she said.

I went about washing my hands. "Thanks," I said. "Got them off the market in Leeds, only fifteen quid they were."

The girl turned down the corners of her mouth. "They look dear to me, don't look like snide."

I knew, that no matter what I said or the way I said it, the conversation was designed for one thing only, to start a quarrel, to begin the process of showing who was boss, whose turf it was.

To be honest, despite my earlier nerves I wasn't scared, I was more concerned that this sideshow could spoil our other plans.

Right on cue, the loo door opened, and in walked blondie's mate. She was shorter, heavier, black leggings, boots, big boobs.

I made to leave but both women blocked my exit. The blonde stood slightly to my right, her mate got in close and eyeballed me like a boxer before the bell rings.

"I reckon she's a copper, Kylie. What you reckon?" said Boobs.

"Might just be right there, girlfriend," added the blonde in a stupid American accent.

There was no point in attempting to reason with people who were plain fucking stupid.

With my left hand, I grabbed the heavier girl by the larynx, my thumb and forefinger digging in hard. I knew she wouldn't be able to breathe and her natural reaction would be to try and prise my hand from her throat. Despite my recuperation from injury, I was still way too strong for her. As I held tight with my left, I let my right arm drop and the ASP slid into my palm. With a flick of my wrist, the kinetic energy needed extended the baton in a split second.

I gave blondie a swift crack on her collarbone, not hard enough to break it, but enough to cause considerable pain. She fell backwards, clutching her shoulder, cracking her head on the wall on her way downward to the pee-covered floor.

Boobs was gasping for breath. She'd gone a funny colour and her legs were beginning to give way. I increased the pressure on her throat and guided her down to sit beside her mate who was checking the back of her head for blood.

Both looked up at me with a mixture of fear and bewilderment.

I prodded each of them in turn with the ASP.

"Listen, you two fuckwits, me and my man are here to do some business with Jimmy London. You heard of him?"

Boobs nodded furiously. "Jimmy, yeah, course, everyone knows Jimmy…why didn't you say? I mean…"
I cut her off.
"And I mean, it's none of your fucking business eh?"
Both women looked at each other and then at me.
"No," they said forlornly.
I touched each on the mouth with the cold steel of the ASP. "So, when you go back to the bar, you keep them shut…Okay?"
More nodding.
I smacked the tip of the ASP hard on the counter to collapse it. Pushed the weapon up my sleeve, checked my lipstick, and went back to my beer feeling much better.

Des watched me walk to the table. He was checking me over.
"You look pleased with yersel," he said, before drinking the last of his pint.
As I was about to reply, the two shoe admirers tottered from the Ladies, looking pale.
Des watched them find their seats and smiled. "Not lost yer touch then?"
I picked up my Stella and put the glass to my mouth. As I felt the cold beer on my tongue, I saw a black Range Rover pull onto the car park. Black car, black alloys, black glass.
"Jimmy's here," I said.

Des Cogan's Story:

From our position I could just make out the driver, a skinny guy, dressed in a white top with MCFC embossed in pale blue letters on the front. The Range Rover swung in very slowly and eventually reverse parked next to our Golf.

From our intel, the slowcoach driver was a positive ID for Jimmy's cousin, Kevin London. He dropped down from the driver's seat, a small, bird-like man with a thick, black crew cut that resembled Lego-man. As I watched him stand in the carpark fumbling in baggy black trackies, the reason for his slow driving became apparent. He lit what looked like a half smoked joint, took a long drag on it and stretched himself.

As I expected, Jimmy's security stepped out of the passenger side. The brute of a man had a brief gander at our empty Golf. It was probably the first time in months another vehicle had been left in the vicinity and he checked it inside for bodies.

He was indeed a big old unit. Well over six feet, and broad-shouldered with it. In some ways he reminded me of Dougie McGinnis. More muscular, but just like his psychopathic countryman, he seemed to have gained his strength from his genes, rather than a gym.

Unlike Dougie however, this boy looked switched on.

"So, that's Paddy Devlin then," said Lauren, stating the obvious.

I gave her a look, pulled my phone from my pocket and hit Rick's speed dial.

Holding the phone to my ear and squinting into the half-light outside, I watched the carrot-topped bodyguard walk to the rear door of the Rover and allow his second charge into the fading light.

Jimmy entered the fray exactly as Rick had described him, all Beatle cut and Army and Navy store catalogue. He sauntered over to Kevin, took the joint from his cousin and treated himself to a pull.

At least that was two out of the three that would be placid.

My eyes were drawn back to the big fella. Finally, a light came on in my thick Scottish head.

Paddy Devlin. Of course, when Rick mentioned his name, I had it in my mind I'd heard it before, and now, peering through glass that hadn't seen a window cleaner in months, I understood why.

In 1997 Rick had fallen off the perch, was drinking himself to a stupor, and was taking on half of Manchester.

Me? I'd been sent to Bosnia as part of a training and recognisance mission. There were three new guys that formed part of 22's crew on that job, and one, was an ex-2 Para guy. A big red-haired Northern Irishman…Patrick Devlin.

Now, ten years on there he was, holding the car door open for one of Manchester's most infamous and dangerous criminals. His fall from grace was not surprising. Paddy had issues. His love of Queen and Country was there for all to see, and despite his name being of infamous Catholic descent, the Ulsterman's father was actually Grand Master of an Orange Lodge. It wouldn't have surprised any of our team out there, if Paddy wore Union Jack pyjamas to bed.

Being someone that 'kicked with the other foot' so to speak, quite a rarity in the British Army I might add, I steered well clear of Mr Devlin on my travels.

Bosnia was his first and last job with the Regiment. There were lots of hard men in the Army, they lived with violence all their lives, yet they were trained to control their aggression. Paddy had slipped the net when it came to selection. There was no doubting his physical abilities, or indeed his bravery. The problem with Paddy was, he enjoyed inflicting pain and relished firing that final round that ended life.

He was a dangerous combination, capability without credibility.

For what it was worth, Lauren and I had worked a little plan between us. She would take control of Paddy and Kevin, much like the cops would. Keep a safe distance, hold them at gunpoint, get them down on the ground, hands behind head, that kind of thing, whilst I dealt with Jimmy until the cavalry arrived.

Of course, when the cops took on someone as dangerous and as unpredictable as our three souls, they usually had a good number of guys at their disposal and used the concept of overwhelming force to their best advantage. We, on the other hand, were only two. Had we to take down a going-to-seed ex-Para, then we had a chance. Controlling Paddy Devlin was going to be a whole different ball game.

I checked the screen of my Nokia.

Rick wasn't answering. In fact, his phone wasn't even ringing.

No fucking signal.
Didn't I say this was a shit job?

Lauren North's Story:

Didn't I say I wanted a run through? Didn't I say we needed checks and balances?

I pulled my phone from my bag as I hurriedly followed Des toward the door and an uncertain future.

One bar flickered on the screen.

There was time for a one-word text before I pushed it back in my bag and wrapped my hand around the Colt. Saying a little prayer that the technology would do its job, I took a deep breath and walked into the night.

I remember Jimmy and Kevin were sharing a joint and talking as they sauntered toward us.

Rick was right about the way that Jimmy walked. Okay, it wasn't just Jimmy, it was this Manchester vibe, or street cred, or whatever. The way his knees seemed to stick out to the side as he bounced along on the balls of his feet. To me, he looked like he'd forgotten to wipe his arse. Des was off to my left making a beeline for Jimmy, our target.

Paddy Devlin had locked eyes on me the second my feet hit the tarmac. Yet the moment Des's hand moved toward the small of his back, the Irishman's lecherous gaze left me and he changed tack. He stepped in front of Jimmy, his massive frame blocking any chance of Des getting close.

Adrenaline coursed through my body. My skin prickled with it. When they say that putting yourself in danger is like a drug they are right. The endorphins hit you so hard, it's almost like a sexual encounter.

The fact that Devlin was Northern Irish only served to shatter my nerves further. McGinnis, McDonald and Findley flashed in my subconscious. I gritted my teeth and put recent history to the back of my mind. I was not going to let Des down.

With our targets just twenty feet away, Paddy's eyes locked on mine again. It wasn't like I'd just left the pub and he was a bloke looking an unfamiliar female up and down, he was taking me apart with his gaze, asking the question. I wanted to avoid his eyes, to appear nonchalant, simply a customer leaving the pub on the way to her car with her partner, yet I felt he could read my thoughts, see inside my head and anticipate my every move.

Ten feet away.

Now or never, girl.

I pulled the Colt from my bag, punched it forward in my right hand cupping the bottom of the grip with my left; feet apart, knees slightly bent, the classic police handgun shooting position. Not in the manual, however, was the fact that I had my finger on the trigger and the safety off.

There was no point in following the usual cop protocol and screaming orders at the big Irishman. Firstly, it wouldn't worry him if he thought I was a detective, and secondly, I didn't want half the pub rushing out to his defence.

"Hands on your head, Paddy," I said quietly. "Don't be a hero, big fella."

He sneered at me, but he knew he was too far away from me to grab my weapon, or reach for his without taking a round or two.

He stood stock still and gave me a death stare.

Knock yourself out, son.

Des had drawn his own gun and was barking at Jimmy to lie on the floor. In turn, the mop-haired gangster was informing Des, in the broadest of Manchester accents, that he was a 'dead man' for daring to take him on in 'his' city. The Scot got in close and gave Jimmy a crack with the butt of his SLP for good measure.

This seemed to quieten Jimmy momentarily, and gave Des the opportunity to grab him by the hair and stick the muzzle of his SIG in his ear.

Jimmy was going nowhere for a minute or two.

Kevin was rooted to the spot, shitting himself. It seemed he wasn't so brave when his opposition wasn't a sixteen-year-old kid with her clothes torn off.

I kept big Paddy in my sights.

All we needed now was Rick and JJ. Trouble was, they were nowhere to be seen.

I couldn't check my phone, to see if my text had sent. Not knowing was the worst part.

Exactly as Des had predicted, as the seconds ticked by, both Jimmy and Paddy realised that this wasn't a hit, but a kidnap.

Jimmy began to scuffle, knowing Des wasn't going to pull the trigger, his confidence growing, feeding his violence.

I felt increasingly concerned with each passing second, and as I risked a glance toward Des, Paddy took instant advantage of my loss of concentration and lurched forward.

He swung a massive hand toward my outstretched weapon, his connection sending it spinning from my grasp. The small silver pistol looped in the air, before clattering along the tarmac toward the gloom and clutter around the builders' skips.

Paddy was amazingly quick for such a big, strong man. He reversed the swing of his powerful arm, intending to hit me square in the jaw with the back of his hand.

A year or so ago, he would've knocked me unconscious, but not now. I was already on the balls of my feet, and rather than do what all my instinct screamed at me to do and duck my head, I rolled my torso backward from my waist, the way a professional fighter would, taking me out of his range. Without the connection of a solid object to stop his swing, Paddy's bodyweight propelled him to his right.

For a split second, he was out of control and off balance. My hand found the ASP in my bag and I grabbed my opportunity. Shuffling in an arc, just as that same fighter might, looking for his opportunity to find a telling punch, I flicked the baton open and swung it at the Irishman's head.

Somehow, Paddy managed to raise a massive forearm and block the blow.

Even so, there was a sickening crack as the tensile steel connected and he cried out in pain.

"Fucking bitch!" he bawled as he made a grab for the ASP, attempting to pull me in close where his superior strength would tell, and easily overpower me.

I was having none of it, I was too nimble, too quick. Any lingering fear, any doubt in my abilities, had vanished the second he'd failed to connect with his first swing.

Now I shuffled left and forward, dropped my shoulder and took an almighty swing at the Irishman's knee.

He grunted as his leg gave way beneath him. The concentrated dynamic energy of the blow from the baton devastates the nerves around the joint, rendering it temporarily useless. As he hit the deck, rolling in agony, I took my chance and scanned the floor for the Colt.

Sometimes, you win one.

The chromed body and pearl inlayed grip stood out in the gloom, like a lost diamond.

Within seconds, I was armed.

Paddy rolled onto his back and pushed his hand toward the inside of his jacket.

I checked the Colt was still ready to fire and pointed it downward at the prostrate Irishman.

"Don't be a hero," I said.

Paddy glared at me, the pain in his arm and knee clouding his judgement. "Fuck you," he spat, pulling his own Berretta from a shoulder holster.

There was no time for a second warning, no time to try another way. I fired.

Two to his chest, both grouped within an inch of each other. Paddy's body bucked at the impact as the 9mm rounds entered the cavity to the left of his heart.

His eyes met mine again, burning with hatred. He tried to speak, small blood-bubbles escaping from the corner of his mouth as he struggled to inflate his ruined lung.

I shook my head, "You don't have to do this, Paddy. That piece of shit Jimmy isn't worth dying for," I warned.

The Irishman snorted and managed a smile, displaying bloodstained teeth. Then slowly, agonisingly, moved his gun toward me.

Some people never learn.

I put a third in his head and it was over.

Rick Fuller's Story:

As the time approached 2000hrs I began to worry.

The unusually hot weather had made for an uncomfortable fifty minutes or so, in the confines of the Escort van.

Both JJ and I were wearing jackets to hide our weaponry.

JJ noticed my concern. "Why don't we have a drive-by and see what happen?"

"They'll call," I said unconvincingly. "Anyway, we don't want to spook Jimmy's crew."

JJ sat back. He was not a man well suited to sitting around.

"I don't like," he said flatly.

Neither did I, and I was about to fire the engine, when my phone buzzed on the dash.

I looked at the screen, it was a text sent from Lauren's phone, just one word, 'Go.'

More of a worry, it was time-stamped 1952hrs.

"Fuck," I said, and fired the engine into life.

Lauren North's Story:

In my peripheral vision, I could see that Des had Jimmy down on the ground, he was sitting astride him and appeared to have control. I was about to turn and join him, as two meat-heads came barrelling out of the Anson door. Obviously the sound of gunfire had drawn them out, like moths to a flame.

They both saw Paddy Devlin dead on the tarmac and swore under their breath before turning their attention toward me. I pointed the Colt.

"Nothing to see here, boys…go finish your beers," I instructed. "Unless you want to join him down there, that is?"

One put his hands in the air, faster than an Italian infantryman, the second growled the usual threats toward me, but stepped backward when he heard the safety click off.

Happy I had bought a minute or two, I spun again toward Des and our quarry.

We had another problem. In all the excitement, I'd forgotten about Kevin. I scanned the carpark for him, and there he was, struggling with a lump of concrete the size of a football he'd obviously got from the contractor's excavations.

Before I could call out a warning, the skinny little shit, lifted it above his head and dropped it squarely on Des as he held Jimmy on the floor.

It hit the Scot with a sickening crack and he slumped forward, unconscious on top of Jimmy's prone figure.

The gangster immediately pushed Des off him, clambered to his feet and started to drag his skinny cousin toward the Range Rover.

For a split second, I was unsure of what to do.

By the time I'd reached Des's still body, Jimmy and Kevin were opening the doors of their Range Rover. I felt a sudden urge to kill them both.

I pointed the Colt at the Rover and was about to pull the trigger when I heard Des moan beneath me.

"Will you stop fucking about and help me up," he said.

Buoyed by the sound of his voice, I pushed the Colt into my jeans and helped him to a sitting position. Blood poured down the side of his scalp, pooling in his ear and dribbling down his neck, soaking the collar of his shirt. I pulled a handful of tissue from my bag and applied direct pressure to the scalp wound. Des held the makeshift dressing in place with one hand and found his SIG with the other. There were louder and more disgruntled voices from behind, as the seasoned Anson drinkers began to grow in confidence and step into the carpark.

Des read my thoughts. "Forget them," he gestured toward the Range Rover. "It's those fuckers we need."

Pulling the Scot to his feet, I found the Golf's remote and popped the doors. Within seconds I had Des bleeding over the back seat, and fired up the engine.

Kevin had bounced the big British 4 x 4 out of the car park, and pulled a left toward the centre of the estate. No doubt heading for home and a whole lot of trouble for us, in the shape of the remainder of the London gang.

The Golf set off like a scalded cat, as its Audi 20 valve engine re-mapped to over 200bhp laid the power down to the front wheels. I turned in behind the Rover and shouted over my shoulder to the Scot.

"You okay?"

Des responded by winding down the rear window and throwing his lunch out into the night.

"I'll take that as a 'no,' then?" I quipped.

Des wiped his mouth with the back of his hand and pulled his SIG from his jeans.

"Just get up close to those wee bastards, hen," he spat. "I'm about ready to dish some out."

"We need Jimmy in one piece," I reminded him.

"Aye…maybe," he said through gritted teeth.

Although the Golf was quicker, Jimmy's Range Rover had a definite advantage as we ploughed on into the sprawling estate. Every fifty yards or so was a speed-hump the size of a small mountain range. The massive ground clearance of the Rover coped admirably, even at speed, whilst our little boy-racer, with its lowered suspension, sent sparks flying into the night with every failed attempt. If the lad who'd modified this hot hatch had fitted an expensive exhaust, we'd left most of it outside the pub.

Des was hanging out of his window, his SIG in his left-hand whilst doing his best to stem the flow of blood from his head with his right. Each time the Golf hit a hump, he swore blue murder.

"Come on, hen," he bellowed. "Get right up his arse."

Flooring the Golf, I closed in on Jimmy and Kevin until I was almost touching his bumper. The engine screamed as it revved to the red line.

Des opened fire.

Double taps. One set, two, three. Finally, the Rover's nearside rear tyre blew and the big car slid to the right, clipping two or three parked vehicles. Sparks flew in all directions and pieces of the eighty-grand motor sailed over our car.

With my own window down, the sound of metal on metal was almost as deafening as the report of the SIG behind me. The Rover had lost a mirror and most of a bumper, but Kevin managed to straighten her up and keep the vehicle heading homeward.

Des had most of his upper torso fully out of the car. As we hit yet another hump, he cried out, close to being thrown into the road.

"Shit...just ram the fucker," he shouted.

Within the next fifty yards, the rear tyre on the Rover had cut itself to shreds on the massive alloy rim. Shards of rubber flew toward our car and slapped on the windscreen and roof, causing me to duck instinctively.

"I said...ram the fucker!" repeated Des.

"You sure?" I bawled over the engine noise.

The Scot responded by opening fire again, this time shattering the rear window of the Rover.

I stamped on the accelerator and the Golf responded, eating up the gap between us. Within seconds we made contact, the impact sending glass and plastic flying in all directions.

I hung onto the wheel for grim death as the collision forced the Rover left and Kevin lost control, mounting the kerb and smashing into a low garden wall.

Des dropped from his elevated position onto the back seat, blood pouring down his face, all thought of stemming the flow forgotten. He opened the mechanism of his weapon, allowing the empty mag to fall from the butt, found his first spare inside his jacket and slid it home.

"Let's finish this," he said.

I grabbed my Colt, knowing I had only three rounds to play with, pushed open my door and rolled into the street.

Jimmy was already out of the Rover, kneeling behind the car's massive engine-block. Before I could even think about taking aim, he opened up on us with a large calibre automatic.

The hi-velocity rounds slammed into our car, cutting through the metal with ease.

Des had exited and had fortunately rolled underneath the Golf finding relative safety. He attempted to return fire, but Jimmy had prime position, good cover and superior weaponry, it was a matter of seconds before he would make his advantage count.

In the words of the poet, we were fucked.

Des Cogan's Story:

I lay under the Golf. Big calibre rounds were slicing open the tarmac in front of me, sending sparks into the air and getting closer with every burst. I couldn't see where Lauren was, but I presumed she'd have the sense to be behind the engine compartment, as the solid cast block was about the only thing that could stop what Jimmy was firing at us.

I could just about see the bastard's feet as he knelt, firing short three-round salvos in our direction. Taking a pot shot at his wee toes wasn't the best of ideas. The chances of hitting him were slim, and only likely to reveal exactly where I was.

It was a shit state of affairs, and I could imagine that cowardly little backstabber Kevin cowering in the foot-well, on his mobile, whining to his security team to get here and finish us off.

Jimmy let go three more, just as headlights appeared behind our car. I heard a vehicle stop and two doors open. I risked a peek and said a Hail Mary as I saw Rick and JJ de-bunk the Escort van.

About fucking time eh?

Rick opened up on Jimmy in an instant. He moved along the kerb edge, keeping low and firing in short bursts to keep Jimmy down, unable to return.

I shuffled around to see JJ in a crouch behind the Escort's engine block.

As Rick kept Jimmy busy, to my horror JJ rolled over the Escort's bonnet into the centre of the road.

At first, I thought the Turk was either tactically naïve, or just plain crazy. He was completely in the open. He strolled toward the Rover as he screwed the suppressor onto his MP7, stopping just feet away from his target.

Then I saw what JJ had done, because of the angle he had created, Jimmy had no choice but to move, fire or be fully exposed by either shooter.

He chose to try and fight his way out and popped up from behind the car, teeth gritted, his Kalashnikov at waist height.

JJ let go a full 22 round mag. The near-silent MP7's specially made ammunition cut Jimmy to pieces.

For a moment there was silence, before Jimmy's ripped and shredded body slid down the bonnet of the Range Rover, hitting the pavement with a nasty slap.

I rolled from under the Golf, still bleeding like a stuck pig.

Rick stood over Jimmy's body, shaking his head.

"We needed him alive, JJ."

The Turk shrugged. "I no like him," he said.

Rick Fuller's Story:

With Jimmy now dead, his right-hand, Kevin would just have to do. All we could hope for was that he too had the information we needed to find Red George.

JJ took control of him, before Des beat him to death there and then in the street. The Turk quickly gagged, hooded and plasti-cuffed the skinny Manchester City fan, before throwing him in the back of the Escort.

Des turned his attention to the Golf. He had no intention of leaving his DNA all over the back seat for the cops to find.

We'd failed to bring any incendiary grenades along, so, after removing a dropped mag from the back seat, the Scot resorted to the old-fashioned petrol and match method.

As our old Escort rattled over the speed humps, away from the Anson estate and toward the A6 with the four of us and our prisoner packed inside, the Golf burned bright.

Curtains would twitch on the street tonight. Dozens of residents would have seen the violent events play out. The news that Jimmy London and Paddy Devlin were shot dead would have hit the jungle drums of Longsight even before the first police patrols made the scene. Yet there would be no witnesses. The word would be, a rival gang had hit the London empire in its own backyard, and that this new and more ruthless crew were going to take over the business. No one would want to upset this fresh and yet unseen criminal element.

CID and forensic teams would visit the pub and the street where Jimmy lay, make house-to-house, run ballistic checks, look for CCTV or ANPR evidence, yet none of it would lead to a suspect. On the Anson, there was only one thing worse than lying dead on the pub carpark, and that was being a grass.

The unit that Kostas Makris had loaned us for the interrogation of Jimmy London, now hastily changed to his cousin Kevin, was located at the end of a row of seven other small industrial premises. I jumped from the Escort, unlocked the tall chain-link gates and waited for Lauren to pull the van inside.

Access to the unit itself was via a side door, protected by a metal roller shutter. This was motorised and opened by a key. Once we were all inside, I closed the shutter behind us. With the Escort parked around the back, any passing police patrols would find nothing out of place. The unit would appear empty.

Ignoring the warehouse area on the ground floor, we climbed a set of stairs which led to an office, a small kitchen, and a staff changing area complete with washing facilities.

Des headed straight for the shower, whilst Lauren looked for a first aid kit.

JJ and yours truly dragged the increasingly uncooperative Kevin into the kitchen. It was a typical working staff canteen; a large metal-legged table took centre stage with eight plastic covered chairs surrounding it. The small kitchen area boasted a sink, fridge, and a couple of units containing various mugs, cups, plates and cutlery.

JJ dumped Kevin on one chair and fastened his wrists to the bottom of the backrest using a second set of plasti-cuffs.

He removed our prisoner's hood and pulled the gag from his mouth. Kevin coughed and spat out bits of fabric for a few seconds before launching into the standard Mancunian gangster tirade. Spending time around his Oasis-obsessed cousin had obviously rubbed off on the lad. If you closed your eyes you would have sworn it was Liam kicking off in the chair.

"You guys are fuckin' dead. You hear what I'm sayin' here, dickhead? You think you can come to the Anson and just take over? This is fuckin' Longsight, pal…it's why they fuckin' call Manchester, 'Gun-Chester' eh? Forget the Moss dudes, them blacks ain't got nothin' on our crew. Jimmy will find you and shoot you in the fuckin' mouth, man, you hear me? In the fuckin' mouth."

I hadn't occurred to me that Kevin wouldn't have seen Jimmy's bullet-ridden body lying at the front of the Range Rover. Of course, as he'd cowered in the thickly carpeted foot-well of the luxury car, he wouldn't have even heard the suppressed MP7 slicing his cousin in half. Then, he'd been instantly hooded as he was pulled from the car, and was therefore blissfully unaware of his cousin's violent demise.

This would be interesting.

JJ removed his Col Moschin Delta fighting knife from its scabbard and laid it on the table in full view of our increasingly irritating charge. It shut Kevin up briefly.
I got a much-needed brew on.

Des Cogan's Story:

I stepped out of the shower, wrapped a towel around my waist, watched my blood swirl around the plug hole as it made its way to the drain, and told myself this was becoming a far too regular occurrence. Lauren was straight into the room, fussing around me.

"Sit here, let me have a look at this wound."

I did as I was told, and she gently parted my hair to inspect the damage done by our Kevin.

She drew in a sharp breath.

"This is deep, Des. I have a nice view of your thick skull. You were lucky, you know, that lump of concrete could have killed you."

I was going to state the obvious, that it was probably Kevin's intention to do just that, but I let it go. She began to clean the cut with wipes from a first aid kit she'd found in the unit.

"Any dizziness?"

"Nope."

"You sure, you're not just being all macho?"

"Sure."

"Pain?"

"I've a head like Birkenhead, if that's what you mean."

She laughed at my quip.

"Funny guy…this needs an X-ray, Desmond, there could be a fracture, Kevin could have…"

"Yeah, could've killed me, you said, but there won't be time for that, hen, and you know it."

She ignored me.

"How about blurred vision?"

"Nope, now the blood is out of my eyes, I can see just fine."

She tutted.

"Well, I can steri-strip it now, and stitch it once we get back to the lock-up, but you'll need to take it easy until it's stitched or it will bleed like hell again."

"Okay, Sister."

She smiled and lit up the room, before humming a little tune as she worked on me.

"You did good back there, Lauren," I said. "Back to your old self eh?"

"I think I took a massive risk…could've gone either way. What if I'd caved?"

"Nah, I knew you'd be okay. You faced your fear, it's the best cure." She smiled again and the room went silent for a moment.

Something had been bugging me for days. I had to ask, it had been burning me up inside. It was one of those things. You know you should just leave it alone, and there's never a right time, but out it came anyway.

"The Old Monkey," I said. "Been lately?"

Our eyes locked and a thousand unsaid words passed between us.

"The Old…?" she began.

"Monkey, yes," I snapped. "The pub on Princess Street on the way into China Town. I asked had you been lately."

I could see anger in her face. Was it anger at being caught out? Anger at being questioned? Or was it that she thought that I had been following her?"

Her mouth turned into a sneer.

"What is this about, Des? Asking me questions that you already know the answer to? Why not ask the question that you really want to? The one that tells you what you don't know?"

I'd opened the door and there was no closing it.

"Okay, fair enough, I will. Why were you holding hands with that copper outside the Old Monkey the other night, when you're supposed to be head over heels for the guy in the next room? I saw you…."

Her anger spilled out of her.

"Saw me doing what? Saw me talking to another man? Is that not allowed in macho ex-soldier world?"

"I didn't mean to…"

"Didn't mean to what, Des? Spy on me? Upset me? Accuse me?" She calmed slightly and pulled up a chair.

"If you are asking, am I having some kind of relationship with Larry, then the answer is no. I told the truth in the meeting. When I said, I got Colin Reed's name from a reporter, that was legit, I did, but I couldn't get his address. I tried the prison and walked the pubs around Strangeways to talk to the PO's, but got no joy. Larry was the only place I could think of, so I used him. I used him to get information for us…End of…okay, Colombo?"

I was open-mouthed. "He gave you the address? He helped us? Well…you anyway?"

She nodded.

"I went to see him at his station. We had words at first, but he finally decided to help me. Now I won't lie to you, Des, he has made it clear that he has a bit of a thing for me, and he came to my flat earlier. He…well he actually wants me to walk away from all this."

"And what do you want?"

Before she could answer, Rick pushed the door open with his elbow, carrying two mugs of tea.

"How's the wounded soldier?" he said breezily.

"He'll live," answered Lauren with the smallest smile.

Rick dropped the mugs on a small table. "Excellent, well, me and JJ are just about to get into Kevin's ribs about Red George."

Before either of us could reply, he'd turned and was gone, apparently only one thing on his mind.

Once the door closed behind him, Lauren took my hand, her eyes shiny, close to tears.

"Me? I want what I don't think I can ever have," she said.

Rick Fuller's Story:

Kevin was giving it large. One long diatribe of street-shite spilling from his mouth, describing all the different ways we were going to die at the hands of his 'gangsta' mates.

He was slight in every way, narrow-shouldered, thin pock-marked face, long nosed. He wore a Manchester City T-Shirt and the obligatory black shiny tracksuit bottoms, that matched his Puma trainers.

Of course, no self-respecting Longsight gangster's outfit would be complete without thick gold neck-chains and a couple of sovereign rings. Our Kevin didn't disappoint.

Despite his wealth, he dressed like a street thug and had pulled his grubby cheap white socks up over the bottom of his joggers. This seemed to be a growing trend amongst the wearers of sportswear, who never indulged in the pastime.

He looked a proper twat.

Kevin may have been slight, but he was as violent as any brute in his own way. Egghead's intel was full of instances of Kevin's viciousness. That said, since his incarceration for his part in the murder of a teenage boy, he seemed to have turned his unwanted attentions on local women, who were too scared to come forward and make complaints against the London crew. When it came to his amorous advances, Kevin was a lad who didn't understand the word no.

Interrogating him reminded me of a time when I did a little job for the sadly deceased Tanya Richards; some nasty piece of work called Alfie Summers had murdered one of her runners and stolen five grand from the family. Stealing from the Yardies and killing Tanya's cousin in the process, was as good as signing your own death warrant.

I recall, Alfie Summers was going to 'shoot me in the mouth' too. He ended up eating his own bodyweight in the latest designer drug and dying of carbon monoxide poisoning up on Saddleworth Moor. The only person who actually 'shot me in the mouth' turned out to be Stephan Goldsmith. How things come around eh?

Now, it was Kevin's turn to tell us what we needed to know, lead us to Red George, and eventually to Goldsmith himself.
Sitting in front of the punk, I put him in his early thirties, which would undoubtedly mean he'd visited the Hacienda club in his time.
"You ever heard of a guy called Freddy Garret, Kevin?"
Kevin curled his lip. "Fuck you, dickhead, I don't know what you want, but I'm sayin' nothin.'"
I managed a thin smile and pressed on.
"Yeah, you must've been to the Hacienda back in the day, Kev, eh? Dropped a few E's, done a few lines?"
Kev shrugged. "So, the fuck, what? Who are you? The fuckin' Five O? The fuckin' drug squad?"
I ignored his question and kept my voice quiet.
"So, Kevin, my old son, whilst you were there, you must've seen Freddy. Big time Charlie he was, loved his sniff, proper little rich boy, liked to hang around with the bad lads."
Kevin's right knee bounced up and down nervously.
"I might have seen him yeah, always had a blonde bird with big tits with him."
"That's the boy, Kevin, yeah…remember what his nickname was?"
Kevin's face fell.
"Erm…yeah, they called him Four-finger Fred."
I picked up JJ's Col Moschin fighting knife from the table and tested the weight in my hand.
"I got him that name, Kev. I cut off his finger with a pair of tin-snips, right there on the street, outside the club. You know why I did that, Kev?"
The boy looked nervous for the first time. He shook his head and stayed quiet.
"Because," I whispered. "I wanted the diamond ring he was wearing"
I brought the knife closer.
"Now… I could have punched him unconscious and stolen it, couldn't I?
I could have even pulled the gun I was carrying and robbed him, but I didn't…you know why?"
More shakes of the head, more knee bouncing.
"Because, Kevin, I was sending out a message, a very important message to very important people. I snipped off his pinkie, stole his

diamond ring, and his twenty-five-grand Rolex, popped the lot into a plastic bag and made myself five large, from one of the biggest faces in town."

I rested the knife against Kevin's skinny chest.

"But, Kevin, do you know what cutting off Freddy's digit did for me? What it told those powerful, rich faces about me?"

We locked eyes. I gripped the knife and plunged the blade into Kevin's shoulder socket.

I shouted over his screams. "That I'm fuckin' ruthless."

I knew he was in agony. I also knew he wasn't going to die or bleed out anytime soon. The razor-sharp fighting knife was buried halfway into Kevin's shoulder about an inch under his clavicle, the blade separating the ball and socket of his shoulder.

JJ was in Kevin's ear.

"He crazy, you know? He cut off your fuckin' arm unless you tell him."

"Tell him what?" Kevin screamed.

Of course, we hadn't asked the boy anything of note, or even hinted about why Kevin the unfortunate was even fastened to this particular plastic chair in the arse end of Stockport.

It was the way we were trained in the field. Make your presence felt first. Ask questions later.

I added the merest twist to the knife. Kevin went very pale.

"Red George," I said. "I need to find him."

Kevin shook his head.

"F...fuck you," he managed.

I twisted the blade further, sending rivers of pain through Kevin's shoulder.

"I will slice you apart, piece by fucking piece, son...now... Red George?"

I could see Kevin was already struggling. He was one of those that could dish it out okay, but wasn't too clever when it came to taking it. Sweat poured from him, his shirt instantly soaked. He stank of fear and shuddered with shock, his body in all kinds of turmoil.

"Okay...okay..." he spluttered. "I know where he lives, but...but, he's...he's not at his flat, he's gone, man."

I eased out the knife and slowly wiped it on Kevin's saturated white shirt. Although a trickle of blood seeped from the wound, I knew his pain would be reduced ten-fold.

"Okay, son...I'm liking the fact that you are being nice and co-operative. So, he's gone. Where the fuck is he?"

Kevin looked at JJ standing over his shoulder and then back to me, his face a mixture of pain, fear and loathing.

"We ain't seen him for days, weeks, man, honest...Jimmy needed him for a job himself, but George knocked it back. He said he'd had a big payday, said he'd done some big job for some foreign bloke, and he was fuckin' off somewhere for a while."

"Foreign bloke? Who?" I pushed.

Kevin shook his head, "I don't fuckin' know, honest I don't."

I moved to insert the knife again.

He tried to squirm away from the blade, but JJ stepped in and held him firm.

"No! No! Please...Don't do that, man...I mean...okay look... he said something about this bloke needing him abroad and that was it, man. Honest it was, he just knocked the job back and he was off. Just like that. That's all I know...honest."

I held the tip of the knife at the entrance to his existing wound.

"You're fucking lying to me, Kevin, I know you are."

Kevin pissed himself, his yellow urine stinking the place out as it splattered on the tiled floor.

"I'm not! No...no, I'm not...look, fuckin' hell, I don't fucking know any more than I told you."

The boy was losing it. His body shook uncontrollably. Physically he was still in good shape. I mean, he hadn't had too much punishment. It was just his lack of bottle.

I found that wasn't rare amongst his kind.

I tried to be reasonable. "You know, Kevin, in my experience, people in your position always do and say the same things."

He shook his head.

I gave him a smile. "Oh, yes, Kevin, they do. They always talk total shite before the truth comes out...so."

I pushed the blade in and twisted hard enough to open the socket.

Kevin screamed so loud, I had to raise my voice again.

"Then of course... there's the begging, Kev, isn't there?"

He tried to twist himself away from the blade, but once again JJ held him down. I was right in his face, my nose touching his.

"That's next, isn't it, Kevin my son? All the, 'oh please don't hurt me, I don't know anything' shite, all the 'it wasn't me, boss, it was me cousin bollocks'…all that nonsense will come out son… I fuckin' promise you."

I pulled the knife out again, releasing him from his agony, dropping it on the table in plain sight.

He was blubbing like a baby. The next thing would be asking for his fuckin' mother. Lifting his chin in my hand, I forced him to look me in the eye.

"Look at me, Kevin…now stop your whining, lad…look at me. You will… tell me everything, son. This is just your shoulder; this is fuck all. I mean, wait until it's your cock and balls… And from what I hear, Kevin, you do like to use that cock and balls of yours eh? Like to dish it out to the young ladies eh? What about that poor little schoolgirl you stuck your smelly little cock in?"

He tried to avoid my gaze and turned toward JJ for help.

"Hey, come on, man, I mean…them bitches, I mean…look no one believed them slags eh? It was just a bit of fun, come on, please, don't…I mean okay…yeah? Right, look, I'll tell you all I know yeah? And I mean everything, yeah?"

He gave me a manic nod, a pathetic attempt to make me mirror him. I didn't oblige.

"Go on," I said, releasing his chin and collecting the blade. "Impress me."

Kevin took deep breaths. "Okay, good, man, cool yeah, look…All I know is, George…when he was abroad, he met this guy who would take any number of Mercs from us, yeah? Some fucker from where he used to live in Polak land or whatever."

"This guy's name? "I pressed.

Kevin shook his head. Tears rolled, and our pointy-nosed rapist began to cry again. "I dunno, honest, boss, I dunno, Gold something, Goldstein maybe."

I felt my heart rate lift. "Goldsmith?"

"Maybe…yeah that's him, Goldsmith…look, the guy always paid cash for the cars, we never met the dude yeah?"

"Go on, Kevin," I said. "Your cock is safe for now."

The boy looked relieved. He took a deep breath. "Well, like I said, we never met the guy. George just took the cars over, collected the cash and brought it to us…now he's working for this Gold guy over there, that's all I know, man."

"Where is 'over there' exactly?"

Kevin shook his head. "I don't know, man…I mean it, I don't."

I sat back and addressed JJ.

"You know what I think, mate? I think that this piece of shit isn't telling us where this customer is, because he thinks we want to steal the Merc buyer from him. What do you think, JJ?"

The Turk stepped to the side so he could make eye contact with the lad. Those black lifeless pools of his would frighten anyone.

JJ curled his lip. "I think if we cut his balls off, he'll tell us."

"No!" bawled Kevin, desperately attempting to tear his wrists from his ties. "I mean it, man. I don't…fuckin'…know."

Kevin threw his last dice.

"Look…you guys are already in the shit, man…I mean, if Jimmy finds you, it's all over eh? If you kill me, man, he'll find you. He's a big player in this town, man…the biggest. Why not just let me go, and we forget all this?"

I leaned in. "Jimmy's gone to the big scrapyard in the sky, son…do I need to let that little gem of information sink in to your thick fuckin' skull? Dead in the fuckin' gutter along with big Paddy." I tapped my temple with my finger. "If I was clever like you…you dumb fuck, I'd be worried that half of the Moss isn't already planning a move on your little empire. You know the saying, Kevin…The king is dead, long live the king."

I picked up the knife and pointed it down toward his groin. "Now, Kevin, one last time…where… is Red George?"

He didn't know.

Lauren North's Story:

I couldn't help but hear the screams from next door. With everything I'd witnessed and been through, it certainly wasn't time for me to become all squeamish and judgemental, but as I walked into the canteen area to see JJ wrapping Kevin's corpse in a plastic sheet, I did feel a tad uneasy.

"Jesus, lads," I said.

The mood was sombre. Des walked in and helped JJ down the stairs with Kevin's body as if it were the most normal thing in the world. He nodded at the gangster's blood-soaked torso and addressed the Turk.

"Must have had a dicky ticker, eh?" he said.

I watched them, speechless.

Rick followed my gaze, his voice, matter of fact.

"Red George is with Goldsmith, but we don't know where," he said.

"What now?" I asked.

Rick blew out his cheeks. "We go back to the lock-up, get some food and some rest."

"And?"

He looked into my eyes.

"Food and rest is good enough for now eh?"

"I suppose."

He held me by the shoulders. "Look, at least we know there won't be any more bodies turning up now he's out of the country At least Reed was the only one."

My unease grew.

"Even so, Rick, there are three people dead, now, tonight…I know they were bad guys, killers and all, but…well it just seems a high price to pay, just to know that Red George isn't in the country anymore."

Rick glowered at me.

"I'll tell you one thing, sweetheart." He spat. "When the news comes out that James and Kevin London are dead, the parents of Paul Long, the poor innocent kid they beat to death, will be dancing around their living room."

He pointed toward the stairs. "And that piece of shit beat and raped a sixteen-year-old girl, then threatened to kill her sister if she testified in court. Oh, yeah, proper little choirboy he was."

He stomped about the room, obviously as pissed off as the rest of us. "Look…no one cares about ordinary people anymore. No one gives a shit about the little guy, the Mr Average that goes to work and pays his taxes, obeys the law. Nobody gives a flying fuck about him eh? The cops have their hands tied and people like Jimmy and Kevin just walk over the good guys… Well I'm not having it!"

He turned for the door and snapped.

"So, if you don't think you can hack it, maybe you should accept Larry's offer and walk away."

As he disappeared from sight, I thought my heart would explode. He must have been behind the door all the time I was talking to Des…must have heard it all.

Everything, every word.

I stood in the centre of the room, feeling sick, unable to move. My tears fell silently, soaking my cheeks and dropping from my chin. What had I done? My stubbornness, my anger, had brought us to this.

I heard his footsteps fade, stop, and then ever so slowly turn and re-climb the stairs. As they came closer my pulse raced until finally, the door opened.

Rick stood there for the longest time. I wanted to run to him, to wrap my arms around his neck, to kiss his face, to tell him how I felt, but nothing came. I was as stone.

He walked the last steps to me, bringing him intimately close. I could feel his breath on my face, smell him. He raised his hand, wiped my tears, and kissed me.

"Come on," he said. "It's been a tough day…Let's go."

Des Cogan's Story:

Me and JJ used the Escort to drop Kevin's body in a spot where it would be found easily, whilst Rick and Lauren picked up a third car we'd left close to the unit.

Within the hour, we were all back in the lock-up.

Lauren stitched me up and dispensed some painkillers, but my head still banged like a bass drum on Orange Day Parade.

That said, Rick was preparing grub and it smelled delicious. Home cooked food had not been high on my list of priorities of late, so my stomach rumbled in anticipation. Considering our shit position, Rick looked relatively pleased with himself as he drained pasta over the sink.

Despite the late hour, we were all ready to eat. The adrenaline rushes had subsided and our bodies were telling us that it was time to refuel.

Lauren tapped away at her laptop.

She suddenly stopped typing and held up her hand, like some school kid with the right answer,

"Erm…Rick…guys…erm…oh shit, oh no!"

We all huddled around her, squinting at the screen.

"What is it?" asked Rick impatiently.

Lauren shook her head slowly. "An email from Rupert Warwick."

"Rupert who?" I asked.

"The guy from the *Manchester Evening News*, the reporter who gave me Colin Reed's name, the guy who was investigating prison suicides at Strangeways."

"And…what about it?" asked Rick.

"Red George," she began. "No wonder he's left the country…Colin Reed wasn't the first on his list …he was the fucking last."

Rick Fuller's Story:

Red George had all the time in the world to find the people he'd been searching for. I had failed to think the way I needed to, and once again, missed the obvious.
Lauren had it in one. Reed had been given the Albanian torture treatment, not because he was the first, but because he was the final victim. It was a warning to anyone Goldsmith may have missed, and a final attempt to find out further names.
I read the email for the second time.
In addition to Colin Reed on the 13th June, three other people who had worked at Strangeways had seemingly committed suicide over the past days:

June 9th, Len Blakely 42yrs (Hospital Orderly)
June 11th, Jenny Simmons 31yrs (Police Surgeon)
June 12th, Mark Cross 23yrs (Prison Officer)

Quite rightly, Rupert Warwick would have his reasons to be doubtful about the initial conclusions of the police reports; the prison officers' union may be up in arms; and Rupert's readers would be outraged, yet I knew nothing would be done…not yet anyway.
I knew that every official statement would describe each demise as a terrible loss to society. Yet, even though the crime scenes were essentially forensically flawed, officially there would be no suspicious circumstances.
Why?
I found my mobile, and dialled the number from memory.
It was answered in seconds.
A familiar cultured voice answered. "Ah, Richard…finally."
"Hello, Cartwright," I said.
The spy came straight to his point.
"Richard, you really must be more prompt when replying to my messages."
I was about to complain, but he was already on a roll.
"Richard, the most insecure devices ever known to mankind are the computer and the mobile phone, and I am appalled that both appear to be your regular mode of communication. However, time is indeed of the essence, therefore, I shall be brief.

I need to see you urgently. I have booked you into the Prince Alexander Suite, Claridge's… tonight, and yes, I am fully aware of the current hour. That sporty little number you bought recently will have you there sharpish…so your arrival time will be, say 0230hrs. Use the valet parking. Your personal butler is called Francis. You can trust him."

The phone went dead.

Lauren positively scowled.

"Cartwright…what has he to do with this…I thought we were away from all that shit?"

I held up a hand. "Like I said, there was always the possibility that the Firm or the CIA had done a deal with Goldsmith and that he had been in their protective custody at some point. Cartwright is just a hired hand like the rest of us. I need to find out what he wants."

Des strode to the kitchen, dumped a mountain of pasta and Arrabiata sauce on a plate and cut the room silent. "And the old boy got you home alive, Lauren, eh? It's only fair we find out the script."

I played peacemaker.

"He got us all back, Des…Anyway, he wants me, in London…asap."

Lauren shot Des a look, stood and walked over to me, searching me with her eyes. "And this is about Goldsmith?"

"I think so, yes." I said.

"If it isn't," said Des, his mouth full of pasta. "Ma dick plays tunes."

There was no time to return to my apartment, therefore I was forced to select my mode of transport and clothes from what was available in the lock-up.

My chosen vehicle was one I'd not driven in years. It had lounged in the corner of the lock-up, covered in linen, for almost as long as I'd owned the premises.

In 1998, when I'd won her in a game of poker, she was worth a couple of grand. Today, nine years on after a total restoration, well, add another zero. The 1988 Porsche 944 Turbo S was a future classic. A vehicle that wouldn't be out of place in Mayfair, yet quick and comfortable for my motorway trip. Indeed, pleasurable enough to keep me awake.

Finished in stone grey metallic with black leather trim, the Turbo S was one of a limited run of cars based on the Cup Racers M030 option code. An uprated turbo, gearbox and shocks, a limited slip diff to cope with the extra power, together with 928 S4 four pot upgraded brakes ensured it went like a scaled cat, and stopped on a sixpence.

The German marque gleamed under the glow of Manchester's sodium lighting as I pushed her toward the M60 and did my best not to think of Lauren, of Larry, and most of all, of Stephan Goldsmith. On a positive note, I'd managed to pack a charcoal Paul Smith two-piece, and white button-down collar Thomas Pink shirt that I'd left in my lock-up wardrobe.
However, I was forced to travel in chocolate Duck and Cover Chinos and a cream Ralf Lauren Polo.
Claridge's would just have to understand.

The hotel itself stands on the corner of Brook Street and Davies Street in Mayfair. It opened in 1812, then called Mivart's. Since then it had been rebuilt and now boasts a hundred and ninety-seven rooms with just eleven suites. Cary Grant and Audrey Hepburn are listed amongst its celebrity guests.

The moment I pulled up outside, a valet took charge of the 944 and I strode into the lobby. A very attractive Eastern European receptionist had barely time to greet me before Francis, my personal butler, was at my shoulder.
"Good morning, Mr Fuller," he beamed, grabbing my bag from my hand. I wasn't too concerned as it contained nothing but clothes and toiletries. I'd decided on borrowing Lauren's little silver Colt, the pistol she'd put to such good use outside the Anson and it sat, somewhat uncomfortably, velcro'd to my right ankle.
"Please allow me to show you to your accommodation."
Francis was extremely tall, maybe six foot six, lithe, dark-skinned and definitely of African origin, yet he seemed accent-less.
My suite, the Prince Alexander, was just under a hundred and fifty square meters in size.

Drinking in the sheer opulence of the sitting room, I couldn't help but recall the house I lived in as a kid, a two up two down job, at best half the size of this very hotel room.

I had everything a wealthy man could ever need, including a full size Broadwood grand piano. Stepping over to it, I lifted the lid and tapped a key or two.

Although Francis didn't let it show, it was obvious I wasn't Elton John.

"Should you wish to play, sir," he said. "The hotel will supply complimentary sheet music for all ability levels."

"I don't think you would have my level," I muttered half to myself, closing the lid.

Francis had the unnerving habit of holding a permanent beam on his face.

"Quite," he said through perfectly whitened teeth.

Desperate to please, he added, "Maybe sir would like a drink or some other refreshment, I realise you have had a long drive. There is complimentary champagne."

I walked over to him and dropped my hand on his shoulder.

"Francis, pal, we both know, that on this particular occasion, everything here is complimentary, so, with that in mind…inside that case you are holding is a suit and shirt, I'd like them pressed and brought back to my room…Is there a gym in this place?"

Francis was already removing my clothes from the bag. "Yes, sir, of course, our Spa and Techno Gym are situated on the top floor. You will find a mixture of cardio vascular and resistance machines, together with a selection of free weights…it's comp…"

"Complimentary, yes, I guessed that, Francis. Good…I'd like breakfast in my room at eight-thirty. That will be bran cereal with a fresh ripe banana and skimmed milk, a four-duck-egg omelette, no cheese, with green pepper and tomato, fresh orange and a double espresso."

Francis looked relieved that I'd given him something to do that he was comfortable with.

"Certainly, Mr Fuller."

He made for the door, my clothes over his arm; as he opened it he turned, rummaged in his inside pocket, removed an envelope and dropped it on a nearby table.

"Your instructions, sir," he said, his smile gone.

I read Cartwright's handwritten note, showered in my very impressive bathroom and slipped between the deliciously crisp sheets.
As usual when things were difficult, I slept like a baby.

Waking before my 0630hrs alarm, I pulled on my training gear and found the lift to the rooftop gym. It was sufficient for my needs, although the heaviest free weights were 25kg.
I was alone, except for a young red-haired woman who ran 10k on a treadmill at a very respectable pace. Under normal circumstances, despite her excellent figure, she wouldn't have registered, but as I was about to meet one of London's top spies, the chances were he would have someone keep an eye on me, even in the gym.
Red was a spook.

I returned to my room to complete my ablutions. Francis had laid out my suit and shirt on the newly made bed, whilst breakfast was warming under solid silver domes.
It was excellent, and I ate wrapped in the softest of bathrobes whilst watching the BBC morning news, none of it good.
Slipping down in the comfiest chair ever, I closed my eyes again.

By 1145hrs, I was dressing and my butler came calling.
"Sir, the dress code for luncheon in the reading room requires a tie. I noticed that you had neglected to pack one, so I took the liberty of bringing a selection from our shop."
I tied my brogues.
"And just how did you know I would be taking lunch, Francis? Did you read my 'instructions' perhaps?"
The guy straightened his strikingly tall frame.
"Certainly not, sir. Although, I am party to all bookings made in the private dining area and, of course, the identities of the diners."
I took a swift look at the selection of neckwear. "I'll take the Salvatore, thank you, Francis."
His manic smile reappeared. "Excellent choice, sir."

By 1230hrs I was shown to a private table in Claridge's Reading Room. Cartwright was already in place, his sharp blue eyes matching his hand-tailored Saville Row suit.

There was a hint of a smile. "Richard, it's good to see you looking so well. How's the wound?"

I sat. "I'm as well as can be expected, Cartwright."

"I'd considered inviting you to my private club," he said. "But they have a new luncheon chef. French, I believe. Garlic before dinner is unnecessary, don't you agree?"

"Awful," I managed.

"So," said the spy, spreading his Le Jacquard Français napkin, and spectacularly missing the irony. "I hope you don't mind, but I have taken the liberty of ordering for us both, Cornish crab salad to start, followed by truffle ricotta tortellini."

"I'm hungry," I said.

Cartwright gestured toward Francis, who was standing discreetly out of earshot.

"We need a drink, my man," said the spy. "Two Sapphires... easy on the tonic."

I leaned in and positively snarled, unable to contain myself, "If you are going to tell me that you had something to do with keeping Stephan Goldsmith alive, I think you should make them large ones."

As you might expect from an MI6 agent who had lived beyond his sixtieth year, Cartwright was unimpressed by my aggression. He studied my face for a moment.

"Stephan Goldsmith was a very useful asset to Her Majesty's Government, Richard."

His response was exactly as expected, but it still hit me like a train. I took a moment and did my best to keep my voice level.

"A fucking asset?"

Cartwright waited for Francis to put down our G and T's and resume his post.

"Yes, Richard, you really must start to look at the big picture."

I took a sip of my ice-cold drink, the bitter gin intensifying the already tart taste in my mouth. "I'm listening."

Cartwright drained half his glass.

"Look, Stephan's father was very close to the Americans, I mean, any deeper in bed and a divorce attorney would have been required.

He had been party to some of the most clandestine CIA operations that had ever taken place internationally, including sorties into the UK, particularly Northern Ireland. They trusted him far more than they trusted us Brits. Therefore, we were keen to establish if, in more recent times, the Yanks had shown the same amount of faith in Stephan as they had in his infamous father. It turned out they had, and therefore, it was essential that we got to him before the CIA could 'persuade' Goldsmith the younger to join them over the Pond."

"I thought we were allies, the Americans and us?"

"We are, old boy."

"Just not that friendly?"

"It's a long story that goes back a long way, Richard, and one we haven't time for today. The fact of the matter is, we did get our man, he did give us what we wanted and in turn, we gave him a… a new start."

"You faked his death."

"Suicide, old boy. Smoke and mirrors as they say. We were quite pleased with the result, actually. The Americans were fucking furious."

The spy finished his drink and waved his empty at our butler.

"And that was that, Richard; no one would ever have been the wiser; until…until someone started snooping about where they weren't wanted."

"Someone?"

He gave me a disappointed look. "You, Richard…You… you and your sense of misplaced bloody loyalty. It was you who persuaded that poor girl at the Registry to obtain a copy of Goldsmith's death certificate wasn't it?"

"Not me…"

The spy turned down his mouth in derision, his tone changing in an instant. "Don't fuck with me, Fuller. The moment that document was accessed the alarms went off in Canary Wharf like a fucking air raid siren, and I knew it was you."

I did my best to hold onto my glass. My anger rose to boiling. "Don't fuck with you? I can't believe I'm hearing this, Cartwright. Goldsmith was an animal, a vicious, murdering, drug dealing, child killer…And you…you and your Saville Row cronies decided to do a deal with him, didn't you? You sat in your air-conditioned, bulletproof offices and decided that what Goldsmith knew was more important than what he'd done."

Cartwright shrugged.

"And your problem is what, Richard? The British Government have done deals with ne'er-do-wells since time immemorial. Let's face it, in modern history, Saddam Hussein, and Mohammed Abu Minyar Gaddafi spring to mind immediately. Not forgetting that Mrs Thatcher was a close friend and confidant of General Pinochet. As I recall, they used to take luncheon together at this very table, the little sweethearts."

A history lesson wasn't going to let him off the hook so easily. "Oh, alright then, so because it's been done before, you figured it was good practice to sponsor another murdering psychopath?" Two more gins arrived. Cartwright leaned forward, hands animated. I sensed the point was coming.

"As soon as we knew the death certificate was compromised, it was standard operating procedure to move our asset. I had one of our chaps pay him a visit…to tell him about the issue and make the arrangements."

"And?"

"And …well, maybe we had taken our eye of the ball somewhat and we found that Goldsmith had forged a good business for himself. Together with a man you know as Red George, he'd carved out a nice living in stolen cars. The bottom line was, he wasn't prepared to leave his location. He said he wanted to stay put, and, more worryingly, he intimated that he would deal with the issue himself."

"And?"

"And we, of course, informed Mr Goldsmith that his preferred course of action was not advisable."

I gulped my own drink, suddenly needing fuel. "So why not just slot him? Stop him from 'dealing with it,' killing poor Spiros and all those other innocent people...you could have topped the bastard and walked away, but you didn't. Why was that, Cartwright? Were you still hopeful he would furnish you with more titbits about the Americans? Is that it?"

I pointed an accusing finger. "From where I'm sitting, I'd say, rather than just dispose of Goldsmith, you lot did the square root of fuck all."

Cartwright screwed up his face to a scowl. "Don't give me that shit, Fuller. The moment Goldsmith started to get bigger than his shoe size, the order was given to remove him. The trouble was, there was a one-time opportunity…and my man missed him…simple as."
"What exactly do you mean by 'one time opportunity'?"
"It's political," said Cartwright.
I gave an exasperated look. "Political?"
"Times are changing, Richard. You can't just wander into someone else's backyard these days and start shooting their residents."
Cartwright laid his palms on the table. "Look, Goldsmith is in Albania…Albania is no longer a Communist state, it is a democracy, a member of NATO. It's even on the list to become part of the EU, God help us."

I wasn't surprised by that news. Red George's connections to Albania were well known, and those boys always had been keen on the odd knock-off motor, particularly the odd Mercedes. Even so, to have it confirmed sent a shiver through me.
"Listen, Cartwright, don't give me that as an excuse, Albania has one of the highest murder rates in the Western world. One more would hardly make the papers."
"Blood feuds, Richard, the silly buggers are still topping each other over things that happened two hundred years ago."
"Sounds like Ireland," I muttered.
Cartwright ignored me. "Look, Richard, Goldsmith has become somewhat of a celebrity in Tropojë. He's ensconced himself firmly with the locals; lots of nice German cars provided to the Albanian Mafioso, either FOC or at knockdown prices did him no harm at all. Indeed, it ensured he got his foot firmly in the door. Then, of course, there was his wealth of drug smuggling contacts in the US …Have you ever heard of the Rudaj Organisation?"
He didn't wait for my answer.
"It's the New York arm of the Albanian Mafia, with links to the Gambino family."
"Big hitters," I said.

Cartwright demolished his second gin.

"The biggest. We knew Goldsmith was using his knowledge of the US Mafia to grow the profile of Rudaj in the States…to get them business. This only increased his popularity locally. In fact, he became a fucking hero."

"No wonder he didn't want to leave Tropojë," I said. "They must have been slaughtering a goat for him on a daily basis."

Cartwright looked down into his empty glass and rolled the ice around the bottom.

"We missed him once, Richard, and now the Albanians have closed ranks. Goldsmith is better protected than the fucking President of the United States of America. To hit him now, would cause far too much of a row. Politically, it's a no-no."

I sat back and shook my head in disbelief. "But, in giving me his location, you know that I will go and kill him, and once again solve your problem."

The spy shrugged.

"The crab is here," he said.

We ate the excellent food in silence. Finally, Francis appeared and cleared our dishes. Once we were alone again, Cartwright leaned forward.

"I take it that the mess in Manchester last night was your doing, Richard?"

I didn't offer a reply. Cartwright didn't need one.

"Come on, an ex-Para executed on a pub carpark by an attractive brunette. My man's little jaunt into the estate finds James Stuart London sliced in half by automatic gunfire. The casings left at the scene were brass jacketed 4.6 x 30mm, bespoke to the MP7 I believe, and currently your weapon of choice."

I cocked my head quizzically. "You had us under surveillance?"

I was ignored. He barely took breath.

"Three hours ago, James London's cousin, Kevin, was discovered on a canal towpath with his testicles in his top pocket. Bit harsh, even for you, Richard."

I shrugged, "Try telling that to the parents of the sixteen-year-old he raped. Maybe it was a revenge killing."

He shook his head and ploughed on.

"I gather that was your rather bullish attempt at finding Gjergj Dushku, the 'go-between', the man who worked for the London crew and provided Goldsmith with the hot motors. You figured that if you followed your nose, Dushku would lead you to Goldsmith…correct?"

Cartwright again waved his empty glass at our butler.

"You could, of course, have saved yourself a great deal of trouble. Had you answered my original telephone call, I could have given you all the information you needed."

"We prefer to work alone," I said flatly.

"Yes, of course you do," said Cartwright, accepting two more G and T's.

I took my fresh glass. "Tell me something. How come your man missed Goldsmith anyway?"

"A cock-up, old boy. I'm sure you've been party to the odd one in your time. Bad intel, wrong move at the wrong time, that sort of thing."

I held a cube of ice in my mouth before crunching on it. "And what did the head-shed have to say about this 'cock-up'?'"

Cartwright caught my gaze but didn't speak. Over his many years, those eyes had told a million lies, and a thousand truths.

It took me a moment to work out, but I got there. Whatever had happened, it was bad news for him. "You're in the shit, aren't you?"

"You could put it that way, Richard."

"Why?"

The old spy gave a shrug. For a moment, he looked all his sixty plus years.

"The rule book is a funny thing, Richard. Sometimes we go by it, then on other occasions, we consider that we know better."

"Meaning?"

He let out a long sigh. "Meaning that maybe, I could have…should have moved earlier, nipped it all in the bud so to speak."

I shook my head. "So, you could have stopped him earlier?"

Cartwright pursed his thin lips and nodded.

I felt my anger rise again. "You could have saved those poor people, those prison officers, maybe even Spiros… but you knew best eh?"

The spy's eyes flashed. "Don't fucking patronise me, Fuller. We've all broken the rules believing it to be for the greater good. Sometimes we pay the price, sometimes we don't…just like you."

"And what is that supposed to mean?"

Cartwright was as cold and calculating a man as I'd ever met. "Remember the Shankhill Road, Richard? Of course, you do…twenty-seven years on, and I'd wager you recall that day as if it were yesterday?"

"And what about it?" I sneered.

"You were just a kid then, Richard, a kid, supposedly guided by a more experienced hand. Unfortunately, you were given that buffoon Wilson as a partner, who was more interested in brawling with the locals than doing his job…remember him?"

How could I forget? I was about to speak, but Cartwright held up a hand.

"You broke the guidelines that day, Richard. You disregarded the mantra of the rules of engagement believing that you needed to do so, in order to save further life, did you not?"

"Correct."

The spy tapped the table as he spat out the words.

"Never fire at, or from, a moving vehicle…That is the rule, is it not? Yet you decided to shoot at the driver."

"I did…yes I shot the driver…and the player with the Armalite, to stop…"

"…To stop them killing innocent people. Indeed, you did, and they gave you a medal, I believe, the first of many."

Cartwright paused. "Do you recall the name of the child who died that day, Richard?"

My guts churned. "Yeah, I remember, he was called Peter…Peter Black, yeah…he was six, he…"

Cartwright stopped me dead in my tracks. "…He was killed by one of your bullets, Richard. You shot Peter Black."

My head spun as the spy ploughed on.

"It was your stray round that was pulled from that child's body, Fuller. Always a dangerous thing to do, isn't it…fire a high velocity weapon in enclosed spaces? No doubt it was a vicious ricochet off the Provo's vehicle, or maybe a nearby building, that turned your bullet around and sent it on its fateful course toward the innocent babe."

He lowered his voice.

"We couldn't hang you out to dry, Fuller, could we? Even though you had disobeyed your rules of engagement. The press would have had a field day. Imagine it. A British soldier shooting an innocent child. We needed heroes back then, Fuller, not villains. Jesus only knows we'd had enough bad publicity…easier to let the IRA take the blame eh? So, you got your medal, and no one was any the wiser."

I felt sick, grabbing the table edge to steady myself. I'd watched that kid bleed to death in his mother's arms, heard her wails of sorrow, felt her pain of loss.

"You're a liar, Cartwright." I hissed. "What is this? Why did you bring me here?"

"No, Richard, I'm not a liar. I'll tell you exactly who I am…I'm the man who got on a plane to Belfast, broke into the evidence room of one of the most secure police stations ever built and swapped your bullet for one fired by Donal Greenhalgh, the Provo who you shot on the Shankhill Road that day.

"Do you know what they would have done to me had I been caught? Do you think the Firm would have held up its metaphorical hand and admitted I was one of theirs?

Of course, not. I would have been hung out to dry as a common criminal.

Don't you understand, Richard? We are the same animal me and you. We may have been born on different sides of the tracks, but we are the same."

"No!"

"Yes, Richard. We've both spent our lives doing others' bidding, doing our best, doing the 'right thing'. Jumping when told, even when we knew, deep down, that what we were jumping into was evil. Yet, if we were to complain or show dissent, well, there was only one punishment. It was our turn for the bullet in the head or the freak car accident."

He pointed.

"I've known about you since you were seventeen years old, Fuller, since you were a spotty youth with a bad attitude. The only difference is, today, you also know me."

Cartwright finished his drink.

"You pride yourself on your loyalty, don't you, Fuller?

Well…because of me, you didn't go on trial, didn't go to jail and didn't end up face down in the communal showers.

I saved your skin, old boy, now…I need you to save mine."

Des Cogan's Story:

JJ had slept most of the day whereas I'd spent it in deep conversation with Lauren. We'd gone over the whole Larry business and as I'd suspected, it was all something and nothing. The fact that Rick now knew about it made me feel even better. Keeping a secret like that from your best mate is never easy.

We'd also got around to the subject of Anne and her decision to leave me Hillside Cottage. With Lauren's guidance, I'd made up my mind that when all this was over, I was going to sell the place. With the money from the sale, and what I'd got put aside, I would officially be a millionaire. They say that money doesn't bring you happiness, and they are right, but it helps eh?

I'd also told Lauren about another big decision.

After this little job, I was done. I would retire for good.

For me, the city is okay for a visit. I'd been born and bred in the heart of Glasgow, seen all that the big smoking sprawls had to offer, and more, but my heart had a yearning for the old place on the Loch; peace, quiet, and a spot of fishing seemed a million miles away, and was where I needed to be.

I'd been happy there before Rick came calling.

It was great to see him doing okay again, and, of course, I would miss the cantankerous bastard, and the action. You can never replace that.

This past year or so had been like being twenty again…Gibraltar and Ireland had been just like the old times. The problem, was, I wasn't twenty anymore, I was firmly the wrong side of forty. I'd recently had my head staved in by a half-stoned Mancunian carrying a brick the size of his fireplace. If I couldn't see him coming…I reckoned it was time to call it a day.

When I'd first met Rick Fuller he, like myself, had completed three tours of Ireland and returned with a medal or two. We were some of the youngest recruits that had ever applied, and made it through the toughest physical and mental assessment, that is selection for the Special Air Service.

Rick's visits over the water had turned him from a lanky youth into a fine physical specimen. Whilst the other lads were pouring Guinness down their necks like it was going out of fashion, Rick was getting the miles under his belt. He liked a pint or two, and he liked the ladies of Belfast, but he liked the idea of passing selection even more.

I was the same, it was an obsession. I've always been slight of frame, and standing a tad over five feet nine, you could hardly call me tall, but I had wire in my blood back then; nothing could touch me, I was invincible.

Selection was not about what you had to do, it was about what you wanted to do…needed to do.

The mind-numbing, foot-destroying runs every morning, increasing in difficulty as the days went on, were all part of the process of seeing what your body and mind could endure. Dozens failed on the first day, dozens more as the days passed.

As my legs burned and my feet faltered, I would see Rick tabbing in front of me. Taller and heavier than me, he had to work even harder on the marches, yet it never showed. To me he was, and still is, a machine.

So it came somewhat as a surprise when, a little after five o'clock, the fucker staggered into the lock-up, looking more than jaded and smelling like he'd bathed in Gordons.

We all stopped what we were doing. Seeing Rick drunk was a total shock.

He still had enough of his shit together to function, and gestured for us to join him at the table.

"Come 'ere," he said quietly.

He dropped into his chair and rubbed the top of his head with his palm, an action I'd seen him do on many occasions, mostly when he'd been bolloxed.

"Tell me you didn't just drive here from London?" I asked.

Rick shook his head. "Train," he muttered. "Got the train…left the motor at the hotel."

Lauren leaned in. "Are you okay, Rick? You look…well you look drunk."

He laid both hands on the table, and took a deep breath. There was the merest hint of a slur. "Never mind that, listen up...Goldsmith is very much alive. He's in Tropojë, with Red George and half the Albanian Mafia for company."

I shook my head. "And, let me guess, the Firm knew all the time?" Rick gave a half smile, but it didn't reach his eyes. "This is a fucking beauty, pal. After the Gibraltar job, MI6 took a keen interest in Goldsmith...they believed he knew where a few CIA bodies were buried, and managed to get their claws into him before the Yanks could whisk him away. Apparently, they struck the jackpot in spy currency. The bastard turned out to be the font of all knowledge when it came to our special friend's misdemeanours, both home and abroad, especially over the water during the troubles."

He took another deep breath.

"So, no sooner had Stephan spilled his guts, than a deal was cut. He was transferred to Strangeways. As you are all aware, once there he 'died' before rolling away the proverbial stone and coming back to life as a used car salesman in Tropojë Province.

Cartwright had the balls to call it, smoke and mirrors.

Bottom line is, they got him away, gave him a new identity and set him up in Albania."

"Bastards," spat JJ.

Rick sneered.

"Ah, there's more...the best bit is, according to Cartwright, all this shit is my fault. All, was apparently well, until I accessed Goldsmith's death certificate."

"And why did you do that?" asked Lauren.

There was more head rubbing.

"Because I promised Spiros proof that Goldsmith was dead. It was what he wanted, his price for helping us out. After Stephan had killed his girl, it was all he could think about. He needed closure...I gave it to him. Trouble was, the moment the document was accessed, it was flagged up at Canary Wharf."

"And?" pressed Lauren.

Rick gave her a look. "And...that, and the fact Spiros had decided to undertake his own investigation, pushed MI6 into action. Once he started snooping into Goldsmith's death, the Firm's SOP was to instantly warn their 'asset' of an impending threat."

I couldn't hold my tongue.

"So, move the fucker, come on, Rick, how many people have we 'moved' whether they liked it or not?"

Rick pointed. "Exactly, and that is what was supposed to happen, but for some reason, only known to Cartwright, it didn't. Goldsmith basically told the Firm to go fuck themselves, and he would sort out the problem himself."

I was straight back in. "So, slot the fucker."

Rick hunched his shoulders, and slurred. "They tried…allegedly."

I felt the need for a drink myself and strolled to the fridge, cracking a can of Guinness. "Sounds like a fucking cop-out to me, pal."

Rick squeezed his eyes shut. "It was…I mean… is…Cartwright thought he had the measure of Goldsmith, but he didn't. By the time the old fucker realised that Stephan was slotting witnesses back in the UK, he was too late. Goldsmith was well protected."

"Sounds like the old spy is in the shit," I said.

Rick stood. "He is…and he expects us to get him out of it."

I took another mouthful of beer.

"So…we're going to hit Goldsmith in Albania? You do realise how hard that will be?"

He caught my eye. "You know, I know and most probably, Goldsmith knows. Look, I need to see Kostas before we do anything…tell him what we've found out. I owe him that."

I stood. "Okay, pal, fair enough, but I think I should drive."

Rick shook his head. "Tomorrow, mate, not now, I'll see him tomorrow."

He walked to the bathroom and opened the door. "I have to be somewhere else tonight."

Rick Fuller's Story:

I took the late Aer Lingus flight. It was full of people drunker than me.
I think the hostess was grateful to have at least one passenger who was drinking coffee and not on a stag weekend.
By the time we landed, it was dark and I was mentally exhausted.
I asked the cabbie to take me to a hotel close to the Shankhill. He took me to an Ibis. After Claridge's, you could say it was a come-down. I didn't give a fuck. I lay on the bed, fully clothed and begged for sleep.
Once it came, it tortured me in ways only nightmares can.

The next morning, I walked to the Shankhill.
Not knowing any better, my first port of call was the old graveyard.
As I arrived, there was a fucking tourist bus dropping off a gaggle of Yanks, all searching for their long dead relatives. I quickly learned that the cemetery had stopped taking burials in the early Fifties, so I left Fat Brad and Fatter Marline to their dreams of being Irish rather than American.
Some clumsy questioning of a local newsagent left me with a flea in my ear and on my way to Belfast City Cemetery.
Run by the council, it has a sunken wall to separate the Catholics from the Protestants. This little gem of information didn't sink in at first. Then I realised that the wall was sunken so it separated the dead, not the living. I mean, you wouldn't want a pesky Catholic coming knocking on your coffin in the middle of the night eh?
Insanity ruled back then; now, it just has a seat in Parliament.
During World War One, they buried all the Commonwealth soldiers who had died in combat in the place. They had to move the graves of the British lads due to constant desecration of their headstones. Last year, 2006, they buried a former IRA player here. He was murdered shortly after being named as a British spy. His burial in the City Cemetery rather than in the Republican plot of Milltown was the Provos' final punishment for his treachery.
If Peter Black was buried in Belfast, I had the feeling he would be here.

There was no doubt that Cartwright had chosen to reveal the truth about the child to ensure I would do his bidding. He already knew about our sortie into Jimmy London's turf, and my commitment to the Makris family so it was a mystery why he thought airing the tale necessary, and the first flaw I'd ever found in his reasoning.

I walked the grounds without any idea of a plan and chastised myself for my stupidity. Almost a quarter of a million had been buried in the council-run cemetery since 1869. I was nothing but a busy fool.
The clock found eleven and I was forced to remove my jacket as the early summer heat pricked my skin. I trudged about, no nearer to finding who I sought.
I knew I would have to get myself together, and begin to think like a soldier again.
Finally my mind allowed me to think straight, and I mentally sliced the Protestant area into sections. This time, however, I noted and checked off each quadrant as I walked.
Three hours later, I found him.
There were no stone angels for Peter; no cherubs sitting above grand marble slabs.
A small, once white, arched stone bore his name, his birth date… and the day I killed him.
Grass grew long around the grave, almost covering the inscription from view. At some point, someone had added a black urn that should have contained flowers in front of the tiny headstone, but that too, was empty, rusted and overturned.
I'd known the instant Cartwright revealed his secret what I had to do. I had to visit Peter. But to say what? To do what? To ask forgiveness? I haven't a religious bone in my body. I don't believe in God, ghosts or things that go bump in the night.
Yet something deep inside me brought me to this place, to this unkempt patch of Irish earth that covered the bones of a small child.
I pinched my nose to prevent it running, but there was no stopping my tears.
Falling to my knees, I grabbed handfuls of grass, and began to tear at the overgrown foliage around the headstone. Sunshine warmed my back as I worked, yet the grass and soil were cold damp and clammy to the touch. Peter's frozen soul chilled my fingers as my nails filled

with dank earth, yet I couldn't stop. Finally, I sat back, pouring with sweat.

A deep, controlled voice came from behind me. "That's very kind of you, sir."

Startled, I wiped away what was left of my tears, streaking my face with mud. In that moment, I felt Peter's age, a solitary child playing in the dirt. I must have looked a real picture.

"What?" I croaked.

The voice had emanated from an elderly man, well into his seventies. Despite the heat, he sported a thick tweed jacket and trousers, a well-worn trilby hat and Wellington boots. Bright yellow Marigold gloves protected his hands. Gripped in his right was a small trowel. Most noticeable of all however, was his black shirt and white clerical collar.

"Are you a relative?" he asked, his pale, watery eyes searching my face.

I shook my head whilst doing my best to wipe dirt from my face with my sleeve.

The man tilted his head, obviously waiting for a rational explanation as to why a stranger would be tending the grave of a long dead child to whom he was no relation.

I used the old trick of turning his question into my own.

Clearing my throat, I asked, "Why is the boy's grave in such poor condition, Father?"

The man smiled kindly. "It's Pastor actually. I'm from West Kirk Presbyterian, on the Shankhill Road. And to answer your question, the reason poor Peter's grave is in such need of some love and care, is because he has no living family left in Ireland.

We try, as a church, to keep on top of the graves as best we can, but I'm afraid our congregations are dwindling, and with them, our volunteer gardeners."

The pastor jutted his thin chin toward an even older guy who was struggling with a small wheelbarrow a dozen plots away.

"Eric is eighty-two. He gives a couple of hours each day when the weather and his arthritis allow."

I stood, briefly towering over the pastor. He took a step away to regain his personal space.

"We could do with a couple of chaps built like you, sir," he managed.

I held up my hands.

"There are no green fingers here, Pastor."

The old man gestured at my crude handiwork. "However, not bad for a beginner… Mr?"

I thought for a moment before my answer, after spending far too long hiding my identity this side of the water.

"Fuller," I said. "Richard Fuller."

"Well, Mr Fuller, as you are not a relation, and not a gardener, what is your connection to Peter Black?"

I studied his eyes, found no malice but again remained silent, mainly as I didn't know what to say.

Finally, I managed, "You say Peter has no living family?"

The pastor seemed happy to talk, even if he wasn't getting the answers he wanted; I suppose, in his line of work, he'd found many of his parishioners were reluctant to admit their sins straight away. Patience was obviously one of his virtues.

"His grandparents," he began, "William and Maud are both long gone. They are laid to rest just a little way from where old Eric is working now, pushing that damned wooden barrow."

My mind played horrible tricks on me as my last memories of Peter flashed in front of my eyes. "What about his mother?" I asked.

The pastor pursed his lips and chose his words. "After Peter was killed, his parents decided that they should emigrate. They had seen too much death, too much hatred. The Troubles had worn them down you see. They had two other wee ones…did you know?"

I shook my head.

"Emma and Joyce," he said. "I seem to recall that there was an uncle who lived in Canada. I think he sponsored them to go, and well, in their situation, who would not? To lose one child to the violence, to the terrorists, is heart-breaking enough. I'm sure you'd agree?"

The pastor locked eyes with me, studying this strange man he'd discovered tearing lumps of grass from a near thirty-year-old grave. He knew…Of course he knew.

"You were there, that day, weren't you?" he said softly.

My tears had betrayed me.

"How old are you, Mr Fuller? Forty-six? Seven? You've been a soldier I'd say, yes, no doubt about it. Even an old man with

cataracts can see that. So…back then…you would have been…
what? Eighteen…nineteen that day?"
"Something like that," I said.
He nodded and examined me again. "It was you, wasn't it? You
were the boy soldier they talked of. The boy that saved the day, the
hero. The one who shot the Provos on the Shankhill Road and saved
those people?"
I felt a lump the size of a tennis ball in my throat.
"Peter wasn't saved though, eh?"
"No," said the pastor. "Sadly, not the boy. But you must take heart,
Mr Fuller, indeed you must. God helped you that day, he put his
hand on yours and helped you shoot straight and true."
I turned to leave, but the old man grabbed my arm.
"Don't turn your back on the Lord, Mr Fuller. Maybe you should
visit the church before you go…It's good for the soul, you know."
I pulled away my arm. "It wasn't your God, or anyone else's, that
steered my hand that day Pastor, it was the Devil himself…and my
soul is long past saving."

I pulled notes from my pocket and pushed them into the old man's
jacket. "Sort the kid's grave, Pastor…and buy Eric a new barrow
eh?"

An uneventful flight back to Ringway, followed by a tedious, traffic-
filled cab ride, found me outside the home of Kostas Makris.
He was in his considerable gardens mowing the grass. The man
obviously loved his work. The lawns were immaculate, and the
flowerbeds were bursting with colour. Of course, unlike the pastor,
he could easily afford a guy or two to tend to his plot, indeed they
would probably cost half what he was paying the brute of a minder
that sat a discreet distance away in the shade, watching his boss
sweat. Kostas obviously enjoyed his labour, and the fruits of it.
Birds sang overhead and the oaks and chestnuts they perched on
shaded the Greek from the late sunshine. Their ancient boughs
painting shimmering pictures on the pathways below. Had I not been
in such a sorrowful mood, I would have described the scene as
idyllic.
Makris saw me before his bodyguard did, which was a worry.

The Greek gave his paid muscle the hard stare and walked over to his electric gates. He hit the 'open' button, wiping the sweat from his head with a rag.

"You missed my brother's funeral," he said flatly.

Mildly irritated, I countered, "As I recall, you are paying me to find his killer, not to spend time mourning him."

He jutted his chin. "You are one hard-faced bastard, Fuller."

I was in no mood for tantrums. "He was my friend, Makris. If I could have been there, I would, but things have moved quickly."

Kostas looked about him, turned and walked toward his imposing house.

"You like lemonade?" he said, pulling out his mobile and dialling. "It's home-made."

A short walk saw us sitting on a beautiful stone patio overlooking the garden. A cast iron table with a thick glass top sat front and centre. Moments after we settled into our chairs, an attractive blonde woman in her thirties delivered a pitcher of ice cold lemonade and two glasses without acknowledging my presence.

Kostas took a long drink of his juice and licked his lips appreciatively.

"My sister-in-law," he said, nodding toward the retreating woman. "Spiros's wife."

I took a sip myself, finding the drink delicious. "I never got the chance to meet her."

Kostas shrugged. "I know this."

The Greeks hate the English for stating the obvious. We do it more than you think. He changed the subject.

"You enjoy my lemonade? I import the lemons from Kavadades, a small village on the island of Corfu, the place I was born."

"It's very nice," I said, before gulping down half the glass.

"The best," he said proudly, before changing his tone. "Now...I presume you are here because you have found Spiros killer, no?"

I nodded. "We know his identity."

"And?"

"His name is Gjergj Dushku, a Kosovan of Albanian descent. He killed Spiros on the orders of Stephan Goldsmith."

Kostas turned down the corners of his mouth. "So, the bastard is alive after all."

"He is."

"How can this be?"

"It's complicated, Kostas…political."

The Greek poured himself more lemonade.

"You mean he paid some rotten politician for his freedom?"

"You could say that. Goldsmith turned out to be valuable to the Secret Service. He turned informer to buy his new life."

"A new life…you mean a new identity, he is in the programme eh? Witness protection?"

"He was."

"So how come he was able to send this Albanian pig to kill my brother? How can this happen when he is under the gaze of MI6?"

I shrugged. "Well it did, and it was not just your brother, there were other innocent victims…it's a mess. And now Goldsmith has got himself ensconced with the Albanian Mafia, and he's well protected."

Kostas's eyes grew wide. "They are in Albania? My God, this is very bad. These people are crazy, they will kill a man for one Euro."

"I know all about Albania, Makris, and I want Goldsmith dead just as much as you do. I don't care where he is. I'm going to find the fucker and kill him. Simple."

Kostas shook his head.

"My brother said you were crazy, and I think he was right, but this I tell you, a man could go to this place with an army and not come back alive. The Albanian will fight you with their bare hands until the last is dead. Do you understand this?"

"You want me to give in? Let sleeping dogs lie?"

Kostas closed his eyes for a moment, before holding my gaze. "I will pay any fee you ask. I want this bastard's head on a plate, Richard."

"I'll send you a picture," I said.

Des Cogan's Story:

Rick's return to the lock-up was all business as usual. There were no signs of his alcohol-induced weakness, although he did baulk at the £700 fee Claridge's charged to bring back his motor.
I'd no idea what had been the matter with him, and there was no point in asking. If he wanted me to know, he'd tell me in good time.
Our intel wasn't exactly comprehensive, but it appeared that after a bungled attempt by the Firm to slot Goldsmith for his misdemeanours, the gangster had left his safe house in Tirana and gone to ground in a fortified location, to the north in Tropojë. This province of Albania, close to the Kosovan border, had a long reputation as one of the wildest and most lawless regions of the country, virtually out of control of every government Tirana had ever produced, Communist or republican.
Tropojë was also the home of Red George's biological family, and the base he'd used to move weapons and fighters over the border to Kosovo during the crisis of 1997.
Like many others of his ilk, George had taken advantage of the humanitarian disaster in the Balkans and sought asylum in the UK. As Britain and its NATO partners did its usual impression of the whole world's policeman, and went to war with Serbia to save Kosovan Albanians from alleged repression and atrocity, thousands of Red George types poured into Britain.
In truth, most had nothing to fear from the regime across the Yugoslav border, but the Albanian Mafia were never one to miss a golden handshake. They saw a lucrative opportunity, and the cities of the UK were a cracking place to build their empires. People trafficking, prostitution and in George's case, murder, mayhem and knock-off motors were all part of their little business plan.
Now it appeared he was back home where it all started, in the closest place to the Wild West he could find.
We couldn't just rock up and start snooping about in Tropojë province. The Albanians are a notoriously violent people, and still kill each other over family arguments that have been rolling on for centuries. If we were to try wandering in any town heavy-handed, we'd be dead before the day was out.

Our options included flying into Tirana, or taking a ferry to Sarande posing as holiday makers. These were relatively safe. Tourism was slowly taking off in Albania and was welcomed by the locals. The problem with this choice was, as soon as we made any move north away from the main tourist track, the jungle drums would start and we'd be visible.

As with all countries that are in flux politically, and Albania was most definitely in that category, the governing body and their associate parts are all subject to the odd issue. The main one being, they are all as bent as a nine-bob note.

The bottom line was that anyone could be connected with the Mafia in Albania, from a waiter in Sarande to a cop in Tirana. They wouldn't drop the dime on a British tourist for money, they would do it out of loyalty…making it a very dangerous place to go if you had our kind of intentions. No, we needed to enter and leave the country without leaving a trace, and that is never easy.

Kostas Makris was a Corfiot, and the island of Corfu was less than one nautical mile from Albania. Our plan was to fly to his birthplace and travel to the north-west coast.

Once there, we would meet with Kostas's cousins who ran a bar in the holiday resort of Arillas.

We were reliably informed that they could supply us with weapons and a small boat to complete the short hop across the water. With transport and weapons, we had a place to start.

What could possibly go wrong?

Lauren had been given the task of booking our flights. Rick flatly refused to fly with either of the big two budget airlines, which meant flying business class with a foreign carrier. I wasn't going to complain, the ticket included grub and complimentary drinks, and anything that is free-gratis is a plus in my book, pal.

Increasing this pasty Scotsman's pleasure further was the fact that the Greeks had one speed when it came to organisation, so the planning of the short trip across the Ionian Sea to bandit country was going to take a while.

This could mean only one thing, a few days of sunshine, scantily clad women, and cold beer. All good, before the real fun started once we got across the water.

Bring it on, pal.

en North's Story:

The three of us had tiptoed around Rick for the first hour of his return, but it quickly became apparent that he wasn't going to mention whatever had caused his obvious distress. Indeed, he seemed more focused than ever on our task ahead.

He'd showered, changed, eaten heartily and then set us all about organising our trip to Corfu and ultimately Albania.

With his dark disposition apparently behind him, he'd regained that confident swagger that so attracted me to him in the first place.

I had to admit, the thought of spending a few days on a sun-kissed Greek island with Rick for company did make my tummy flutter somewhat.

I'd booked us all with Austrian Airlines. Annoyingly, they had a thirty-minute stopover in Vienna, however, AA promised Rick the legroom he desired, so we all had to endure the inconvenience of a longer flight to ensure His Nibs could stretch out and enjoy his cabin service.

Despite this, the mood in the camp had been as relaxed as I'd known it. Even though we were about to travel to one of the most lawless countries in the world to assassinate a man who was about as dangerous as a wounded lion, everyone went about their tasks with a smile on their face, and banter filled the lock-up. I swear I even saw JJ smile.

I'd visited my flat to recover some more of my summer wardrobe and, even with no fighting kit to pack, I'd just managed to bring my case in under the 22kg weight limit that AA demanded. Mr Fuller, however, was a good 4kg over and would need his credit card at the check-in.

The black cab dropped us outside Terminal One and Rick and I dragged our suitcases along to the express desk whist Des and JJ, who had opted for the hand-luggage only option, wandered straight to the Escape Lounge and the complimentary drinks.

If we looked and acted like tourists, then that was not only the idea, but a fact. None of our party had ever visited Corfu, and with the possibility of a few days' grace before we would have access to weapons and our boat, it was time to relax.

Meeting the boys had made me realise that soldiers or troupers of whatever regiment or corps knew how to use the time they had to its maximum advantage. There was no point in sitting around worrying about what might happen next. When you had a day or two to have fun, you made the most of it.

As Rick and I wandered into the VIP lounge, Des and JJ were already sitting comfortably and tucking into the cold meats and cheeses that were part of the buffet. I found a comfortable leather sofa and ordered drinks from a very handsome and friendly Polish waiter.
Guinness for Des, Peroni for JJ and myself, and an Evian for Rick. Well, some things never change, eh?

We took off on time and I had to admit, the in-flight service on AA was excellent. As for the stop-over, well it was hardly an inconvenience, as I slept through it, so comfortable were our seats. By the time we were making our final approach into Corfu, darkness had fallen. The aircraft passed over Mouse Island, and all I could see were the twinkling lights of the hotels and tavernas that sat alongside the solitary runway.
As we landed Rick took my hand in his, and, despite the pending danger, for the first time in many years I felt truly happy.

A short taxi ride saw us to our digs for the night. The Siorra Vittoria Boutique Hotel was situated on the edge of Corfu Old Town.
The 19th-century mansion used to be a private dwelling until the Sixties. It had been empty for many years until the new owners fully restored it, turning it into charming accommodation. Our rooms were typically Greek, simple and clean with classic wooden furniture, oak wood floors and marble bathrooms. Each room had plenty of personality though, with elegant furnishings and wooden beamed ceilings.
Des and JJ dropped their rucksacks and were keen to hit the town. Rick insisted on hanging his clothes and changing into a clean Dolce and Gabbana shirt before we could leave.
As I said, some things never change.

Des Cogan's Story:

A nice wee flight with free beverages, a hotel that was smart as, and seventy-plus degrees in the shade all made for a happy wee Desmond.

With my bag dropped, I considered it was time to find a good pub and settle in for the night.

As we waited for Rick to ponce about, JJ stood in the lobby muttering things about Greek-Turkish relations, or the lack of. I figured I may need to keep an eye on the wee short-tempered Turk.

Rick appeared, gave him the hard word about behaving himself, and strode off toward the town with Lauren at his side.

JJ shrugged. "I suppose we follow the love-birds eh?"

We did.

Rick pointed out the need to get our bearings, so we made for the Old Fortress via the Spianada, a patch of grass that had been seeded by the British in the 1800's. The local kids often played a game of cricket on it, smashing hell out of the nearby parked cars with the ball.

Despite the time being well past beer o'clock the temperature was still up there, and as we crossed the sea-moat and climbed the ancient fortress battlements that overlooked the harbour, we all had a sweat on.

Once there, I realised what Rick was doing.

We stood in silence for a moment, as from our elevated position we had the perfect view of the Albanian mainland, our ultimate destination. The mountainous landscape towered behind the berthed cruise liners in the port.

"So, that's Albania," said Lauren. "It looks…well it looks scary."

Nobody argued.

I caught Rick's eye. I'd seen the look before. This was going to be a tough one.

As we walked beneath the New Fortress ramparts, we were all surprised to find a synagogue there. JJ pointed out that the Germans sent thousands of Corfiot Jews to Auschwitz to be gassed during the war, then destroyed a quarter of the town, including fourteen churches.

He was becoming a proper little historian.

I pointed out that in more recent times, the most dangerous thing the Teutonic types did was take up all the sunbeds at six in the morning, whilst the Scots were still sleeping off there fuckin' hangovers.

Fifteen sweaty minutes later, found us back at the cricket pitch and the Liston, a promenade of arcaded terraces and fashionable cafés. It had been built by the French, when Corfu was part of the First French Empire. I was beginning to ask myself just who hadn't successfully invaded this island, until JJ pointed out it was his own race.

I made another mental note to keep an eye on our tetchy Turk. It was like dragging a Rangers fan around Celtic Park.

Finally we flopped in a café, guzzled cold beer, forgot the foreboding mountains of Albania and Greek-Turkish relations, and talked shite until the wee small hours.

My kind of night, pal.

Rick Fuller's Story:

I liked Corfu town. It had everything, great history, architecture, food and hospitable people. There was no doubting the Corfiots' love of the British, even if we'd done our best to destroy the relationship in recent years by being, well, just by being Brits abroad.

Fortunately, Peter Black hadn't visited me in the night, indeed I'd somehow managed to square what had happened away in my head. Of course I would never forget the kid, or my error, but I wasn't going to beat myself up over it any more than I already had. I'd broken the rules, I'd saved lives. End of.

That said, I think visiting his grave had been a positive experience for me, and given me the closure that I needed.

Once again…Time heals, they say.

The next morning, whilst the others slept off their hangovers, I hired a nice-looking Audi Q7 S-Line 3.0L turbo. It was big enough to take the four of us in comfort and at 229bhp, the Quattro had enough grunt to take our party around the notorious hairpins of Corfu Island. It also had a tow-bar.

By 1000hrs we were on our way out of town, and on the Paleocastrista road.

We quickly realised that getting around the island was a little tricky, as once you ventured outside Corfu Town, there were no road names or house numbers. It was just a question of following the map and asking directions when you got there.

Within forty minutes we were winding down the final hill toward our destination. The Q7 swept silently between fragrant cypress trees and olive groves, whilst dealing admirably with the shocking road conditions. After one very tight right-hander, we were treated to the stunning view of the bays of St George and Arillas.

"Now that's bonny," said Des, sticking his bare feet out of the rear passenger window and popping a cold can of Greek beer.

"Bit early, isn't it?" I commented.

Des took a deep swig and handed the can to JJ. "Fuck off," he said. "You need to lighten up, I'm on ma fuckin' jollies pal. Can you recall the last time you had a holiday?"

I tried to remember, and shook my head.

"I can," said Des, prodding me in the back to make his point. "Fucking 1986, pal…that's when. Where was it now? We went to Benidorm…you remember?"

JJ drained the rest of the can. "You should have visited Turkey, Rick, it is wonderful country, so much better than Spain…or Greece."

I shook my head at JJ's persistence.

Lauren looked over from the passenger seat. She was beautiful in a lemon Karen Millen shirt, white Levi cut-off shorts and Gucci sandals.

"Maybe it's time you had a break eh?" she said quietly.

"Maybe," I said, knowing she was right.

Arillas was popular with the hippies during the late Sixties and early Seventies. According to the locals, the place still retained spiritual qualities. Some tour operators made small fortunes selling package holidays that promised unworldly adventures to middle-aged Europeans seeking divinity in the sands of the resort.

Our hotel, however, boasted no guru or group meditation sessions, just quality rooms, a nice pool and a beachfront location.

The Horizon was a casual hotel of quality and I liked it, and the resort of Arillas, instantly.

Our four rooms all overlooked the sparkling Ionian Sea, and fortunately faced west, away from Albania. This ensured we could relax, enjoy the view and forget the malevolence of the dark coastline that awaited us.

That afternoon we swam, ate, drank and laughed together, and it was good.

Des Cogan's Story:

On our second afternoon in Arillas, Lauren and JJ took the Audi to Acharavi, a medium-sized town by Corfiot standards, situated on the north coast. Their task was to source some comms for us, nothing fancy, just some F27's and G shape earpieces. They are a basic walkie-talkie with a decent range and more importantly, as we would be getting wet, the handset is waterproof.

As for Rick and me, well, we were off to meet the extended Makris clan, Pericles and Konstantinos.

The guys owned one of only two late bars in Arillas, The Coconut. It was a short stroll from our hotel and when we arrived Pericles was just opening up for the lunchtime drinkers. He was a smartly dressed guy and wore chinos and a polo shirt. His short-cropped hair was receding slightly, but this did not detract from his handsome features.

Having no idea who we were, or the reason for our visit, the guy greeted us as he would any other thirsty tourist.

"Give me a minute to open eh, boys," he said. "The *malakas* (wankers) didn't leave here until five-thirty and I am still asleep in my head huh?"

He seemed a good bloke, instantly likeable and straight-talking. I held up my hand. "You take your time, pal, no hurry."

Peri pushed open the folding doors to reveal a room that would hold maybe two hundred people. There was a long, well stocked bar off to the left and a stage and DJ booth to the right. As we stepped inside, I saw climbing plants crawling across the ceiling and large old fashioned fans whirring above out heads.

Peri clicked on the lights, switched on the TV screens and pressed play somewhere behind the DJ booth.

He reappeared and gave me a big smile.

"So, you are Scottish, my friend, yes?"

The boy knew his accents. "Aye, from Glasgow originally, pal."

Rick had remained silent. "And your quiet friend?"

"London," said Rick climbing on a bar stool. "But we all live in the north of England these days."

A light came on in Peri's head. "Ah, so you are Richard and…?"

I held out my hand. "Des…I'm Des. Our friends Lauren and JJ are out shopping."

Peri pulled two frosted glasses from a chest freezer and started to fill them with ice cold Mythos. "Then you have the better of the two jobs…beer okay?"

"Beer is fine," said Rick. "Where is your brother, Peri? You cousin Kostas tells me, he can help us with our …issue."

The boy gave a shrug, a movement common amongst the local men when faced with any issue that involved any modicum of difficulty. "My brother? Now? He was here till close also…so he will be asleep or having sex. And yes, if Kostas tells you this, then it is true. Me? I run this bar, look after my family, and keep my nose out of these matters…understand?

We nodded.

Peri handed over the beers. "So, boys, have a few drinks on me and relax, I will call Konstantinos shortly."

Shortly, turned into two hours.

Peri obviously had no intention of disturbing his brother's slumber or sex life before two in the afternoon, and by the time Konstantinos pulled up outside The Coconut in his BMW, we were four beers deep.

The two brothers couldn't have been more different. Konstantinos stepped into the bar wearing nothing but red shorts and mirrored sunglasses. He was lean and muscular with long dark hair that touched his shoulders. He displayed hawkish features, and when he removed his shades, unveiled eyes that held a touch of madness in them.

I got the instant impression that Konstantinos was not a man to be messed with, and made another mental note to keep him and JJ apart. He strode over, gave us a beaming smile that only made him look even more insane, and shook our hands.

"Hello, boys," he said in a sing-song voice. "I take it you have come to see your boat?"

The drive to San Stefano harbour was just over a mile. Konstantinos drove like a fuckin' madman and spent the whole journey on his phone. I was very glad to step onto the jetty, I'll tell you, pal.

The Greek pushed his sunglasses onto the top of his head and pointed at a fiberglass pleasure boat with a 30hp outboard that bobbed up and down in the dock. The hull appeared to be a quarter full of seawater.

"Don't worry about this, we will fix the leak before you go," he said, waving his Aviators in the general direction of the very tired looking craft. "And anyway, it is not far where you go."

He then slapped Rick on the back, a movement that I considered as dangerous as any ride in a knackered boat.

"And it is not likely that you come back anyway eh?" bawled the Greek, before bursting into fits of laughter.

Mercifully, Rick managed to stop himself from throwing Konstantinos into the water and we wandered back to the Beamer and suffered another white-knuckle ride back to The Coconut.

Once in the bar Konstantinos led us through the back, up a rickety wooden staircase and into a storage area.

The Greek rooted about in a large wooden chest and removed a rolled-up blanket. He placed the blanket on the floor and proudly unfurled it.

Inside were the weapons we had been promised.

There were two handguns. The first was a WWI German Officer's Luger PO8 pistol.

The Luger was famous with weapon aficionados, for its 9×19mm Parabellum cartridge. This name came from the Latin, *si vis pacem, para bellum*, meaning, 'If you seek peace, prepare for war.'

Personally, I didn't give a shit about the Latin meaning, the gun was over a hundred years old.

A quick inspection revealed just one round in the chamber and three in the cartridge.

The second handgun was a little newer, but equally Teutonic. The Walther P38 was intended to replace the Luger, as it was cheaper for the German army to buy. Even so it was a WWII weapon. It had an eight-round, single row, detachable box magazine, but just as worrying, ours had only five rounds to its name.

Lying at the side of the two handguns were two single-barrel sawn-off shotguns. All manufacturers' names and serial numbers had been ground off, but I figured them to be cheap, and older than me. A box of 24 cartridges came with them, loaded with 00 buckshot. At least they were man-stoppers.

Konstantinos looked us both in the eye, his broad smile fixed in place.

"Good, yes?"

I thought Rick may strangle him.

"When was the last time these were fired?" he said managing to keep his voice level.

The Greek looked at us like we were mad. "Easter of course."

The Greek was unusually stating the obvious; in addition to smashing pots and urns worth thousands of pounds during the Easter celebrations, the Corfiot men felt it necessary to fire any old firearm into the air at random intervals and hang the danger to everyone else.

I could feel Rick's temper rising. "Easter when? Fucking 1939?"

It appeared that either Konstantinos didn't realise or didn't care what physical danger he was in. The smile remained firmly in place and he committed another mortal sin by placing a reassuring hand on Rick's shoulder.

"Don't stress, Richard, these guns are cleaned all the time and fired every year."

Rick stepped away from the Greek's touch. His dander was up and I was beginning to worry that I wouldn't be able to control him.

"So," he began, his voice almost a whisper. "You expect us to launch an assault on a fortified compound containing any number of armed men with two antique pistols, no ammunition and a couple of sawn-offs?"

The Greek looked puzzled. "Don't be silly, boys...Look, I speak with my cousin Kostas, yes? He tell me that you come here to borrow my very nice boat. Then he say to me that you need guns too, no? I tell him, 'what you think we are here, gangsters?' He say, don't stress, just give the boys what you have and the address of Arjan Bajrami in Sarande. There, they will find all the weapons they need."

I asked a stupid question.

"Bajrami? Is a mate of your cousin?"

The Greek's manic smile reappeared. "Of course not. He is a sworn enemy of the Makris family. He steal thousands from my cousins

Spiros and Kostas, they sell many guns to this Albanian malaka, but he never pay."

Rick was in. "So why didn't you sort him out yourselves?" Konstantinos eyes grew wide. "Are you crazy? Go to Albania and kill an Albanian?"

He went to put his arm on Rick again, but Rick was too quick and stepped backward, The Greek shrugged, obviously thinking this behaviour strange. He continued. "Richard, we live next door to this fucking place full of crazy mother-fuckers. Every third guy that walks past my bar is Albanian. So…we go over, kill this robbing bastard Bajrami and recover my cousin's money? Then what?"

We waited for the punchline...it came.

"We all dead the next day."

I was doing all the maths in my head. That cheeky fucker Kostas was paying us to top Goldsmith alright, but he was settling another score at the same time. Before we could move on Stephan, Red George and his crew, we would have to sort Bajrami.

I looked over to Rick, who was shaking his head in resignation. He picked up the Luger PO8 and gave it the once-over.

"You know how much this is worth, Konstantinos?" he said quietly laying the gun back in position. "More than your BMW, pal."

The Greek looked doubtful. "Really?"

"Really," said Rick.

"Fuck," muttered the Greek. "I need to change my price."

"Your price?" I asked.

It was Konstantinos's turn to shrug. "Of course, mean, really, I tell Kostas you are insane but he doesn't listen. Like I say to you on the dock, I am very sorry for this, but the truth is, I will never see my boat, these guns or you again eh?"

He gave us both his trademark smile. "But hey…fuck it, let's have a beer."

Rick Fuller's Story:

Konstantinos wasn't such a bad bloke. Once you got past the manic eyes, the matching smile and his constant attempts to touch you, he was okay.

And it wasn't that he was being awkward either. Kostas Makris had called on his cousins out of the blue and dropped our little problem in their lap. To be fair, neither he nor Peri had anything to do with the shadier side of the Makris business. They ran a bar, end of.

By the time, I'd made it to San Stephanos jetty the following morning, Peri and Konstantinos had the boat out of the water and were patching her up.

"She will be a good as new, Richard," shouted Peri as I scrambled over the rocks to the beach where the boat was upturned.

They seemed to be doing a reasonable job by Greek standards. After three short days on the island, I'd already learned that the Corfiots never threw anything away until it was truly dead.

As Peri plugged the considerable holes in the hull with fiberglass resin, Konstantinos was re-waterproofing the joints, with what looked suspiciously like a tube of bathroom sealant.

"Nice," I managed. "Is the engine in good order?"

Both brothers spoke in unison. "Perfect!"

Konstantinos dropped his tube and wandered over.

Annoyingly, once again he insisted on putting his arm around me as he spoke. "Look, my friend. Don't worry, the boat will get you where you want to go. It is now just a question of when, yes?"

He wore a concerned frown.

"Now…two things, Richard; first, you need to cover the boat with something dark coloured, blankets maybe, and second, you need cloud. I tell you this, if you make the crossing in the moonlight, the Albanians kill you dead before you see land."

I looked into the clearest blue sky. "And when are we due clouds?" I asked.

The smile and the shrug said it all.

Thankfully the Greek let go of me before lighting his roll-up. He exhaled a large plume of smoke as he spoke.

"The clouds will come…we tell you when. Anyway, the good news is, to find this Albanian bastard Bajrami, is not so hard. This pig who steal from my cousins, his house is near to the coast and will be easy to get to."

I'd already been onto our tech guru in the UK, and Egghead had solved some of our mapping issues by somehow obtaining images from a Russian military satellite that passed within a mile or two over Bajrami's gaff. I'd downloaded them overnight on my PAYG phone, and sent the stills to a little print shop in Sidari. This stuff, together with the official MI6 file on Goldsmith's hideout, that Cartwright had provided, meant we were looking a bit healthier in the intelligence department.

Other than that, we were on a bit of a wing and a prayer. Once we recovered the alleged weapons and ammunition from Bajrami, we would then have to travel by road from Sarande to Tropojë. In Albania, the further north you travelled the more you encountered bandit territory, and once we got to Tropojë, there was the small matter of taking on a fully armed crew of Stephan's followers, including the formidable Red George.

Nice easy trip eh?

I gave Konstantinos a wry smile. "Finding this malaka's house is the easy part, my friend. Taking his life and getting away without detection, is quite another."

The Greek nodded.

"Your boat will be ready tonight… and I think maybe soon, you have your clouds."

Lauren North's Story:

Forget Richard Fuller, I was in love with Arillas.

Okay, I'd been to prettier resorts with more spectacular views and the five-star life.

But, Arillas was for living, relishing, savouring, like a fine wine. And the more you drank, the more it gave you.

People talked about the place as having mystical qualities. Well, I'm not certain of that, but it did have something I just couldn't put my finger on, something enchanting.

I instantly belonged, and I never wanted to leave.

After Rick and I had spent most of the previous evening dancing around each other, neither knowing quite how to behave, I was happy to spend the morning alone. Our relationship seemed to have progressed to the occasional knowing look.

The hot, passionate, sun-kissed romance was not exactly going to plan.

After breakfasting on Greek yoghurt, honey and pomegranate. I put the big oaf to the back of my mind, bought a large bottle of water and began my planned walk from the resort of Arillas to the hillside village of Kavadades.

It hadn't seemed too far away on the drive in, so I figured that I could power-walk, and get some exercise in at the same time. Maybe it would offset the wine?

I hadn't quite realised quite how the searing heat would hurt my progress; climbing the hills was tough, and my leg and guts complained bitterly. Gritting my teeth, I realised I wouldn't forget what the O'Donnells had done to me, in a hurry.

I dropped down the final hill, stopped, pulled a small towel from my bag, dried myself off as best I could, and strolled into what can only be described as the centre of the village.

Kavadades centre comprised a bakery that sold bread, a closed post office with a digger parked outside, and a Cafeneon.

It was wonderful.

A Cafeneon is a café-cum-shop-cum-bar type place. They're hidden away in most Greek villages, and tend to be where the locals drop in to pass the time of day.

My resting place was called Angelika's, and stocked everything from windscreen wipers to Uncle Joe's Mint Balls. However, from the age and look of the packaging, she didn't sell too much of anything except coffee, booze and the occasional bottle of milk.
The place boasted a couple of outside tables perched precariously by the edge of the road. I selected a fine Formica-topped model, slipped into my seat, ordered an ice-cold Amstel…no glass…and settled down to people-watch.
Halfway down the bottle, my mobile buzzed. It was Des, there was a team meeting planned for the afternoon.
He had his serious head on, and I got the impression my holiday was all but over.

On the stroke of 1400hrs we were all together in Rick's hotel room. Spread across his bed were aerial pictures of two separate dwellings, one larger than the other, together with enlarged sections of maps of Albania. Egghead had provided some excellent intel on our first goal, which was the home of a local arms dealer and all round pillar of the community, Arjan Bajrami. Much to our surprise, Cartwright had given in to Rick's persistence and finally sent over everything he had on our primary target, the residence of Stephan Goldsmith. Stephan's place looked more like a fortress than a holiday home, and I began to feel a little uneasy.
For the next two hours, we worked on our plan. Just how we would disguise our boat, where we would land, how we would enter the first house, and finally, by what means we would find and kill Stephan Goldsmith.
All we needed now was the right weather.

By the end of the briefing, I felt the need to chill out. Des and JJ attempted to get me to The Coconut for 'Happy Hour' cocktails, but I resisted. Rick went all quiet when I suggested a drink, so I left him pondering his maps.
I ventured no further than next door, to the seafront restaurant, Thalassa.
I flopped in one of the old-fashioned deckchairs that faced the sea, ordered myself a large glass of Pinot and let my mind wander.
One glass turned into two, and the sun commenced its slow descent. People were leaving the beach and heading off to their

accommodation, to shower and change before their evening meals. The rolling sea began to take on a mercury-like quality, shimmering and flashing all the way to the horizon. Some children, reluctant to leave the beach, still played, silhouetted in the shallows.

Then I saw him.

I couldn't mistake the frame. He must have sneaked by me as I lounged with my wine. Rick was sprinting between two unseen points on the beach. Shuttle runs are hard in the gym, but on sand they are a killer. I watched him push himself left and right, twisting his torso and powering forward, before twisting again.
If Rick was testing his groin, he was doing a fine job.
Feeling slightly light-headed, I dropped cash on the table next to me and wandered across the road to get a closer look.
As I drew nearer, I could see the sweat pouring from his body and hear his breathing as he worked himself to exhaustion.
My feet hit the hot sand, I was no more than twenty feet from him, his muscular upper body framed against the iridescent waves.
Without noticing my presence, he turned and ran for the sea. Before he was thigh deep, he dove forward and disappeared below the shimmering water. Then he was up, slicing through the waves, his powerful arms plunging forward, driving him out, deeper and deeper.
I watched as he turned for the beach and finally strode from the water, dripping wet, his swim-shorts clinging to every curve of his frame.
Daniel Craig, eat your heart out.
He wiped his eyes, saw me, and smiled.
The wine had given me the courage I needed. Taking a very deep breath, I walked to him. Lifting my arms, I clung to his neck, pulling him close, the chill of his wet skin and solid strength of his body making me shiver. His eyes drew me closer, and there was nothing in the world that was going to stop me kissing him there and then.
I felt him take me in his arms and tasted salt on his lips. Cold droplets of seawater dripped from his forearms down my back.
My world was instantly perfect.

Then, somewhere behind us, was a Scottish voice. "Put her down, Romeo…Peri says we'll have cloud by midnight."

Rick Fuller's Story:

Once again, we all stood around my bed and packed the kit.
We wanted to leave the hotel looking like tourists, so everything we
needed for the job had to be taken out of the rear of the hotel.
Konstantinos and Peri would see to that.
Until we hit the first target we were desperately short of firepower.
However, when Lauren and JJ had travelled to Acharavi to source
our comms, purely by chance they'd stumbled across Corfu's
version of a US survivalist store.
It had proved to be a veritable Aladdin's cave, and their discoveries
had cheered me up no end, especially after the shock of the Makris
brothers' antique German pistol presentation.

Admittedly, they'd paid an extraordinary amount for a pair of cheap
Chinese night vision goggles, but they'd practically stole everything
else. Combats, ammunition vests, half decent boots and socks,
balaclavas, meds, even some dried field rations. The guy didn't have
body armour, but he did have eight enamel back and breast plates
that had been removed from old NATO sets. So, with a bit of handy
needlework that problem was solved too.
JJ…yes JJ, had sewn pockets into the front and back of the ammo
vests. This meant you had to pull them over your head, but they were
almost as good as full armour and, more importantly, the enamel
stopped a Kalashnikov round.
Apparently, JJ's skill with the needle had come from many hours of
watching his wife work. However, his sewing didn't hold a candle to
his best find. The pièce de résistance had come when the Turk had
been rooting around the store.
Under a pile of sleeping bags he found a 1930's Swiss Karabiner
straight pull, bolt action carbine.
Admittedly the rifle was almost as old as the Makris brothers'
pistols, but was in fine condition. Sometimes old Swiss carbines had
rotten stocks, due to the troops stacking them in groups of three in
the snow when on patrol, but this one was mint. The Karabiner had
been the rifle of choice for the Swiss Army until the late Fifties and
used a 7.5 x 55mm Swiss-made cartridge, very similar in power to

our NATO 7.62 x 51mm. When issued to each soldier, the carbine came complete with a six-round box magazine.

So did this one, and miraculously it was fully loaded.

Adding to our good fortune, attached to the weapon was a Kern 1.8 x 9 scope, good for 1000 yards. Having seen JJ take half the head off Seamus O'Donnell from a similar distance through a window the size of a biscuit tin, I considered this a fucking godsend.

The guy who ran the shop was a Finn by birth who had followed his hippy friends to the north of Corfu, and never left. Lauren said he was built like a brick wall.

As they packed all the gear into two Bergans, the guy counted his wad of cash and asked, "What are you going to do with all this stuff, man?"

Lauren smiled at him. "We're going to Albania to kill some gangsters."

"Cool," he said.

Des Cogan's Story:

We hooked up the boat and trailer to the Q7 and pulled out of San Stefano harbour. All our ID's, passports, driving licences, medical cards, the lot, had been left behind in the hotel. If things were to go tits up, the longer it took the Albanians to identify us the better.
As Rick drove, the crew went quiet. The easy banter that had been ringing around the hotel room as we packed had vanished faster than a Scotsman out of a taxi, and we travelled in silence, each alone with our thoughts.
It took just over forty minutes to get to a small jetty, north of Kassiopi. This was our jump-off point; from there Albania was just over one nautical mile away.
As we stood on the shore, we could make out Sarande, the lights of its hotels and tavernas twinkling in the distance, warm and welcoming. Our destination was a few clicks further north. There would be little in the way of a warm welcome there. You didn't need to travel far from the resorts to discover real poverty and real danger in Albania.

By 2300hrs, the boat was loaded and in the water. Despite the partial cloud cover, we draped it with old grey horse blankets to prevent light reflection, changed into our fighting kit and shoved off.

Our first target, was the home of arms dealer, Arjan Bajrami. Konstantinos's intel suggested he lived with his cousin in a small one-storey dwelling in the town of Bregas, just over 10k north of Sarande. The Greek described him as a 'man who fucks goats'. Thankfully, Egghead's intelligence material was more helpful. He had given us an exact GPS location of the gaff and some photographs of the building. We couldn't be exactly sure, but it looked as if the windows on the house were barred. This, of course, wasn't surprising. If you were a gun runner, you had things worth stealing.
In addition to the main house there appeared to be two outbuildings in the garden, one the size of a garage, the other about as big as a shitter.

One thing was for certain, Bajrami's gaff was far too close to other dwellings for us to go steaming in with the sawn-offs.

There was no way we could risk being detected, after all our second port of call, Tropojë province, was three hours away by car, and that's a long way to be chased by the cops, or worse still, the Albanian Mafia.

I'd already cleaned and checked all the weapons we had. Rick had selected the Luger 08, whilst Lauren had chosen the Walther P38. Rick had manufactured noise suppressors for each pistol by cutting the tops off two plastic bottles. When the time came, you pushed the necks over the barrels of the pistols and secured them in place with tape. The idea being, you got in close enough to press the open end of your Diet Coke bottle against your target, and pulled the trigger. The bottle was supposed to muffle the ambient noise.

It made you look a proper twat, like you were carrying a kid's plastic ray gun, but I'd tried it before in Gib and it worked a treat.

Unsurprisingly, JJ had found himself a knife to play with. A WWII double-edged knuckle-handled trench knife, to be precise. It was a beast of a thing, about the size of a British Army issue bayonet that was held by a handle-cum-knuckle-duster type arrangement. He'd spent most of the last couple of days sharpening the fucking thing. Just looking at it made me wince.

As Rick was determined to keep the Swiss carbine in reserve for our assault on Goldsmith's place, I was left with a shotgun…which I wasn't allowed to use.

Happy days.

Once the boat was out of the shallows I dropped the motor into the Ionian and tried to start it. The ancient Yamaha coughed and spluttered before rattling along like an old steam train. Within ten minutes, all ambient light had gone.

I was so dark, you couldn't see your hand in front of your face. JJ pulled on the night vision binos he and Lauren had sourced in Acharavi and directed us toward our landing point by tapping the port or starboard side of the boat indicating that I should edge left or right.

Forty silent minutes later, I killed the motor and let the little craft coast to a tiny shingle bay.

We were in Albania unscathed and undetected.

Taking great care, we dragged the old tourist rental boat from the water, and took even greater care with the ancient Jap engine. After all, it wouldn't be good to damage the prop and find we had to swim back eh?

This time we covered the craft completely with the blankets and added a few bits of driftwood to complete the picture. Our feeble attempt at camouflage wouldn't pass any proper scrutiny, but anyone offering a casual glance from the top of the ridge above, or a passing patrol boat in the channel, probably wouldn't notice her.

We each pulled on our makeshift body armour and checked each other over for loose kit. It was down to JJ and me to carry the Bergans as Rick and Lauren were still trying to gain full fitness. Finally we donned our balaclavas, which were thankfully lightweight cotton and not the Scottish woolly variety, and commenced the ascent of the rocky outcrop that led to the road.

Once on level ground, we began our tab to Bregas. Rick had meticulously planned the route, ensuring it took us away from populated areas and main roads. This meant fifteen kilometres over rough terrain to achieve ten by road. Rough was one thing, but our Rick hadn't counted on the locals' obvious love of a good drainage ditch.

Now I wasn't too clued up on the Albanian year-round weather, but, believe me, one thing was for certain, if it rained, the bastards were prepared. After 5k, I began to feel like I was on some kindae fuckin' rollercoaster.

Add to the fact, that it had been a while since I'd done any real tabbing and, I'll tell you straight, I was blowing out of my arse after 10k no bother.

Blowing or not, as the home of Arjan Bajrami came into sight the time was 0152hrs, and we were eight minutes ahead of schedule.

Rick Fuller's Story:

Bajrami's house was a single-storey block and render job, very similar to many Greek houses we had seen on Corfu. However, this one had bars on the windows, as opposed to nicely painted shutters. Thankfully, the metal grill to secure the front door was ajar. Maybe the boy had visitors?

Either way, the whole look of the gaff was more reminiscent of the Anson Estate in Manchester, rather than Arillas' shabby-chic. To add to the British industrial revolutionary feel, it had an outside toilet.

The property was set on a large plot, of maybe 1000 square meters. The white face (front), comprised of a wooden entrance door with small windows either side, black face (rear) had a patio-style slider, whereas red sported one small window, too small for a man to exit from, and green, no access at all.

The outdoor loo was adjacent to green face so could be covered from black.

What we had identified as a garage from the aerial shots, was no more than a roof on stilts that shaded a very shiny Mitsubishi L200 Animal pickup, from the heat of the sun.

Bajrami the unfortunate didn't buy that from the profits off his two goats and six chickens.

JJ, Des and I used his near-new truck as cover for a brief LUP (lying up point) as it gave us a safe place to give one final brief, and had a decent view of the property. I have to admit, we didn't have much of a plan, but sometimes a wing and a prayer was as good as anything else you might have in your pocket.

The secret to this little escapade was going to be aggression, and we had that in spades.

Lauren would cover black face, and the outside shitter, in case we lost a player. Her sole task was to slot anyone who managed to make it out of the patio doors.

To keep our presence a secret, she would have to get in close and use the plastic bottle suppressor, but after O'Donnell and Belfast, I had every faith in her.

Our intel was that we had two males in the house, Arjan and his unnamed cousin. As far as we knew they would be armed and most definitely dangerous.

So, just how would you coax an Albanian out of his house at two in the morning?

Send a Turk to knock on the fucking door of course.

Lauren North's Story:

I left the boys talking tactics at the L200 and made my way to the rear of the house. I needed some cover to sort myself out, and surprise, surprise, not ten feet from the back door was a drainage ditch. My legs were so pleased to see another one, they burst into a cramp spasm the second I slid down the bank and hit the bottom. Much to my disbelief, this one had water in the bottom that smelled so vile I almost threw my breakfast.

Still, beggars couldn't be choosers, and it did give me a clear view of the rear patio door and the outside loo from a position of relative safety.

I did my best to ignore the stench, and stretched my aching muscles. Rooting in my combats, I found a ration pack that would replace the salts I needed. Ripping open the packet, I squeezed the contents into my mouth. It didn't taste too good, but was nowhere near as revolting as the shin deep, slimy water I found myself in. There was no doubting the outdoor toilet that served Bajrami's house had a connection to my ditch somewhere along the line.

Not content with ensuring I was wading in ten inches of shit, the Lord in heaven had sent my favourite creatures to join me in my venture.

Rats.

Dozens scuttled around my legs in the darkness, slashing about in the fetid water.

I'd pushed the empty ration sachet back into my combats; after all, it wouldn't have been prudent to leave litter in Mr Bajrami's garden, or indeed any evidence of our presence. Trouble was, the odour from the packet, must have smelled like a full-on Sunday dinner to Mr Ratty and his pals. Within seconds, one fat brown lump of vermin decided he was going to retrieve it, ripping at my trousers with his razor-sharp teeth.

I desperately wanted to check over my comms and weapon before taking up my position, but the thought of being bitten by a rat that lived in that stinking cesspit made up my mind for me, and I clambered out, quick sharp.

Seconds later, I stood with my back to Bajrami's rear wall shaking with revulsion. I pulled out the Walther, and gave it the once-over. The magazine would usually hold eight 9mm rounds and one in the chamber, but we were terribly short of ammunition. I had just five ancient shots to my name.

The Walther indicated a chambered round with the presence of a small pin that jutted out, just above the trigger, but with little light I needed to make sure, so I slid back the action and physically checked that the WWII bullet was actually there. Belt and braces and all that.

Then, pulling my home-made silencer kit from my pocket, I pushed the plastic device over the barrel and used a small roll of insulating tape to secure it.

After firing up my comms I connected my earpiece, and was delighted to hear the relevant clicks to confirm we were all in position and ready to go.

I felt much better.

Rick Fuller's Story:

I'd been first out from behind the L200, keeping low and using the garden's many bushes for cover. I reached the furthest away of the two small windows that sat either side of the front door, and knelt below it. Pulling the P08 from my combats, I checked it and fitted the plastic silencer. Seconds later Des was in the kneel, under his window. He held one of the single-barrel sawn-offs the Greeks had given us, toward the door, but I knew he was more likely to use it as a club than pull the trigger. If that baby went bang, the neighbours would be on our backs in seconds, and the shit would really hit the fan.

I shouldn't have been surprised, but as JJ appeared from behind the Mitsubishi I saw that he had removed his body-armour and balaclava. The Turk casually wandered out of cover wearing his black T-shirt, combats and a big grin. He stood calmly at the door, and I shook my head in disbelief when he ran his fingers through his hair as if he was about to meet his date for the evening. At least when the bloke looked through the spyhole, JJ would look the part. However, the big difference was this late-night visitor was an angry Turk with a big fucking knife strapped to his thigh and he wasn't there to get a kiss goodnight.

Some kind of Russian or Balkan gangster rap tune rumbled from inside the house and there was the faintest smell of cannabis in the air.

Nothing changes wherever you are, eh?

JJ looked at me and gave the faintest nod, we all gave a single click on our comms and waited for Lauren to do the same, confirming she was in position.

The Turk wasted no time and hammered on the door with his fist. We waited…nothing…JJ tried again, this time he shouted, "*zgjoheni ju derra yndyrë.*"

He later told me this roughly translated as, 'come out, you fat pigs.' I'm not sure about that, but it definitely did the trick.

There was the scraping of chairs, raised angry voices and the door was almost ripped off its hinges by an angry-looking bloke with a very shiny Tasco 7ET9 sub-machine gun in his hand.

It was similar in size to the Israeli-made Uzi, and I'd only ever seen a picture of the Ukrainian-built weapon. Allegedly it was notoriously unreliable. However, I had no desire to find out if this one was in full working order.

JJ was in like a flash. I'd never seen such lightning speed and technical brilliance hand to hand. Elbows out, he twisted his torso, as you and I would do to stretch before exercise. But as his body pivoted, he allowed his left arm to loosen, drop backward toward his thigh, and locate the scabbard that held his knife.

His right arm, however, had stayed in the horizontal. As he rotated his body back to centre he grabbed the underside of the boy's Tasco. The speed and energy of this movement pushed the machinegun upward and toward the face of his opponent preventing him firing. In perfect concert, his left hand flashed forward, and with the grace of a fencer's riposte, JJ plunged the razor-sharp blade into the boy's throat.

The Albanian made a funny gurgling noise as his legs gave way. The Turk let his blade slip from the boy, stripped the Tasco from his grasp and threw it to a grateful Des.

The second JJ stepped back I was through the door, with the Scot at my shoulder.

Just like old times.

Lauren North's Story:

I heard the entry, the unmistakable sound of conflict, and a body fall. Raising the Walther, I set myself and waited for the patio door to slide open and for my target emerge. The kill would be as simple as a single step forward, safety off, and pull the trigger.
A single muffled gunshot reverberated from inside the house. I figured that it had come from Rick's Luger, and our second guy would be accounted for. Ten seconds later, my comms burst to life and I heard Des give the all clear. Someone with taste turned off Bajrami's music, and the night was instantly silent.
Feeling my body relax, I started to tear at the tape from the muzzle of my Walther, so I could remove the bottle top silencer and slip the weapon back in my belt.
I was impressed. Rick's idea had worked. I mean, you could hear his shot from the garden, but it wasn't loud enough to wake the neighbours or anything.

It was, however, loud enough to be heard by the guy who'd been sitting in the dark on the outdoor bog all the time.
It was a fucking schoolboy error. I'd had the time to clear the outdoor loo. So why didn't I? It was an obvious thing to do…so bloody obvious, I'd missed it.
The guy had sprinted toward me in the darkness, and by the time I knew he was there, it was way too late.
He smashed my body against the wall, knocking the wind from me. Gripping tight onto my useless, now un-silenced Walther, I attempted to twist away. I did my best to use my elbows and knees, hoping to catch his chin or groin, but he was too strong, too quick. He cuffed me up the side of my head with a massive hand, rocking my senses and sending bright sparkles into my sightline. In the same movement, he pulled off my balaclava, and for the briefest moment, he inspected me.
The guy was a brute, well over six feet, huge shoulders and arms. With a vice-like grip, he held me against the wall by my throat, cutting off the blood to my brain. He fumbled around with his other, trying to grab my pistol as I did my best to keep it from his grasp. I knew that within seconds I would be unconscious and this guy would not be concerned about waking the locals. On the contrary, he

would gleefully empty the Walther into me, as if he'd come across a rabid dog in his yard.

Once again, I tried to fight him, but he just batted my efforts away like a grown man would a child.

He finally gripped the barrel of my pistol and gave me a sickening smile as he now had total control.

To my surprise, he momentarily slackened his hold on my neck, deliberately keeping me conscious. He leaned in close, and his lips touched my ear as he whispered to me in harsh rasping Albanian. I could smell his sour breath.

Sweat poured down his face, he sounded measured; yet there was a hint of panic in there. His eyes bulged as he waited for an answer, I had none of course, I didn't understand.

He squeezed my neck again and said in English, "How many are you?"

I considered his red round face; despite his size, fear filled his eyes, fear of the unknown and the identity of his attackers. My guts churned, but I was never going to show my own anxiety. I'd seen and been through too much for that.

I didn't know any Albanian, but I knew that he would understand one Greek word.

I eyeballed him and managed a grin.

"Enough to kill you, malaka," I said.

The guy flew into a rage, drew back a huge fist, and went to punch me full in the face. This was, as they say in the north, shit or bust time.

I had just enough movement, just enough strength and the last of my wits to tear my head to the left. His blow glanced my cheek, simultaneously sending spikes of pain upward toward my eye and down into my teeth, rattling my already dulled senses.

However, big boy had punched more concrete wall than Yorkshire lass. The pain in his hand must have been horrendous. So much so, he released his grip on my throat.

You need space to fight anyone. Being pinned against a wall by man-mountain was not conducive to a fair contest.

I took my chance.

Slipping to my right, I had some clean air in which to move, and miraculously still held the Walther. With his good hand, the brute swung another haymaker in my direction, but this time I was easily able to avoid it and he was instantly off balance.

I knew I wouldn't have enough weight or power in my upper body to cause any real damage to such a heavy guy.

I would have to use my most powerful muscle group.

Lifting my right knee to my chest, I powered my foot downward toward the Albanian's knee joint.

This was a one-time opportunity. The move needed accuracy, speed and power to work. Miss my target, and I would simply fall into the arms of my opponent in a heap.

I drove down my boot with everything I had, following in with my upper body so that all my weight and kinetic power would be concentrated on my target, the inside of the knee.

I connected.

Because your opponent's standing foot is planted, the sheer power of this blow opens the joint, tearing the anterior, medial and lateral ligaments away from the femur and fibular. I'd seen footballers with minor tears of one ligament, but nothing to compare with the devastating damage this move inflicts.

The guy collapsed in a heap.

I knew I only had the time it would take him to draw breath before he would start screaming in agony.

Stepping in, I kicked him in the temple with everything I had.

He lay on his back blowing hard, eyes open but barely conscious.

I walked over to the L200 and found a grubby roll-up sleeping bag tossed in the back, ideal for my needs, then returned to the boy.

He was moaning quietly, beginning to come around. Kneeling next to him, I pushed the barrel of the Walther into his mouth, covered his face with the sleeper, and pulled the trigger.

A dog barked somewhere in the distance then, for a second time that night, all was quiet.

Des Cogan's Story:

The entry had gone as smooth as a baby's bottom.
JJ had dropped the boy at the door with a move fuckin' Bruce Lee
would have been proud of. Rick had taken the point and I dropped in
behind. A nice short hallway with no doors either side, opened up
into one large room.
Standing next to a large wooden table adorned with more drugs than
you could shake a stick at, was a very stoned player, waving a Desert
Eagle around in no particular direction.
I got his attention, just showing him the Tasco, and Rick put one in
his temple with the 08.
Then I'd walked two bedrooms, the kitchen and bathroom, opened
my mic and gave the all clear.
Job done.
Rick and JJ went looking for the weapon stash, and sure enough, the
Greeks had been on the money. Minutes later, Rick emerged from a
bedroom dragging a wooden crate.
"Bingo," he said.
Seconds later, however, a muffled gunshot came from the rear of the
gaff.
"Anyone seen Lauren?" I asked.
In a move any game show host would have been proud of, the rear
patio swished open and in she flounced, sporting a shiner and
smelling like she'd bathed in a swamp.
"Where have you been?" I asked.
She strode past, ignoring me. "Is there a shower in this shithole?"
Rick stood in the doorway open-mouthed.
"Off to the left," he said.
Lauren dropped the Walther, minus Coke bottle, on the table and
headed for the door. "I suggest one of you lot make yourselves
useful whilst I clean up. Albania's answer to Giant Haystacks is
outside with a hole in his fuckin' head...Think you could manage to
move him before the neighbours start breakfast?"
"You okay, Lauren?" enquired Rick.
"Fuck you," she spat, and slammed the bathroom door.

JJ emerged from the second bedroom with more kit wrapped in a blanket.

"Someone's tired," he said.

Rick Fuller's Story:

Leaving Lauren to clean herself up, we all walked out back. Just as she'd said, we found a guy built like a brick shithouse lying on his back, dead as the proverbial. His right leg was sticking out at an unnatural angle. Ironically, he'd been shot in the mouth, the round exiting the top of his head and burying itself in the ground.
Des took the guy's feet, JJ his shoulders.
"Fuck me," whispered the Scot, blowing out his cheeks at the effort. "He's a big bastard...I'll tell you something, pal, if you and that lassie do get it together, I'm not too sure who I'd back in a fight. His fuckin' leg is half hanging off."
They dropped the guy out of sight in a drainage ditch that ran the length of the property. There was a splash as he hit the bottom, followed by the sound of rats scurrying and the shocking stench of untreated sewerage.
I'd seen what rats can do to a dead body. If they didn't find the boy in a day or two, they wouldn't find much at all.

Once back inside we began to take inventory of what we had in the way of weaponry. As expected, the kit was mostly Eastern Bloc. Inside the crate I'd pulled from one bedroom were four brand spanking new Bizon PP19 submachine guns, a weapon developed in the early 1990's by Victor Kalashnikov, the son of Mikhail Kalashnikov, creator of the infamous AK-47.
PP19's were first used by the Russian FSB, a modern off-shoot of the old KGB. However, the FSB were more concerned with the fight against organised crime, drug smuggling and border security, than poisoning people with dodgy umbrellas.
Despite being replaced in 2004 by the Vityaz-SN, the PP19 was also used extensively in combat operations against separatists in the troublesome regions of Chechnya and Dagestan. Thousands had since been illegally sold to the rebels via other friendly countries, and the weapon proved very popular with Eastern European gangsters; probably the reason our unfortunate Albanian friends purchased them.
I was well pleased as this was a cracking little weapon, and boasted a 64 round helical feed magazine that sat beneath the barrel.

To go with the Bizons were a hundred boxes of 9 x 18mm Makarov rounds, giving us twenty- five mags' worth of firepower.

We could do some serious damage with these babies.

The pistols were decent too.

In the same crate were eight Zastava CZ 99's. These compact SLP's had been made for the Yugoslavian police back in the day, and were a similar weapon to the SIG P226 and the Walther P88 Compact. With a 15-round magazine, they were a handy little gun. Again, dozens of boxes of ammunition came with them.

When I saw what JJ had carried out of the back bedroom, I could have kissed him. He unwrapped the blanket to reveal two RMG 27 disposable rocket launchers.

I knew from our intel, and the satellite shots the Firm had given us, that Goldsmith's gaff was well fortified. We would have to go in hard, and once again use the early hour and tons of aggression to get inside and slot the fuckers.

The RMG 27's would be a godsend.

The little launcher carries a tandem warhead. The first penetrates armour or other obstacles, in our case concrete walls or fortified doors, then the main warhead creates a fine explosive cloud that spreads into the interior through the hole, pierced by the first charge. When the cloud ignites, everything inside is either blown to bits, or incinerated. Clever eh?

Des and JJ bundled the two dead boys into one bedroom and closed the shutters. I started loading mags at the table, as Lauren appeared. Her left eye was closing rapidly and she still looked pissed off.

She sat down next to me, picked up an empty magazine and gave me a hand.

I caught her gaze.

"You did well out there, you know. He looked a proper handful." She tapped a full mag on the table top.

"I forgot to clear the loo. He was in the fuckin' bog all the time."

I shrugged, "We've all done it, Lauren…at least you're okay…I'd get some ice from the kitchen on that eye though."

She stood, shook her head, leaned over, and kissed me on the forehead.

"I'll see if I can get a brew on before we go."

Des Cogan's Story:

Lauren had done better than just a brew, and found bread, ham, cheese and gherkins in the kitchen. We stuffed our faces as we loaded the truck, grateful for the fuel we would need for the next battle.

I eventually found the keys for the L200 in the pockets of the big goon in the ditch. A quick note to self…search the fuckers before chucking them into two feet of rat-infested shite.

I washed off my boots and combats in the shower but still stank like a sewer.

Even though the Mitsubishi was a crew-cab and could seat us all, we decided that Rick and Lauren should sit up front whilst JJ and I lay in loading area, covered by a tarpaulin.

Lauren fashioned a makeshift headscarf to complete the look of a local man and wife on the move.

Police patrols were a rarity the further north you travelled, but they were replaced by equally troublesome robbers and bandits.

That said, we would all feel a little easier dealing with the latter.

We'd fallen on our feet with the pick-up as it was full to the brim with diesel and had another hundred litres in jerry cans in the loading area. Obviously Bajrami and his boys ventured north quite a bit…understandable in their line of work.

Tropojë was three hours away, Goldsmith's stronghold being just ten kilometres from the Kosovan border.

We'd already decided that if things went pear-shaped and we got separated, the trip north through Kosovo and the former Yugoslavia would be a decent alternative.

By the time we hit the road, it was 0315hrs. First light would come in just four hours. There was no margin for error, no time for a wheel change, no time for a breakdown.

As I tucked myself under the tarp and the L200 rolled out toward the E853 I did my best to put all negative thoughts out of my head.

Within ten minutes, JJ was snoring.

I must have nodded off myself, until the road surface had changed from decent tarmac motorway to rough gravel road. As we bounced along at a fair rate, I pulled myself out of cover and drank in the fresh early morning air. JJ decided to join me and we both went through the dedicated smoker's routine of attempting a nicotine hit, whilst being bounced around in the back of a pick-up in the wind. Rick must have noticed the flickering lighters as we took several attempts to get our makings lit. He slowed the truck slightly, wound down his window and shouted.

"Don't be long with those…. ETA twenty minutes."

I checked my watch, it read 0550hrs. Again, we were ahead of schedule. "Two minutes, pal," I shouted back.

Rick was as good as his word and fifteen minutes later, just two kilometres from our target, he killed the lights on the L200 and slowed to a crawl.

In typical Albanian fashion, deep ditches ran either side us. This was not the time to test the Mitsubishi's off-road capabilities or get covered in shite again so, with virtually no ambient light, Rick was forced to pull on our solitary pair of night vision goggles to finish the journey.

Ten minutes later, he swung our transport into a cutting in the treeline and killed the engine. We stepped out and stretched ourselves, like a family on a motorway services after a long run. Then, standing in a circle in near total darkness, we pulled on our balaclavas and makeshift armour. The vests JJ had fashioned had enough pockets for extra ammunition, and we all stuffed 16-round boxes of 9 x 18mm Makarov into them, to feed the hungry Bizon PP19's. The weapon itself had come complete with a sling which enabled the little gun to be carried in several ways. I preferred mine to be strapped to my back whilst tabbing. It was a split-second of a job to release it and have the weapon operational. But, if I found myself in the shit, I had two CZ99's in my belt as back-up.

JJ carried his the same, but he had the additional baggage of the Karabiner carbine and that fuckin' huge knife of his.

Lauren and Rick had the extra weight of the RMG27's. I knew she'd never fired an RPG, but the Russian model was a simple, pull a pin, lift the sight and fire job.

Piece of piss.

When we were all happy, we did our usual buddy-up and checked each other's kit for loose flaps, buttons and the like. We would leave a lot of empty cartridges on this job. We didn't intend to leave any other clues.

Rick took the point, and we were off.

Rick Fuller's Story:

Once kitted up, I led from the front using the night vision goggles. The area of Tropojë that Goldsmith and his sidekick Red George had chosen to ply their trade was a wild and unruly place. The ground leading to our target was uneven and covered in vegetation. Roots stubbed your toes and creepers grabbed at your ankles as we snaked through the thick undergrowth. The last thing I wanted was a team member with a twisted or broken ankle to deal with before we even got on plot, so it was slow going.

The intel provided by the Firm described our target premises as a detached two-storey job with four or five bedrooms. The ground floor boasted three reception rooms, together with a large kitchen and laundry room to the rear. To MI6's knowledge, the house itself wasn't fortified in any way other than steel reinforced doors to the front and rear. Adjacent to the main building was a substantial stable block that had been converted into a vehicle workshop. Aerial photographs showed lots of activity around this building, and we identified at least a dozen guys working there. Hopefully, we would be in and out before the workforce arrived for the day.
The same shots also pointed to a working spray-shop toward the front of the gaff; no doubt the paint booth was there to ensure the colour of the stolen car Red George had provided was the preferred hue of the bent government employee who had ordered it.
It seemed that Stefan and Gjergj were forming a thriving business venture in the middle of nowhere.
The compound itself appeared to be simple rough ground with paved areas leading to and from the main buildings. On every aerial shot, dozens of vehicles were dotted about the place. One area to the side of the main dwelling was in the process of being landscaped and laid to lawn, and a couple of sets of patio furniture were clearly visible. We wouldn't be invited for cocktails, I was sure of that.
Outer security consisted of a rusting chain-link fence, which in turn, had a four meter 'clean' area surrounding it. This clear space had all its trees and foliage removed and ensured anyone attempting to attack the premises from the forest or bush would be easily seen before reaching the barrier. Infrared security lights were erected on

twelve-foot posts every ten meters or so, to deter night crawlers like us. The only vehicular access to the property was via a single-track road and through the main gate.

One way in, one way out.

With no suggestion of any alarm systems, and with no further intelligence to indicate any other fortifications, on paper it looked a straight forward job.

However, the intelligence also proposed that it wasn't only the remote nature of the plot that had triggered the spooks' reluctance to attempt a second assassination attempt, it was the suggestion Goldsmith and Dushku had amassed a fighting team from all corners of the former Communist Bloc: Kosovans, Macedonians, Bosnians, Albanians, and Chechnyans, all armed and willing to die for the most powerful and far reaching Mafia in the world. How many would be there overnight, was unknown.

Like I said, easy on paper.

It took us thirty minutes to negotiate the thick undergrowth, and by the time Goldsmith's house came into view, the sky was getting lighter by the minute.

It was time to wake up the sleepy locals, before their alarms went off for another day of playing gangster.

We dropped in together at the edge of the treeline, and checked our comms were operational.

Staying in cover, JJ set off toward the north of the building. This would give him the best view of the compound to the front of the house, and the most height to employ his Swiss Karabiner rifle, with that Kern 1.8 x 9 scope. He only had half a dozen rounds to play with, but I was banking on the Turk's unnerving accuracy with a rifle. Six rounds equalled six kills in my book, even before he got in close.

Our plan had to be as simple as possible.

Me, Des and Lauren, would approach the fence to the south, cut our way in and split left and right. Des would fight alongside Lauren, I would be alone until JJ ran out of ammunition for the rifle, when he would join me in assaulting the front of the building.

In all, I anticipated we would be through the fence in fifteen seconds and would be in our forward firing positions ten seconds later.

On my mark, we would simultaneously fire the two Russian RMG's into the main house. One through the front door, one through the rear.

By the time Goldsmith and his cronies were pulling their pants up, all hell would have broken loose.

The RMG27 was a horrible weapon, and within seconds most of the ground floor would be either decimated or ablaze. The occupants would be like rats in a sinking ship and have no choice but to come running into the compound to escape the blaze. Their instinct would be to run toward the only exit, or parked vehicles.

Unfortunately for them, they would be met with three PP19's on full auto and the Turk with his Karabiner.

Once we'd dealt with the boys in the compound, we would have the more dangerous task of clearing the rest of the building room by room. According to the spooks our ultimate targets, Stephan Goldsmith and Gjergj Dushku, both slept in the main house. An operation to fight in enclosed spaces, with a pair like them waiting for you, was as treacherous as it got.

That said, a similar ploy had worked for us in Ireland; we'd recovered our target there and disposed of the O'Donnell crew, so why not a second time?

I had one issue.

The Firm had assured me that there were no 'soft' targets on the premises. No women or children. With our plan, there would be nobody left to tell the story. I hoped they were right.

Lauren North's Story:

My heart raced and my mouth, the polar-opposite to my wet palms, craved liquid.
The wait for JJ to indicate he was in position seemed to take forever. As the seconds ticked by, my fear took hold of me, as it always did. I knew of course that the moment we moved, I would be fine.
The horror of what might be is always worse than the event itself.
Finally, I heard the double click in my ear to say the Turk was on plot.
I took a deep breath and keeping as low as possible, shuffled in behind Des as we crossed 'no man's land', to the fence.
As we expected, the security lights instantly detected our movements, and we were in sudden, virtual daylight. Other than the change in visibility, there was no suggestion of an audible warning; no sirens, no raised voices. It seemed that the Firm had it right for a change.
Des chopped at the fence with his pliers, slicing an 'L' shape in the wire, before turning the section backward, like he was opening a tin of sardines.
I was first through, then Rick, who in turn held the section of fence to enable Des to make his own welcome appearance.
Once we were all inside the compound, Des sprinted off left to toward the rear of the building and I followed behind him.
Leaving Rick alone tore at my heart. No time for goodbye.
See you on the other side.

As Des and I neared the rear of the main house, I saw the first signs that our little plan was not going to be as straightforward as we thought.
Sitting off to the right of the back door was a large porta-cabin that hadn't been there when the satellite shots were taken.
The door was open, lights were on inside and I could hear a concerned voice that sounded like he was on a phone or radio.
Had Goldsmith added CCTV cameras to the security?
There was no time to worry about it.

We dropped down behind a large Mercedes 4 x 4. I got into the kneel, and set the RMG 27 into fire mode. Rick crackled in my ear, barely audible, but enough.

"On my mark…three…two…one."

Des Cogan's Story:

We were nicely tucked in behind the Merc and had the perfect view of our target. The moment Rick gave the order, I heard Lauren engage the fire button on the RMG 27. There was a whooshing sound, and the backdraft almost took my hair off.

I'd expected the first stage of the warhead to punch a hole in the heavy wood and steel door. Instead it destroyed it, sending razor-sharp splinters and flying masonry in all directions, forcing us to duck down behind the luxury car.

The Merc took the full brunt of the explosion. That said, the porta-cabin that had mysteriously appeared at the side of the rear entrance since the last satellite pass didn't come out unscathed either.

All its windows were gone and part of the gable was missing. Bits of roofing felt fluttered down to earth.

When the second stage of the RMG ignited, it lit the rear compound up like a fuckin' Christmas tree. The explosion shook the ground. Flames billowed from the opening where the door had once been and instantly set fire to the easily combustible cabin.

Four guys came barrelling out of it, one screaming, his clothes and hair alight.

I opened up with the PP19 and put him out of his misery.

The three others were all armed with AK-47's, but their heads had gone. The explosion and subsequent fire had disorientated them and they shot wildly in different directions, missing badly.

I heard Lauren let go several short bursts and seconds later, all four boys were down.

I was about to turn my attention to the main house, when I heard shouting to my left.

We had a different, and very pressing, issue.

MI6 had cocked up again.

It seemed the dozen or so players we'd identified in the satellite shots didn't go home at the end of each shift after all. Goldsmith must have had some kind of living quarters built in rear of the garage and all his little pals had been on a nice fuckin' sleep over.

Of course these guys weren't just mechanics and panel beaters either; they'd been hand-picked from all corners of Eastern Europe, were well trained, well-armed and extremely determined fighters.

In seconds, we began to take small arms fire from the garage crew, 9 millimetre spat and rattled around the already damaged German marque and kicked up dust around us.

A massive guy carrying an AK was splitting the men into two groups. Without a shadow of a doubt it was Red George, who had most definitely not been sleeping in the main house.

Thanks again, Cartwright.

About half of George's crew were going to attack our position whilst the rest, including the big fella, were making to the front of the house and Rick, who was still alone.

I tapped Lauren on the shoulder and pointed in the direction of the threat.

She instantly dropped into prone and started to lay down covering fire, clipping a couple of guys and sending the rest scurrying for cover.

Matters got immediately worse, when I heard glass being raked out of the upstairs windows of the main house.

As I'd suspected, it wasn't good news and multiple shooters opened up from the upstairs. Big calibre rounds slammed into the Merc and we were well and truly pinned down. The bullets pierced the roof and the floor of the luxury car, before burying themselves in the ground beneath our feet.

For the briefest moment, I clocked one of the boys on the first floor. That unmistakable blond hair, that scar, the M16A4 rifle...it was none other than Stephan Goldsmith.

I popped up for as long as I dared and squeezed off a dozen rounds in the bastard's direction. All I succeeded in doing was to push him back deeper into the house and into cover. In a flash, he reappeared and peppered the Merc with 5.56 forcing me back into the dirt.

I tapped Lauren on the leg as she emptied her PP19 in the direction of the approaching garage team.

We were in the shit. It was only a matter of time before the boys in the upstairs got lucky with a ricochet, or a round just sliced through the Merc and took one of us out.

"We need to move, now," I shouted, and pointed toward a large stack of cut logs that would give us cover from Goldsmith's M16 and allow us to return his fire in cover.

I depressed my comms pretzel.

"JJ, we have shooters exiting the garage area adjacent to red face, and approaching our positions."

I heard JJ's rifle crack once, then seconds later, a second report split the sky. His dulcet voice was monotone in my ear.

"Two down," he said. "I kill some more, then go to Richard."

Lauren pulled herself into the kneel and reloaded. I fired short bursts, first in the direction of the approaching crew, then above my head toward the first floor of the house.

It was nothing more than a token gesture, buying precious seconds. Lauren snapped her mag in place, swung the PP19 around her back and pulled her two

Zastava CZ 99's from her belt.

"You go first," she barked. "Then cover me."

As I sprinted for my life to the log pile, I heard her cracking off shots with both pistols, in a desperate attempt to keep both sets of enemy down and quiet.

However, Goldsmith and his pals on the first floor were protected by thick stone walls, and the small windows kept them well concealed. They could almost fire at will.

As I did my best impression of Linford Christy with a rocket up his arse, the boys upstairs had clear shots and although I weaved as best I could, as I reached the logs I caught two rounds.

The first nicked my right calf, tearing my skin and slicing away a nice lump of muscle. I felt the searing pain of the white-hot round as it cauterised the wound in an instant.

The second caught me square in the back, and I went down.

Rick Fuller's Story:

The moment I'd discharged the RMG27 I knew something wasn't right. It fizzed and faltered on its way to target. It did manage to tear a hole in the front doors and did explode, but it was as if only half of the weapon had worked. There was smoke and some flame, but the front rooms of the house remained relatively unscathed.

Nobody had run out toward me in panic. In fact, the whole plan had seemed as damp a squib at the rocket I'd just fired.

Then all hell broke loose.

Two bodies appeared at the upstairs windows, smashed the glass and opened up on my position with AK-47's on full auto.

I'd been kneeling behind a brick wall that enclosed a well, probably forty meters from the main dwelling. It was as old as the house itself and around three feet thick. This was extremely helpful as the AK fires a 7.62×39mm cartridge with a muzzle velocity of 715 meters per second. The boat-tail bullet is powerful enough to penetrate interior walls or the metal body of any standard vehicle, but thankfully, not my wall.

Even so, the sheer onslaught of the rate of fire had me pinned to the ground as shards of brick and cement were torn from the masonry.

I managed to pop up and return fire with the PP19, firing in bursts of three and four. Even though I had a sixty-four-round mag, I didn't want to have to reload any time soon. I'd some success too, catching one guy in the left-hand window full in the face, dropping him instantly.

My comms had been crackling away, and were working about as well as the fucking rocket. I'd heard Des say something about the garage, but it wasn't until I'd caught the crack of small arms, and shouting off to my right that I was aware that we were fighting on two fronts.

Approaching my position were maybe half a dozen guys, all carrying various automatic weapons. These boys were no mugs, and were using the many stationary vehicles dotted about the compound for cover, so they could get around me and finish the job.

They hadn't, however, banked on the Turk.

The closest guy to me was perhaps fifty meters away. He was hunkered down, knees bent, carrying an M16 by its handle and shuffling forward a few meters at a time.

The report of JJ's rifle rattled around the compound like a jet breaking the sound barrier. The boy instantly dropped his M16, and fell to one side, his feet kicking as his brain stopped functioning; half his head was splattered against the passenger door of a silver Lexus.

Less than five seconds later the Turk found his second victim, with the same result. This time the guy was sprinting between two cars.

The Swiss-made 7.5 x 55mm cartridge that the Karabiner used would start to yaw (tumble) at about 700 meters. This gave the weapon its appalling effect on the human body. Surprisingly, you may survive being shot at close range by a high velocity round, but once the bullet begins its little dance in mid-air, and becomes unstable, it will tear you apart inside.

The round caught the boy in the centre of his back and exited through his throat, devastating his central nervous system. It was as if he'd been switched off. He fell and was instantly still.

This gave the others something to think about, and they gave up on trying to make ground on my position for a moment or two.

Then, for a couple of seconds, my comms burst into life and I heard Lauren, there was terror in her voice. "Man down!" she bawled. "We have a man down…Des…Des is down."

I was in shock, my brain as useful as the bloke's who'd just had his splashed all over the Jap car. I squeezed my eyes together, pinched the bridge of my nose and fumbled for my comms pretzel.

Before I could speak, someone very big and extremely strong clubbed me from behind.

I was out cold.

Lauren North's Story:

I saw Des fall, saw the first round clip his leg, saw the splash of blood, saw his body buck as the second bullet hit, then saw him go down. I was instantly consumed by a mixture of blind panic and withering grief. Every bone in my body screamed at me to go to him, to help him, comfort him. But I could not, dare not. I would be cut down just as he had.

Tears rolled down my cheeks soaking the inside of my balaclava. I ripped it from my head, what was the fucking point now?

I waited for Rick to reply to my mayday, but nothing came...nothing, just static. My mind tortured me. Was Rick shot too? Was he dead? I tried the radio again and again, and got more nothingness. All-encompassing fear held me in a vice. My hands shook uncontrollably as I gripped weapons I was too scared to use.

Self-doubt filled my very soul. What had I been thinking? I just couldn't do this without Rick and Des, I just couldn't. I hadn't the physical strength or the mental bottle to do it. They had it all. It had all been about them, all the time. How stupid was I? Without Rick and Des, I was nothing, just a nurse pretending to be something I fucking wasn't.

I sat with my back pressed against the Merc, my knees up to my chin, as salvo after salvo of gunfire rained down on me from the first floor of the house. As their bullets got closer and closer, I almost wished for one to find its target and put me out of my misery.

More small bursts came from the direction of the garage. More men, intent on killing me; all tucked into cover, firing at me. Did they not realise that I was just a frightened, useless nurse?

Their rounds were kicking up the dirt just inches from my feet. It would only be a matter of time before they realised there was no return of fire, and they would be upon me.

Even in that certain knowledge, I could not move. I dared not move.

From above my head the shooting suddenly stopped, and a voice shouted down to me, his accent a blend of American and Dutch, educated yet as callous as a jackal circling its prey. I didn't need to look up to see who the voice emanated from. I didn't need to see the blond hair fall across his face, or the bite mark on his cheek.

"Why are you sitting there, Lauren?" shouted Goldsmith. "Your boyfriend Fuller's waiting for me downstairs with Red George for company. I'm so going to enjoy playing with him. And that funny little Scottish chap, well, you can see for yourself, eh? It's just you now, Lauren. And you haven't fired a shot in a while. Have you run out of ammunition, Miss North?"

Goldsmith's voice became an animal-like snarl. "Or guts? Have you run out of guts, my English rose?"

Ashamed of my cowardice, I let my head fall.
Should I just sit here and wait to be killed, or worse still, captured? Oh no, not that. I wasn't going to be taken again. I couldn't go through that kind of abuse, that kind of torture.
I took deep breaths.
Better to be shot than taken.
Goldsmith taunted me again.
"What's the matter, girly? Cat got your tongue?"
At least two other men laughed somewhere inside the house.
I let the CZ's fall to the floor and grabbed my PP19. Slipping off the safety, I held it to my chest, like a mother would a child. I had never felt such terror, but I couldn't be taken again.
Closing my eyes, I imagined exactly where my primary target was. Even if I didn't make it, at least I would achieve what we came for, to kill that bastard. I could see his scowling face as he leaned from the window, full of smug, self-satisfied confidence. All I had to do was twist my body left, straighten my legs, punch the weapon upward and pull the trigger. For the briefest moment, Rick was in my ear. *Take them all…no messing…no talking…one movement.* Take them all? How could I? I needed confidence, I needed certainty. Forcing myself to believe JJ was still out there, I imagined him running toward the compound. He must be alive. I'd heard his rifle earlier. I'd counted his shots, he had four left. He must be there, would be there.
He would come for me.
I shuffled five feet to my right, tucked my legs under my backside and got ready to push myself into the open.

Rick Fuller's Story:

I managed to open my eyes.

Someone had removed my balaclava, comms and my body armour. I was aware that my feet were dragging in the dirt and that a bloke the size of Shrek was pulling me through the compound by my collar. As more of my brain came back on line, I realised that I was being hauled along the ground, one-handed, by none other than Red George.

I think Shrek was an understatement. I couldn't remember ever seeing such a big guy. I'd seen plenty of soldiers and bodyguards in my time, but never one the size of Gjergj Dushku.

More wires connected in my head.

I twisted my torso to get a better look at where I was going. This movement was instantly met by a slap up the side of my head from Georgie boy and a ringing right ear.

Then I realised, he was taking me to the main house to meet my mate Stephan.

The fucker was striding toward the gaff like he was pulling a shopping cart rather than a sixteen-stone man.

There was no way on this earth, that I was going inside that house with Popeye and Bluto for company. I needed to get to Lauren, and to see what condition Des was in.

I twisted again, expecting the same thug response, and I got it. George swung his massive ham of a hand in my direction, except this time I grabbed his wrist just before contact.

The boy's instinctive reaction at having one hand out of action, was to release his other, and that is exactly what he did.

He let go of my collar and I fell to the floor in a heap.

George inspected me as I rolled in the dust. I think he viewed my pathetic attempt at escape as no more than bad or childish behaviour. It was no big deal to him, a mere inconvenience. After all, he'd stripped me of my weapons, he still carried an AK-47 strapped to his back, he was built like Arnold Schwarzenegger's big brother, and I was lying at his feet with a lump on my head the size of the Isle of Dogs.

On the other hand, he shared a brain cell with his cousin in Kosovo, and more to the fucking point, he was wearing a pair of snide Timberland boots.

What a twat.

He watched me slowly pull myself up into the kneel. I swayed a little as I did so, something he thought funny.

He laughed, "You want to fight me, fool?"

My head was spinning, but I was not going to lose a tear-up with some fat-faced bastard who, despite driving an AMG Merc, shopped on the fucking market.

I eyeballed him.

Kneeling in the shit, I formed the opinion that if George had wanted to kill me he would have already done so. He wasn't going to use the AK anytime soon. Oh no, that would be too clean. I had the distinct impression that Goldsmith had a far more inventive plan for my demise.

Even so, the way people like Red George worked was simple. If his boss said 'don't kill him,' he wouldn't. But that didn't mean he couldn't inflict some pain to his charge in the process. He'd been a bully all his life, he wasn't going to change now.

George decided to teach me a lesson, drew back a leg, and went to kick me in the guts with his £9.99 specials.

Some guys like to try and smother the actual kick when they find themselves at a disadvantage on the ground. Me, I go for the standing leg.

It was like gripping a fucking tree.

From my kneeling position, I pushed myself forward with both feet and buried my left shoulder into his left knee. George's swinging leg only served to make him more unstable and went over like a redwood.

He bellowed like a giant as he fell, crashing into the dirt and slapping the back of his head on the ground in the process. He lay on his back, winded and groggy. I knew I wouldn't have long before he was back on song and able to snap me in half with his bare hands.

Crawling up his body like a demented mountaineer, I smashed my right fist into his nose, once, twice. Then, turning my body and bending my elbow to increase the power, my third punch took out his front teeth. He tried to bat me away with his massive forearms, but I had too much aggression for him. I changed my body position again, so I could twist my torso and use all my upper-body strength. I punched him hard in the jaw with my left…one, two, three, four punches, each one harder than the last. As I connected with his massive square jaw, the pain in my hand shot up my forearms to the elbow, but this was no time to worry about busted knuckles.

Dushku knew he was in trouble and went to grab me, to pull me in close so I couldn't punch, then use his brute strength to roll me over and gain the advantage.

I was ready for the bastard.

As he grabbed me, I didn't fight the movement. Instead, I used his own strength alongside my own, to propel my head forward and butt him in his already ruined nose.

I wanted to push his nasal bone into his skull; smash his nasal bridge, to the extent that the fluid that bathed his brain ran out of his nose.

I drew my head back again and used every last ounce I had to slam it back into the same spot. George's blood covered my face, I could feel the hot spatters each time I brought my head down.

At the fourth strike, George went limp.

A quick check on my surroundings saw me outside the body repair shop some twenty meters from the front door of the main house. It seemed that all the players had moved toward the rear, of the gaff, no doubt hoping to finish Lauren and Des off, secure in the knowledge that Red George would handle me with ease.

How fucking wrong they were, eh?

I wiped George's blood from my eyes and checked his pulse.

He was alive.

I pulled the AK-47 from underneath his body, knocked the action forward and applied the safety.

Ideally, I would've just put a 7.62 into his head, but I didn't fancy attracting the marauding hordes.

Still…where there's a will and all that.

A quick recce of the body-shop armed me with a crowbar.

It wasn't pretty.

Keeping my head down and using vehicles for cover, I made toward the rear of the main house.

As Goldsmith's guys had all approached from the garage area, I tabbed in the opposite direction, approaching Lauren's position from green face. All I could hope for was that JJ would get to the compound anytime soon, and attack the crew from their rear, giving us a pincer movement. But with no comms to guide him in, it was no more than wishful thinking.

As I reached the corner of the main building, I dropped into the kneel and risked a quick look-see onto the back off the gaff. Twenty feet in front of me a porta-cabin smouldered away, obscuring my view of most of the ground floor. What was left of a big Merc was parked about thirty feet adjacent to the back door. I could just see the toes of a pair of black boots tucked in behind it which just had to be Lauren's. And heartbreakingly, lying face down in the dirt, halfway between the car and a log-pile was the unmistakeable body of Des Cogan.

Des and I had gone back a long way and my gut churned with a devastating concoction of sadness and fury.

Someone once told me, 'never fight angry'.

It was way too late for that.

Lauren North's Story:

As I sat finding the courage to move, the rate of fire from the boys who were tucked in between me and the garage slowed, they simply took the odd pot shot in my direction. It appeared that since Goldsmith's tirade, they were confident that they could take their time with me. One shouted from behind a Sprinter van. 'I come get you now, English...I fuck you good. Your boyfriend dead...Red George kill him." His mates found the whole thing amusing and guffawed at his bravado.

I couldn't concern myself with the hired help, or their attempts at unnerving me further.

I knew I had two, maybe three targets hanging out of any of the four upstairs windows above me.

But who was in which?

My head told me, Goldsmith would be the least switched on.

A tormenter, more concerned with taunting me than finishing the job, he had been unable to keep his braggart's mouth shut and I was pretty sure he was at the window, closest to red face.

I told myself he may not even have his weapon ready and in the aim, whereas the other players would be waiting for my head to appear from the cover of the car.

As I had my back to the Merc, I decided I would be twisting my body left as I rose.

Attacking all the upstairs windows, one through four, would require a line of fire approximately sixteen meters in length. My PP19 had a full sixty-four rounds in it, and on fully automatic, the little Bizon would spit them out at around twelve per second.

If my plan worked, I could strafe all four windows in three seconds flat. Left to right.

This meant Goldsmith would get the good news last.

Beggars and choosers again.

Three seconds.

I took a deep breath and turned.

Rick Fuller's Story:

Before I could find a way to indicate my position, Lauren popped up from behind the Merc and let go with the PP19 toward the upstairs windows, strafing the house from left to right.
She wasn't messing about either and didn't take her finger off the trigger until she was happy.
I heard screaming as she found her targets.
Rolling forward out of cover I joined in the party, firing in twos and threes toward the windows above.
It was a pointless exercise, my rounds found only corpses for targets as two very dead men dangled from the openings, their blood dripping down the whitewashed walls of the house, their weapons useless on the ground beneath.
She turned toward the sound of my gunfire, saw me and tapped the top of her head, a signal indicating for me to join her. A split second later she vanished behind the Merc and turned her attention toward the garage area and our remaining enemy.
I sprinted over and hunkered down beside her.
"Jesus, am I glad to see you," she said. Then, looking over toward the Scott lying twenty feet away added. "Go get Des from there, Rick, I'll cover you."
I nodded, feeling the sour taste of grief in my mouth.
"Okay," I said. "I'll drag him behind the woodpile. Once I'm set, I'll cover you and you join me."
Lauren grabbed my arm. "Be careful," she shouted over another burst of gunfire coming from the garage. "...Please."

I held the AK one-handed and fired toward the shooters as I ran. As I approached Des, I dipped down, grabbed his vest collar and dragged him behind the pile of timber.
The Scot rolled over on his back and groaned in agony.
"You took your fucking time," he said.
I had been so convinced the fucker was dead, I nearly shit myself.
I pulled his balaclava from his face. "Jesus Christ, Des, I thought you'd been slotted."
The Scot lay immobile on his back, face racked with pain. He was desperately short of breath.

"I caught one in the leg…then one got me right in…in the back…hit the enamel plate in my vest, think my ribs are busted."

I rummaged in my combats, found a field morphine shot, and stabbed it into his leg. The results were instantaneous. Des blew out his cheeks.

"Fuckin hell…that's…that's better, pal…cheers."

Being hit by a 5.56 round even with full armour is shocking, but our makeshift kit was just a cotton vest with the breast and back-plates sewn in. There was no Kevlar to absorb the shock of the impact. No wonder his ribs had gone. It must have been like being hit with a sledgehammer. Still, it saved his life.

"Well, you have the Turk to thank for still being here to tell the tale, mate."

Des nodded. "Yeah, he's been in the shit himself. I think me and him are the only ones with working comms. He's been trying you and Lauren for the last ten minutes. His Karabiner went fucked on him. He's on his way to the compound."

As if JJ had heard his cue, I heard the very welcome sound of his PP19 rattling out some rounds to the rear of the garage.

Des pulled himself into a sitting position and checked over his own Bizon.

"I reckon I can shoot, but dinnae be askin' me to run anywhere, pal. I was out cold for a while there, and when I came around, I was in too much pain to move. I knew if I started crawling into cover, they'd put another couple of rounds in me and I'd be a goner for sure."

I almost slapped him on the back.

"You get tucked in here, pal," I said. "We've got these fuckers trapped now JJ's on plot. I just need you to keep an eye on the main house. Make sure nobody pops out of a window and spoils the party."

The Scot shook his head. "I didn't see it, but I heard it. I reckon Lauren took them all out. Goldsmith included."

For a split second, I was slightly disappointed.

"Give me your radio, pal, cover those windows just in case, and I'll be back for you shortly."

Lauren North's Story:

The four of us stood behind a big silver Mercedes Sprinter van parked in the centre of the compound. Apart from the birds, there was silence in the yard. The dead lay everywhere, blood soaked the pale ground beneath them, their twisted, grotesque corpses casting long shadows in the early morning sunrise.

JJ had killed four of Goldsmith's crew, before Rick and I even moved from cover. Two with his Bizon, two with his knife.

Between us we'd slotted the rest as they bottled it and tried to run away. You may think it unsporting to shoot a man in the back, but after they have just done their level best to kill you, it makes it a whole lot easier.

A massive guy who Rick identified as Red George lay on his back, close to the front door of the main house. Half his head was missing and a bloodied crowbar lay next to him.

As Mr Fuller's face neck and forearms were still splattered with claret, I presumed it was his handiwork.

Rick was talking us through the house entry as we reloaded our weapons.

Before we got paid for the job, Kostas Makris required photographic evidence that Stephan Goldsmith was dead. There was no doubt in my mind that Rick would have done the job for free, but the deal had been struck, and a quarter of a million pounds was to be split between the team once the picture had been delivered.

At that price, if he wanted a fucking album he could have one.

I knew I'd hit Goldsmith at least twice. I saw him fall, but we'd come too far not to make sure, and after all, he'd risen from the dead once before.

Des rested against the van trying to get his breath. I was so pleased to see him alive, I grinned like a Cheshire cat every time I caught his eye. If he hadn't been in such pain, I would have hugged him there and then.

After a second morphine jab, he was moving a little easier, but the drug made him feel sick and light-headed. It seemed silly to put him through the entry when it was more of a mopping up exercise. Reluctantly he agreed, kept one set of comms and acted as lookout.

Rick Fuller's Story:

I've lost count of how many buildings I've cleared.
For me, there's always been a niggle with the job, and it always gave me the hump when I had to do it.
You are victorious, if you can ever call killing a victory, and for all intents and purposes the fighting's over, the job done...except it isn't, is it?
What's left after all the bangs and flashes, all the smoke, the screams and the blood, are streets, yards, and houses. They were there before your battle, and they would probably be there after you had gone.
Yet lurking in those places was what may be left of your enemy.
I've also lost count of how many good blokes get killed during these 'simple' clearances. People switch off. It's natural in a way, and it was my job to ensure everyone stayed sharp and on point.

Clearing houses in a 'three', was not unusual. It was a simple case of methodical movement and cover. The team made its way through the house room by room, floor by floor, leapfrogging each other, each taking turns on point. It couldn't be done quickly and it was best not to make too much fucking noise. Clearing houses is hot sweaty, dangerous work.

The rear ground-floor rooms had been badly damaged by Lauren's RMG 27. It didn't appear that anyone had been inside the kitchen or laundry room of the main house when the rocket was fired.
Stephan's pet cat hadn't fared too well though.
We cleared the three receptions at the front with relative ease, but then, we had the staircase to deal with
Ask any soldier, any cop... 'what's the worst part of an RI (Rapid Intervention) or clearance?' And they'll tell you it's the fuckin' stairs.

This one was fourteen treads high with a solid wall to your left as you rose. The landing at the top split left and right, then back on itself to give access to the two front bedrooms. Two of the four rear windows that had been so troublesome for Des and Lauren were accessed by the part of the landing we could see.

In each of those windows lay an unidentified corpse. This meant that if Lauren was correct, Stephan Goldsmith's body lay in the rear bedroom to the right of the landing.

I indicated to clear the left rear first.

We climbed slowly and silently.

Our first target, the left room, had its door ajar. JJ took point, went in low, I stepped right, Lauren left. Check under the bed, in the wardrobe.

Clear.

In a line of three, we stepped past the two dead men hanging from the windows, me on point, covering the target door, Lauren and JJ covering the two closed front bedroom doors.

Once we got in close, I held up my hand and we had a good listen.

All quiet.

Indicating that I would take point, Lauren left, JJ right, I grabbed the door handle, pushed, and we were in.

Lauren North's Story:

The room was not a bedroom at all, but an office, and sitting behind a grand mahogany desk, was none other than Stephan Goldsmith. He had both his arms upturned on the polished top. In his right hand, he held a small grenade, in his left, the pin.

His usual pallor had taken on a grey hue and I saw that I had indeed hit him with my PP19, not twice, but three times. He did his best to breathe through his mouth. I'd hit him in the upper chest and jaw, and his lungs were filling with his blood by the minute. Unless he got urgent medical treatment, he was not long for the world.

If he let go of that grenade, neither were we.

"Well, well, Fuller," he croaked. "We finally meet again."

He coughed down his nose, but blood still escaped from the corners of his mouth as he spoke.

"I knew you would come, Richard. I knew the moment my death certificate was accessed by that silly little girl you were fucking in Manchester, that you'd come...eventually."

Rick clicked off the safety on his AK-47.

"Not a good ploy," coughed Goldsmith. "You know what I have in my hand."

Rick stepped to his right and raised the AK in line with Goldsmith's face.

"Oh yes, I know, a Soviet F1 grenade."

The bastard actually smiled, his blond hair falling over his right eye as he spoke.

"Yes, Richard. The Russians call it 'the little lemon', did you know?"

"No," spat Rick. "I didn't."

"Ah," said Goldsmith, wincing in pain. "But you do know its capabilities, don't you?"

Rick remained impassive; Goldsmith had the floor and all the cards. He coughed again, his breathing worsening by the moment.

"It will cause devastation for thirty square meters, Richard, shrapnel travel of up to two hundred. Easily powerful enough to kill everyone in this room. Of course, you understand that the standard fuse on this weapon is three-point-five to four seconds, do you not? More than enough time for the three of you to shoot me, dive for the door and plunge down the stairs to safety…no?"

"No," said Rick flatly.

"No," said Goldsmith, with all the satisfaction he could muster. "Because the fuse attached to my little lemon is different, isn't it?"

Rick curled his lip.

"Yes, it's a Russian MUV booby trap device. A zero-delay fuse."

"Exactly," purred Goldsmith. "Well done, my Cockney wide boy, go to the top of the class. And that, of course means, that when I die…you all die too. See…there really is a God."

"Look, Goldsmith," started Rick. "We both know this is about me and you, why not let these two go, and we'll see this out…just between us two? Me and you…man to man."

Goldsmith tried to laugh, but his pain was too great.

"Ah yes, Richard Fuller the hero. There for the greater good. Always the one to sacrifice yourself for the cause eh? Queen…Country…friend…lover..."

He turned his head and looked deep into my eyes. Despite his imminent mortality, he still gloated.

"Because that is what you are now, are you not, Ms North? His lover?"

I didn't answer.

Goldsmith turned his attention back to Rick. He practically snarled, his voice full of hate.

"You see, Fuller, I'm going to take away what you took from me. I'm going to take away the only thing you love."

JJ was standing to Rick's right. I hadn't seen him draw his knife. He sprang at Goldsmith, plunging the blade into the side of his neck and falling on the grenade, smothering it with his body.

I heard a tiny hissing sound. Rick bellowed, "Get down!" Dragged me to the floor and landed on top of me.

Rick Fuller's Story:

As a result of JJ Yakim's selfless bravery, we had survived the fragmentation of the grenade.

The shockwave from the detonation, however, was a different matter. My nose and ears bled and I felt like Red George had been kicking me in the guts after all. Being in such close proximity to an explosion damages your hollow organs.

I checked Lauren over, she was groggy but conscious. Exactly how much internal damage we had suffered from the over pressure, time would tell.

She rolled on her side, picked herself up and walked over to JJ's body. The blast had thrown him across the room and he was lying on his back under the window. The breast plate of his vest had taken the brunt of the detonation, but his wounds were devastating. Lauren knelt by him and stroked his hair.

Goldsmith was sitting in his chair. Most of his right arm had gone and he bled from both eyes. JJ's knife was still buried to the hilt in his neck. I pulled my phone from my combats, took a shot of his corpse and pulled the knife from his neck. I wiped Goldsmith's blood from the weapon, and joined Lauren at JJ's side.

Des had obviously heard the blast and despite his own injuries, came barrelling through the door with his Bizon at the ready. He stopped in the centre of the room and took in the scene.

He grimaced at the sight. "Oh fuck, no…JJ," he said, kneeling next to me.

Lauren put two practiced fingers on the Turk's throat.

"Oh my God," she said. "He's alive…sheets, get me sheets from the bedroom."

We packed JJ's shocking abdominal injuries, and did our best with the compound fracture of his right femur. We needed an air ambulance, we needed Cartwright to work his magic just as he had for Lauren and me, back in Ireland.

But this was Albania, and no one was coming.

I carried JJ down the stairs. Des reversed the Sprinter up to the front door, and we laid him in the back, Des, a far more competent medic than me, climbed in the back with Lauren.

I drove.

The nearest hospital with a trauma unit good enough to treat JJ was thirty kilometres away in Kosovo. Would there be a guarded border? Would they allow us in the country? Would they treat JJ?

We didn't know the answers, but it was all we had.

I stamped on the gas and headed north.

Des Cogan's Story:

Lauren cradled JJ's head on her knee as we bounced down the rutted Albanian roads. She'd administered the last of our supply of morphine to him as we set off. I held the Turk's hand and talked shite to him, not knowing if he could hear. Looking at the blood pooled in his ears, probably not.

He was a real mess.

"How'd this happen?" I asked Lauren.

She shook her head, fighting back tears. "He did it to save us...me and Rick. He threw himself on the grenade to save our lives."

I had no answer to that one.

We swung a left and the road became tarmac, the ride smoother. As Rick pushed the van to its limit, I felt JJ squeeze my hand.

"Okay, son," I shouted over the screaming engine noise. "You're going to be okay. We're on our way to the hospital now, get you fixed up, good as new, pal."

His eyes flickered open. "...Des," he managed.

"You take it easy now, son," I said.

He squeezed my hand tighter, showing surprising strength.

"Des...look out for my boy... Kaya...yes? You promise me?"

"Listen, mate, come on, I'll not have that talk. You'll be looking after him yourself in a few weeks."

The Turk smiled.

"There's no point... in bullshit, my friend...please, just promise me."

He was right of course. "I promise," I said.

Seconds later, JJ's body stiffened. Lauren looked concerned and checked his vitals. "He's arresting," she shouted. "Come on, Des, start compressions."

Lauren spun herself around, placed one hand behind JJ's neck and the other on his jaw, and began mouth to mouth.

I found his breastbone with the heel of my hand and began the compressions I'd practised so often in my life.

"Come on, JJ!" she shouted between breaths. "Come on, think of Kaya now, think of Grace."

The van suddenly lurched to one side, throwing us off our task.

I bawled through the bulkhead, "For fuck's sake, Rick, take it easy."

I didn't wait for an answer, just got back to work, mentally counting the compressions in ratio to Lauren's breaths. It was roasting in the back of the van. Sweat dripped from my nose onto JJ's chest. My ribs were agony, I struggled for breath.

Finally, a cool hand gripped my wrist, stopping my work. It moved hold my hand tight.
I looked up into Lauren's face as tears ran down her cheeks. She shook her head. No words needed.
I banged on the bulkhead.
"Slow down, mate," I shouted. "Turn around…we've lost him, pal…he's gone."

Rick Fuller's Story:

I pulled to the side of the road and opened the back doors of the van. Lauren was inconsolable. She held JJ in her arms rocking him like a child, sobbing uncontrollably. Des gingerly stepped out into the fresh air leaving her to her grief.
He lit his pipe.
"You okay?" I asked.
The Scot nodded. It wasn't the first time we'd lost guys on jobs, guys we would have called mates, good mates, but I got the impression that this one had hit Des harder than most. He'd stayed with JJ and his missus when Lauren and I were convalescing and I think he'd become close to the kid too.
Despite his pain, he took a long pull of smoke into his lungs. "I'll tell Grace," he said.
I shook my head. "That's my job, it's my team and…"
"I want to, mate," he said.
What was there to add?

We finally prised Lauren from JJ and she sat in the front with me in silence. Two and a half hours later, we found a spot on the coast to park the van, and holed ourselves up until darkness fell.
We wrapped JJ in the blankets we'd used to cover the boat, and, although the moon shone bright, we took our chances and pushed off for Corfu.
The moment we made land, I sent the image of Goldsmith's corpse via SMS to Kostas Makris, and phoned Cartwright.
Konstantinos played a blinder and organised for us to store JJ's body in a small refrigerated room at the rear of the local medical centre in Arillas. The doctor, who was a distant relative, wrote the death certificate, showing the official cause as injuries sustained in a boating accident.
From there the Firm picked up the tab for the rest, chartering a private jet to repatriate JJ's body.
We all flew home separately.

Des Cogan's Story:

On the day of JJ Yakim's funeral, the long hot spell of weather finally broke and the rain poured.

As neither JJ nor Grace had any religious leanings, the ceremony took place at Manchester Crematorium. The place has the look of a church about it to be fair, and housed two chapels, but there was nothing spiritual about this day.

The crematorium did have beautiful grounds to sit in and visit should you decide to scatter your loved one's ashes there, but Grace had other plans that she didn't share with me.

JJ's service was held in the smaller 'New Chapel'.

Grace had contacted the local British Legion, and, despite JJ never having fought under a British flag, four old WWII veterans had turned up and flanked his coffin. The front two carried flags, one with the Union Ensign the second with the 2nd Battalion Para's Standard. All of them looked smart-as, in their regimental blazers, purple berets and their chests full of medals.

The coffin itself was draped in the Turkish flag with JJ's own Special Forces maroon beret having pride of place atop.

Sadly, the chapel was virtually empty. Apart from Rick, Lauren, me and the four old Paras, there were a further eight people.

Grace had explained that neither her nor JJ's family had agreed with their marriage and therefore didn't expect them to show their faces on this day.

Race and religion can be a terrible curse on occasions, can they not? Thank goodness, the RBL don't give a monkey's.

I'd half expected to see Cartwright skulking about at the back of the chapel, but even he had decided to stay away.

Bad form if you ask me.

We sat in silence as Grace took to the podium, her tiny frame almost totally hidden by it.

In a clear proud voice that belied her stature, she began:

"They'll be no prayers for JJ," she said. "No hymns, no priest or vicar here. It's what he wanted, so it's what he'll be having.

But for me, I want to speak in rhyme today, something pretty, something nice, to send him on his way wherever he may be going."

She pulled out a single page from her bag. "I found this…me and Kaya liked it…."

Grace cleared her throat:
"Do not stand at my grave and weep.
I am not there, I do not sleep.
I am a thousand winds that blow.
I am the diamond glints on snow.

I am the sunlight on ripened grain.
I am the gentle autumn rain.

When you awaken in the mornings hush,
I am the swift uplifting rush
of quiet birds in circled flight,
I am the soft stars that shine at night.

Do not stand at my grave and cry,
I am not there, I did not die."
There were quiet tears in the chapel, but none from Grace or the boy.
The most senior looking of the old soldiers stepped forward, took
JJ's beret from the coffin, folded the flag and handed both to wee
Kaya. The lad, dressed in a smart little suit, took the items and
tucked them under his arm before finding his mother's hand again.
The coffin began to roll forward as quiet organ music played. The
curtains closed, and it was over.

The rain had stopped and gaps of blue began to appear in the grey
sky, as I waited outside for Grace and the boy. Finally she saw me,
and walked over.
"I'm sorry, Grace," I managed.
She waved a hand at me, fighting tears now. "Don't be sorry,
Desmond," she said. "JJ was a scrapper, a fighter. You knew that,
and I knew it. He was a scrapper when I met him, and given his time
over, he'd do it again. If he hadn't been fighting with you, he'd have
been working some grotty pub door, fighting the local drunks. That
was him."
She managed a brave smile. "Don't be sorry for me, Des, I was
lucky to have loved him."
I looked down at Kaya.

He held out a very mature hand. I knelt, to match his height, took it and shook.

"Thank you for coming, Des," he announced in his best grown-up voice.

"I wouldn't have missed it for the world, wee man," I said.

The boy hadn't shed a tear all morning, but I could see his lip start to tremble. "Was my daddy brave?" he asked.

I smiled at him. "The bravest, son. Your daddy was the bravest trooper of them all."

At that he threw his skinny wee arms around my neck, buried his face in my chest and broke his heart.

I think he broke mine too.

I walked Grace and Kaya to their car. As she opened the door for the boy, I pulled an envelope from my pocket and handed it to her.

"What's this?" she asked with a hint of suspicion.

"A house," I said. "I mean, the deeds anyway. Anne left me a house…in Scotland…I can't…I mean…it holds too many memories for me and…well I made a promise to JJ… I'd watch out for Kaya and…"

She waved the envelope back at me. "No, Des, I can't accept something like this, it's…"

"It's not for you," I said, as firmly as I could. "It's in trust…for the boy…when he's eighteen. There's a good rental income from it. You don't need to do anything, a company does it all for ye. Please…Grace…I want to do this."

She wiped her eyes, stepped to me, kissed my cheek and managed a smile. "I thought you were retiring? Surely the sale of that house would make you comfortable."

"Maybe it's not my time just yet," I said.

Grace held my face in her small hands. "You're a fine man, Des Cogan," she said. "Don't forget us, eh?"

"You'll be sick of the sight of me," I said.

Rick Fuller's Story:

We sat around our usual table in the Thirsty Scholar and had a drink for JJ Yakim.

It was how it was.

Back in the day, we would always have a drink for the ones who didn't make it back.

Part of the healing process, they say.

I have to admit, I found it hard to accept that the two families couldn't forego their differences on this one day, and attend JJ's service.

A brave man deserves respect.

Des bought a bottle of Jameson's, the Turk's preferred tipple, and we all got steadily pissed.

We toasted everything Turkish we could think of, from the Ottoman Empire to a fucking kebab. The toasts got louder and more bizarre as the afternoon wore on. Martin the Mod, the landlord, fussed around us. I think he was secretly concerned that things might get out of hand, but he'd no need to worry.

We finished the bottle and ordered pints of beer to wash it down.

Des took a big gulp. "Tell, you what, guys, I'm starving, I haven't eaten today," he said.

"Me either," chirped Lauren.

"How about a Chinese then?" I asked.

Des pursed his lips. "I fancy a curry, pal, let's get a cab down to Rusholme, eh?"

"I'll ring one now," I said.

I dialled…and nothing happened. I looked at Lauren. "I've no signal," I said. "You're on my network, aren't you? Have you got anything?"

She checked her screen and shook her head. "Nope, nothing…that's weird."

"Dinnae look at me, pal," said Des standing up with a distinct wobble on. "My phone is where it should be on a day like today…at home."

Lauren stood and leaned on the Scot for support. "Well there's a rank just across the road, I'm sure the walk won't kill us."

I looked at the pair. "Neither of you look like you could walk to the fuckin' bar…you're both pissed."

Des pointed at me, "Oh aye, and you're not eh? Listen to it, you're the one who toasted fuckin' Turkish Delight a minute ago."

We all had a laugh at that, downed our beer as the inebriated do and made for the exit. I stepped out onto the cobbles, the old railway arch above my head, the other two shuffling out behind me like a pair of old soaks.

A black Range Rove burbled away at the kerb. The moment we stepped out, a second one screeched to a halt inches behind it. Standing next to the open rear door of the first vehicle was a smartly dressed man. He was well over six feet, all buzz cut and Ray-Bans, comms in his left ear. I looked behind me to find a further two burly men, similarly attired, jackets open, shoulder holsters on view.

"What the fuck's this?" I said.

The man at the door spoke. He was American, from the deep south, Virginia maybe?

"Mr Fuller," he said politely. "Mr Cogan, Ms. North… ma'am… step into the vehicle, please."

THE END

Printed in Great Britain
by Amazon